The Tyrant King

The Revenge of the Fallen

Michael Robling

Illustrations by Liliana Tikage

For more information, contact:
thetyrantking@michaelrobling.com or visit **michaelrobling.com**

First edition: July 2024

Paperback ISBN: 979-8-9899608-1-1

DEDICATION

This book is dedicated to my wife, Kaitlynn, for always believing in me; to my mom and dad, for their unconditional support; and to my two beautiful children, Adalynn and Jackson, my fellow dinosaur lovers.

CONTENTS

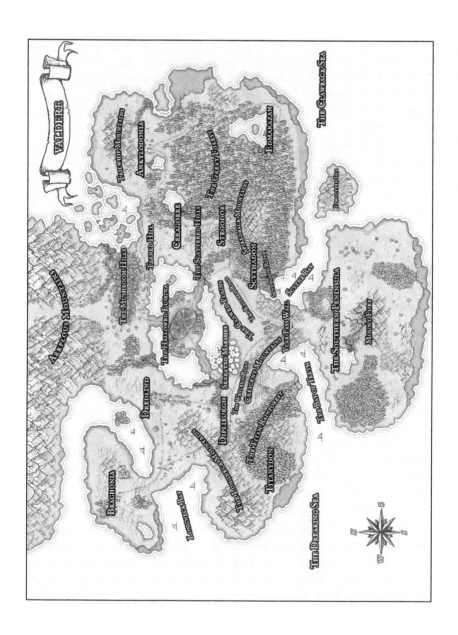

VALDIERE

THE CLAWBACK SEA

THE TRIILWHIP MOUNTAINS
ANYLODONIA
EDMARAZAN

THE GREAT FOREST
CRAGORRE
THE SCATTERED HILLS
STEGODOK
SPLINTERSPUR MOUNTAINS
SOUTHADON
THE MUSHROOM HILLS
TARNED HILL
THE HALLOWED LUMINA
SCUTHEL BAY

ARKILOUS MOUNTAINS
THE GLADE OF SHADOWS
THE SCATTERED PLAINS

THE SOUTHERN PENINSULA
MOUNT FURY

DREDLIND
DIPIERURGH   SERRATED MEADOW
THE WILLESS WOOD
CRESCENT MOUNTAINS
VAST PAST WALL
THE BAY OF HIRTH

BRACHIONIA
THE JOSGOR MOUNTAINS
THE HELEN RAINFOREST
TITANYDON

LONGNECK BAY

THE DREAKING SEA

N
E
W
S

DINOTOLOGY

The Dinotology provides a brief introduction to some of Valdere's inhabitants. Although countless others call Valdere home, the following creatures make prominent appearances in the first part of *The Tyrant King: The Revenge of the Fallen.*

Viridi Tribes: The Herbivores

Scythekin

Description: Shades and mixtures of gray, brown, black, and tan feathers; three, three-foot-long razor-sharp claws extend from each arm; average speed

Size: Length: 35 feet / Height: 18 feet / Weight: 11,000 pounds

Bio: The deadly use of their claws and ability to walk upright positions the Scythekin as one of the foremost enemies of the Carne. A very proud and resilient kin, Scythekin are well respected by the other Viridi tribes due to their actions in the Great War of Extinction.

Stegokin

Description: Various shades of green with brown, orange, or red backplates; strong thagomizer tail that consists of four, three-foot-long spikes; very slow

Size: Length: 33 feet / Height: 14 feet / Weight: 12,000 pounds

Bio: Their thick armored skin and devastating thagomizer make the Stegokin a formidable foe. Although slow, a well-trained Stegokin army can hold its own, even against superior numbers. A very proud and stubborn species, the Stegokin will defend their home to the death. Surrender is not an option.

Trikin

Description: Various shades of gray, red, green, and brown; three facial horns, two of which grow up to three feet long; above average speed

Size: Length: 30 feet / Height: 10 feet / Weight: 16,000 pounds

Bio: With thick armored skin and strong deadly horns, Trikin are feared far and wide. Their horns and speed make for devastating charges in battle. Stubborn to a fault and strong-willed, the Trikin value their lives above all else. If something won't benefit them directly, they will often look the other way.

Pachykin

Description: Shades of orange and brown with maroon back stripes; nine-inch-thick skull with short, but sharpened head spikes; slightly above average speed

Size: Length: 16 feet / Height: 10 feet / Weight: 2,500 pounds

Bio: Although much smaller than many of their Viridi counterparts, the Pachykin fight valiantly. They prefer to ram their enemies, knocking them to the ground, and at times, knocking them out completely. A courageous species, they survived the Great War of Extinction due to their stoic resilience.

Carne Tribes: The Carnivores

Gigakin

Description: Shades of pale green and black, with black or gray back stripes; long and sharp serrated teeth; average speed

Size: Length: 40 feet / Height: 20 feet / Weight: 16,000 pounds

Bio: Among the largest of the Carne, the Gigakin were known for their savagery during the Great War of Extinction. In the present day, the Gigakin are just as ruthless toward other Carne as they are toward Viridi. Girozz and Gwon; however, have proven that not all Gigakin are inherently evil.

Tarbokin

Description: Shades of dark green and gray with black back stripes; conical bone crushing teeth; slightly below average speed

Size: Length: 36 feet / Height: 16 feet / Weight: 10,000 pounds

Bio: One of the larger Carne species, the Tarbokin cause devastation wherever they roam. As one of the most common Carne to assault the Vlax Pass Wall, Tarbokin and Scythekin are used to going teeth to claws. Feared for their aggression and sheer strength. Their apparent lack of value for their own lives makes them even more dangerous. They are content with sacrificing themselves as long as they take their enemies with them.

Carnokin

Description: Shades of red and brown; short and sharp serrated teeth; two small, but sharpened, conical horns on head; above average speed

Size: Length: 30 feet / Height: 12 feet / Weight: 6,000 pounds

Bio: The Carnokin can be described with one word: hostile. Although an average sized Carne, the Carnokin can cause great mayhem and destruction. They often ram their short horns into their enemies first, weakening them prior to latching on with their teeth. Oftentimes irate for no particular reason, Carnokin terrorize everyone and everything they come across.

Allokin

Description: Shades of orange and tan; short and sharp serrated teeth; above average speed

Size: Length: 36 feet / Height: 16 feet / Weight: 5,000 pounds

Bio: Cunning and audacious, Allokin are a worthy foe. A rather mysterious Carne, not much is known about them, as they rarely assault the Vlax Pass Wall. It is said that during the Great War of Extinction, the Allokin were among the most feared Carne; not because of their size, but because of their tenacity.

SEEKING ASYLUM

The vast pass extended between two mountain ranges for about a mile. Only a few shrubs grew scattered across the flat land, allowing for a keen eye to see a great distance in all directions.

The mountain ranges reached high into the sky, scraping the clouds that drifted overhead with their sharp peaks. As the mountains were unscalable, the pass was the only gateway from the Southern Peninsula to mainland Valdere.

This pass, known as the Vlax Pass to those who dwelled there, was the sight of a devastating battle fought long ago. Stories about the Battle of Vlax Pass had been passed down for a millennium, transforming into legendary tales. It was a battle that forever changed the history and very fabric of Valdere.

Following the battle, the victors built an enormous wooden wall as a barrier between the Southern Peninsula and the mainland. Set deep in the land, the Wall was sturdy. It would take significant force to knock it down.

The Wall stood for a thousand years, carrying out its duty of preventing those in the south from crossing the Vlax Pass. Its builders continued to maintain it, generation after generation. The threat those in the south posed grew into but a faint memory, only to be rekindled in the minds of those who guarded the Wall every once in a distant while.

This was the norm until one strange day when an unlikely visitor approached the Wall with his young son by his side. It was a day that those all throughout Valdere could look to for hope; a day that changed the hearts and minds of many.

Until that day, hate festered between those north and those south of the Wall. This hate was so ingrained that its existence was never even questioned. It simply existed…and that was it.

But when the visitor and his son approached, as luck would have it on that fateful day, the leader of those who kept the Wall was also visiting. His presence changed history, and with it, the world.

"My King," said a guard. "We've spotted a Carne slowly making his way toward the Wall. He has…what looks like a child with him."

The King shot the guard a confused look. "What?" he asked. "A Carne child?"

The King made it a priority to visit the Wall. He didn't do so often, but as the King of Scythadon, the kingdom that built and maintained the Wall, he believed it was his duty to ensure the well-being of those who guarded it.

His visit was always good for morale, and he showed appreciation to those who risked their lives to keep the rest of Valdere safe. He was a highly respected king, at least among the Viridi kingdoms north of the Wall. The Carne to the south, however, would have loved nothing more than to sink their teeth deep into his flesh, ending his life in a mere instant.

"I'm just as confused as you are," said the guard. "They're still far away, but what's even stranger is that they appear to be Gigakin. It is hard to tell. Come, look for yourself."

"Gigakin?" the King asked, more confused than before.

The King ascended the Wall with the guard. When he reached the top, he looked out over the pass before him and caught his first glimpse of the two Carne as they approached.

As a fair and just king, he would never have asked something of his subjects that he himself would not do. In this, he had fought many Gigakin at the Wall during his reign. Without a doubt, they were Gigakin, and he knew them to be among the largest and...usually the most aggressive of the Carne.

Their narrow jaws and rigid menacing appearance quickly gave them away. The larger one was remarkably bigger than the child, and their scales were a shade of pale green. The older one had black stripes across his back, while the younger one had gray.

"What are your orders, King Thax?" the guard asked. "Should we run them off?"

As the two Carne advanced toward the Wall, the King couldn't help but notice they didn't look threatening at all. As a matter of fact, they looked peaceful. There had been many Carne in the past that advanced on the Wall, skirmishes breaking out between them and the Scythekin guardians.

King Thax had taken part in a few skirmishes himself during some of his previous visits. He had certainly never seen peaceful-looking Carne before. He had also never laid eyes upon a Carne child. If not for this peculiar occurrence, Carne children might as well have not existed.

"No," said King Thax. "Let's wait and see what they do."

The King gazed intently at the child. His small features and subtle expression became more visible the closer he got. His walk was awkward, most likely because he was not but two or three months in age. They eventually stopped before the Wall about thirty paces away.

King Thax was transfixed by the Carne child and saw something unexpected…unimaginable even. Something that suddenly made him question everything he thought he knew about Carne. He saw innocence. The same innocence he saw in his recently hatched son, who appeared to be about the same age as the Carne that stood before him. The child didn't look evil. He didn't even look hateful. He looked…good. And a fair bit scared.

"Who goes there?" the guard shouted. "What is your purpose here? You know your kin are not welcome!"

King Thax hadn't noticed it at first, but he now saw the distraught look on the older Carne's face. He didn't look vicious or angry, typical traits of the uncivilized Carne. Instead, worry was spread across his face, and he slightly quivered as he turned to look over his shoulder. King Thax looked in the distance as well, but all he saw was barren land.

Worry and distraught weren't words used to describe Carne, nor peaceful or innocent. No, they were violent creatures and wanted to commit atrocities against all Viridi, not just the Scythekin.

They had no alternative agenda other than that of causing despair and destruction. Or had they? In an instant, King Thax felt his world had turned upside down when the older Carne

4

gently spoke. "Please," he said in a heavy accent, almost too difficult to understand. "We've come seeking asylum. We were just attacked. My mate…" He paused briefly, turning to look at the young Carne that accompanied him before returning his eyes to the King. "My mate was killed as were my other companions. Please help us, I beg you."

Feelings of shock, confusion, and pity flooded the King all at once, unsure of which emotion to latch onto. He was caught off guard and uncertain of how to respond. Speaking and acting this way wasn't like the Carne. The Carne only ever wanted one thing: blood. The blood of his kin and all other Viridi.

He considered what to say, surprised with himself that he hadn't already turned them away. As he deliberated in his mind, he leaned toward telling them to get lost. After all, what would happen? Two Carne, Gigakin nonetheless, would live among his kin? Could he really just pretend that the brutal history between their kinds had been nonexistent?

It wasn't an option, nor had it ever been. When Viridi and Carne encountered one another, rivers ran red, fields turned crimson, and families were ripped apart. The King grew conflicted, bewildered, and a bit frustrated. How could he even consider such a thing? The Carne were beasts that looked to harm everyone around them. Weren't they?

Just as the King settled on turning them away, he glanced back at the child and caught his first word before it left his mouth. At the last moment, he changed his response. "What do you mean, you were attacked?" he asked. "By who?"

It was no secret that the Carne fought and killed one another. It was to the benefit of the Viridi that they behaved in such a rudimentary way. If the Carne were fighting among themselves, they had no intention of trying to reinvade mainland Valdere.

The only Carne that ever ventured to the Wall were rogue groups looking for trouble. They weren't typically many—no more than fifteen to twenty. Few enough that the defenders could easily drive them off.

The older Carne looked down at the ground in shame. "Carne," he said as he returned his gaze to the King. "Our fellow Carne attacked us. I'm done with this life."

He looked at the young Carne, who was too young to even know what was happening.

"I want my son to grow up and not have to look over his shoulder every waking minute. His mother was killed right in front of him. That's no way to live."

King Thax became even more confused. This was unlike anything he had ever seen. The sincerity in the eyes of the older Carne seemed genuine, and the fright in the eyes of the younger one was unmistakable.

The King thought about his son and how awful it would be if he lost his mother. He couldn't bear the thought and quickly tried to suppress it. "What is your name?" he asked.

"Girozz," the Carne replied. He gestured to his son with his jaws. "And this is Gwon."

Girozz then looked over his shoulder again. The King looked too but saw no sign of anything for as far as his eyes could see.

So many thoughts were rushing through the King's mind, each one leaving him more perplexed than the last. He then thought of something that finally made a bit of sense. An idea that made him feel better about the decision he had arrived at.

Yes, it would be strange for Carne to live among the Viridi. And yes, it would not sit well with many of his kin, especially those who had lost loved ones at the Wall to the teeth of the Carne.

Yet, he realized the potential benefits of having Carne on his side. This enemy had been so elusive and mysterious for the last thousand years. King Thax, as with the other Viridi leaders, knew nothing of the Southern Peninsula.

All they knew was that the evil and hateful Carne lived there. They didn't know how big it was, nor did they know how many Carne there were. All the questions they had about the Carne might now get answered.

The King signaled to the guards down below to open the gate with a nod and gesture of his right claws. "Let's talk further," he said. "Stay where you are." He then turned around and descended the Wall.

As he made his way through the gate with more than a dozen guards at his back, he came face to face with the two Carne. It was truly a sight to behold, a Gigakin and a Scythekin, within two paces of one another. Neither had any will to fight, nor was there any hate in their eyes.

They were there to talk…and that's all. And talk they did for a very long time. A moment in time for the ages, a moment in time in the story of The Tyrant King.

CHAPTER ONE

STORIES OF OLD

Fifteen Years Later...

Thadarack loved this place. The calm atmosphere, the sway of the tall grass, the rustling of the leaves as the breeze grazed them with its soft touch. He loved how the songs of the birds gave way to the melody of the crickets. This signaled his favorite reason for visiting the valley: the sunset. The beautiful shades of yellow, orange, and red always left him in awe.

He looked across the valley from the overlook and saw harmony, a picturesque view that filled his heart with warmth. He then glanced at his father beside him, expecting to see him also enjoying the view. Instead, the concerned expression on his face was as apparent as the setting sun; although, not nearly as comforting.

"Father," he said in a young, innocent voice. "Are you okay?"

Thadarack's father was no ordinary Scythekin. He wasn't a healer, builder, cultivator, or even a warrior. He wasn't a scout who patrolled the lands or a trader who bartered goods with the other cities of the East.

He was a king. The eighteenth King of Scythadon, and as such, had great responsibilities. Although he tried his utmost to hide it, it was evident that something was bothering him. Thadarack could see it in his eyes.

"I'm alright," said King Thax. "It's beautiful here, isn't it?"

"It is," said Thadarack, as he turned his head back toward the sprawling landscape.

The valley was vast, stretching for a great while before transitioning into forest. It wasn't bare, but it was much more open compared to the dense forest land that surrounded it. Trees were scattered here and there, and lush grass and shrubs dotted its interior.

A winding stream ran right down the center and was full of various kinds of fish. Thadarack loved watching them jump out of the water. The beautiful hues of the sunset glistened off their shiny bodies as they plummeted back into the stream, disappearing from sight. In the far distance, he could see a few Greatdeer grazing, at times visiting the stream for a drink.

"I'm not sure how much longer we'll be able to come here," said King Thax.

Thadarack gave his father a confused look. "What do you mean?"

The King sighed. "The war is getting out of control. I fear that if it does not end soon, we will have no choice but to intervene. It may not be safe to come here if that happens."

Thadarack stared back at his father unnerved. He knew the Stegokin and the Trikin had been at war for the last three years but didn't know why. Having been so wrapped up in his studies and the other more exciting things that young Scythekin did, he never cared much. A good game of Clawball and spending time with his friends was much more fun. Besides, the war was far away...at least in his mind.

Thadarack's father was a good king and had successfully kept the Kingdom of Scythadon out of the war. So, why *would* he have cared before? It wasn't like the war was directly impacting him or those he loved.

"But I thought you said we wouldn't get involved?" he asked. "Did something happen?"

"I've tried my best to appease her," said the King. "But Queen Cerathorn thinks I favor King Sturklan. And if I'm being honest, I can't fault her for she is right. She knows that if Ceragorre gets the upper claw in the war, then I will have no choice but to intercede on behalf of Stegodor."

It didn't surprise Thadarack to hear such things, especially because he knew how close his father was with the Stegokin king. The Scythekin had a deep bond and long-standing friendship with the Stegokin. Although they'd been cordial with the Trikin in the past, the war adversely affected their relations. Many believed that it was only a matter of time before the Scythekin would join the war on the side of the Stegokin.

"Why are they even fighting?" asked Thadarack. "Why can't they just get along?"

"The cause for this war goes much deeper than what we can see on the surface," said King Thax. "Something happened long ago that just couldn't...can't be forgiven."

"What can't be forgiven?" asked Thadarack.

The King didn't answer right away, most likely contemplating his next words carefully. He never told his son much about what happened outside the walls of Scythadon. Although he didn't ask often, when he did, his father insisted Thadarack was too young and that he should enjoy his childhood. "Don't grow up too fast," he always said. "Don't concern yourself with such matters…not yet."

In Thadarack's mind, that childhood was now quickly coming to an end. He had just turned fifteen and in the Scythekin tradition, he was officially an adult. He believed he should now be privy to such information. After all, he was the heir to the throne of Scythadon. Shouldn't he already know such things?

"I suppose it's time you know," King Thax said eventually. "I've sheltered you for far too long from the tough reality of the world. If you're to be king of the Scythekin one day, you must first learn the truth about how things are, not how we wish them to be." He paused for a moment and examined his son. "Yes…it is time."

Thadarack quickly reconsidered his position. Did he want to know? His father's words did little to intrigue him, especially the part regarding the "reality of the world." What did that even mean? Before he had a chance to change the conversation, his father spoke. "What do you remember about the Great War?"

Thadarack *knew* of the Great War and how his kin played a major role in defeating the Carne, but he didn't know the specific details. He knew the Viridi were victorious and that the Carne, to this day, were trapped south of the Vlax Pass. "I know we won," he said. "Why? What does that have to do with the current war?"

"Everything," said King Thax. "During the Great War, in the Battle of Tarned Hill, the Stegokin were on the brink of defeat. The Carne had them surrounded, pinched between them and a cliff. The Trikin army was camped not but five miles from the battle and knew that the Stegokin needed help. Instead of coming to their aid, the Trikin sought safety and marched further away, leaving the Stegokin to their certain demise."

Thadarack stared at his father wide-eyed and uncertain of what to say. In his mind, this was strange to hear. He had heard a few stories about the Great War passed down from the elders around Scythadon. He was always fascinated by them, especially the ones about how his forebears helped bring victory. He believed that without the Scythekin, history would have told a different tale.

What he thought he also understood was that the Viridi tribes worked together to defeat the Carne. Hearing that the Trikin abandoned the Stegokin came to him as a surprise.

After a brief pause, his father continued, "The two sides claim this war is based on border encroachments and broken treaties. But in reality, this act of abandonment has prevailed an everlasting resentment, causing great animosity between them. This is why the war broke out, even though a thousand years have passed."

"But why didn't the Trikin help them?" Thadarack asked.

"I suppose I should start from the very beginning," King Thax said. "The reason is more complex than you might think." He turned away and looked out over the valley.

Thadarack followed his father's gaze just in time to see the last glimpse of the sun as it concealed itself below the distant tree line. He then looked up at the sky as the stars began to appear through the grayish-blue blanket and subsiding white clouds that lay overhead.

"What I'm about to tell you will change your perspective on the entire world," the King said, as he and Thadarack turned back to one another. "In the beginning, before Scythadon was even a thought, there were small groups of Carne and Viridi scattered across Valdere. Many of these were just families trying to find food and survive. The Carne lived mostly on the Southern Peninsula, and the Viridi roamed all throughout the mainland. Eventually, with each passing year, more and more Carne crossed over the Vlax Pass onto the mainland. We don't know for certain what prompted them to do this, but Girozz believes it was due to decreasing food supply and the hardships they faced at the jaws of one another."

Thadarack listened to his father intently. He knew of the Vlax Pass and of the Wall that his kin built to keep the Carne at bay following the Great War, but he never saw it. It was off-limits to all except for the guards who were there patrolling it.

His father never discussed the Wall with him, and even though he heard stories about it from time to time in the city, it almost didn't seem real. The Carne themselves seemed like a myth. Had it not been for Girozz and Gwon, Thadarack might have very well thought Carne didn't exist at all. Only those at the Wall encountered them. Well, the wild ones, at least, that sought to wreak despair and destruction.

"Whatever their reason for venturing further north, encounters with Viridi increased gradually," the King continued. "The Viridi soon realized that to protect themselves, they had to come together. Like Viridi soon joined forces, but the individual tribes remained separate. Very similar to how we still are today. We each have our separate kingdoms, traditions, and values."

Thadarack knew this to be true. The Viridi tribes did have separate kingdoms. The Kingdom of Scythadon was built along the Scythadon River on the outskirts of the Great Forest. It was founded just northeast of the Vlax Pass after the Great War, so the Scythekin, the guardians of the Wall there, could ensure the Carne stayed trapped in the Southern Peninsula.

The Kingdom of Stegodor was about a day and a half walk northeast of Scythadon. Although Thadarack himself had never been, those who traveled there took the Eastern Road, a very long road that began in Scythadon. From there, it ran along the outskirts of the Great Forest and connected all the major cities of the east.

The Kingdom of Ceragorre was about the same distance north of Stegodor, but nobody traveled that portion of the Eastern Road anymore. Thadarack had heard that it was now a battlefield, littered with the decay and bones of fallen warriors.

"The Carne didn't like that the Viridi could now fight back, especially because their newfound food supply became harder to obtain. The Carne shortly followed suit, and instead of continuing to fight among one another as they had always done, they began joining forces. At first, it was the same as the Viridi, only like Carne joined forces."

Thadarack had never really thought about the differences between Carne and Viridi. Having never seen other Carne besides Girozz and Gwon, the fact that they ate meat was foreign to him. The talk around the city recently was usually about the war between the Stegokin and the Trikin, not about the Carne.

"Eventually, larger battles broke out and before long, stationary societies formed. The Viridi tribes no longer roamed

14

and preferred to stay in one place as this proved easier to protect themselves. Fortunately for the Viridi, they outnumbered the Carne and were soon able to fight them off effectively."

King Thax's expression turned to sadness as his eyes shifted toward the stars in the night sky. Thadarack's eyes remained fixed on his father, listening closely to his every word.

"Various Carne tribes began to work together, creating larger forces that quickly overpowered the separate Viridi tribes. Gradually, over time…this turned into one large, single army that terrorized the land. They—"

"But I thought the Carne hated each other," interrupted Thadarack. "I thought all the different tribes fought and killed one another. Why would they join together?"

"That's all true," said King Thax, now turning his eyes back toward his son. "They did hate each other, and they did kill one another. But there was one who was able to unite them. One who nobody dared to disobey. He didn't do it through benevolence or diplomacy. He did it through violence."

"What do you mean?" Thadarack asked reluctantly. "There was one leader of the Carne?"

Although Thadarack lacked deep knowledge of the Great War, it was commonly known that each individual Carne tribe had its own leaders. The same was true for the Viridi tribes. King Thax was king of the Scythekin, and the Scythekin alone. Queen Cerathorn was queen of the Trikin and King Sturklan was king of the Stegokin.

There was no overlord or one supreme leader among them. That same concept, at least Thadarack thought, applied to the Carne as well. Even in the stories he'd heard about the Great

War, none of them mentioned one leader of the Carne.

"There was one Rexkin that fought and killed all the other Carne leaders until there were none left who dared to challenge him. From that point on, he was hailed the High King of all the Carne. The devastating army he amassed ravaged Valdere, subjugating and destroying anyone and anything in its path. He was known far and wide as Orzligorn…Orzligorn the Ruthless."

Thadarack quivered at the name. *Orzligorn*, he thought. *Orzligorn the Ruthless.*

"A lust for power and domination fueled him, as well as all those that served him. Many Viridi tribes were enslaved and forced into breeding, only to be slaughtered as a means of sustenance to the Carne. Any tribes that stood up to such evil were annihilated. It's believed this happened to many tribes, but the only one that *I* know of is the Parakin. We know nothing of them, save for their name, all else sadly lost to history and forgotten. This is why the war has also been called the Great War of Extinction."

Thadarack was so shaken that he had trouble speaking. He cleared his throat and opened his mouth slowly. "So, why didn't the Viridi tribes join forces? Why didn't they help one another?"

"For one, they were too stubborn," said the King. "Just like the Carne, they didn't want a High King. But unlike the Carne, their leaders weren't going to fight one another for it. On top of that, the Carne army grew so strong and the terror it brought with it made the Viridi tribes unwilling to help one another. To you and me it may seem strange, but to them it made perfect sense. Amid such evil, why would they risk their own lives to try to save the lives of others that weren't their own kin?"

Although Thadarack knew that the Viridi were victorious in the end, this story didn't make it seem so. He regretted asking any questions and hoped that his father would reach the conclusion soon.

"For the most part, the only Viridi tribes that were still alive, the one exception being the Longnecks, were the tribes that could outrun the Carne. The—"

"I forgot about the Longnecks," interrupted Thadarack. "What were they doing during the war?"

"Even though the Carne were such a powerful force, the Longnecks were among their greatest rivals," answered the King. "The Carne focused on who they perceived as the weaker links first and planned to finish off the strong after. They didn't want to leave any Viridi tribes alive that they felt could later challenge their dominion over Valdere."

"I'm so confused," said Thadarack. "Why didn't the Viridi tribes help each other? It just doesn't make sense! Why would they let one another die?"

"You have to understand," said King Thax. "Valdere was in chaos. All Viridi were scared, scattered, and afraid that their own family was going to die. This terror continued for years, not just weeks or months. All hope seemed lost as the Carne army swept across the land. It was to the point where one's only chance of survival was to hide and hope the Carne couldn't find them."

"So, what happened with the Stegokin?" asked Thadarack. "How did they end up surviving if the Carne had them surrounded?"

"As I said earlier, the Stegokin were backed up to the edge of a cliff," said King Thax. "It was their last stand and a courageous one it was. The Carne were closing in all around them. Their leader had just fallen, and all hope seemed lost. Until—"

"Until what!" Thadarack interrupted animatedly. "What happened?"

"Until your kin showed up," said the King. "Your ancestor Thrifsaer, with the Scythekin army at his back, unexpectedly charged the Carne from behind. Not expecting such a feat to take place, the Carne were so caught off guard that they quickly fell apart and retreated. Their losses were so heavy that they never fully recovered. And thus, the tide of the war was turned."

Thadarack's emotions completely shifted. He was no longer anxious or frustrated. He was proud. Proud to be a Scythekin and to be related to someone so great. He knew of Thrifsaer, the founder of Scythadon, but didn't know this story about him. He immediately thought about his grave just outside the city, wanting to go to it to pay his respects.

That heroism ran in his veins as a young but determined Scythekin. Deep down, he was unsure if he'd make a good king. He was unsure if he'd be able to live up to the expectations that others set for him. But he was going to try.

"From that day forward, the Viridi tribes and their leaders flocked under Thrifsaer's claws. They now knew the Carne could be beaten, and if they worked together, they could hopefully defeat them once and for all. It took many difficult years, but the Viridi pushed the Carne out of mainland Valdere, all the way to the Vlax Pass. On their way, they freed all those who the Carne had enslaved and captured. In the final engagement of the war, the Battle of Vlax Pass, Thrifsaer threw down Orzligorn. After that, the remaining Carne disbanded and fled back to the

Southern Peninsula."

It would've been impossible for Thadarack to be prouder than he was at this moment. *Thrifsaer,* he thought. *I want to be just like him.* He almost asked his father to walk through the part about Thrifsaer again, wanting to hear how he nearly saved the Viridi single-clawededly.

Thadarack thought about how marvelous the sight must have been. One army of all different Viridi tribes fighting side by side, led by Thrifsaer. Although he was content with the story now, he still had many questions. "Did the Trikin end up helping as well? Or did they still refuse?"

"They helped," said King Thax. "Their leader at the time, Ceraplazz, realized he had made a grave mistake. Once Thrifsaer helped the Stegokin, Ceraplazz was among the first of the other Viridi leaders to join up with him. It's said that not a day went by that Ceraplazz didn't feel remorse for abandoning the Stegokin. From that day forward, he pledged to always come to the aid of his fellow Viridi, no matter what kin."

King Thax shook his head. "That's why this war between the Stegokin and the Trikin is so troubling. They fought side by side together against the Carne in the Great War. If they hadn't put their differences aside and helped one another, they would have both surely fallen."

"So, what happened?" Thadarack asked. "Why do they fight now? It still doesn't make sense to me."

"Generations have passed, my son. Those who fought and died together are long gone. Only those who know the story of the Great Forsaking live among us today. A story they can't forgive, nor forget."

"That's sad," said Thadarack.

"It is," said King Thax. "Fortunately, I received word earlier that King Sturklan and Queen Cerathorn have agreed to a meeting to discuss bringing about a peaceful end to the war."

"Well, that's good news," said Thadarack. "Do you think they'll agree to peace?"

"I'm not sure," answered the King. "But they've both grown weary and tired of all the fighting. Countless Viridi lives have been lost due to such a futile war."

"When is the meeting?" asked Thadarack.

"I am to leave with my entourage in the morning," said the King. "Queen Cerathorn has agreed to meet King Sturklan and me in Stegodor the day after tomorrow."

Thadarack hoped this meeting would bring about peace. He thought about the possibility of Scythekin dying in the war if it didn't, a thought that deeply upset him.

He turned and looked out at the beautiful sight before him and couldn't believe that a war was raging on. Nor could he believe that such a devastating war occurred a thousand years ago.

He began to drift off, staring in awe at the starlit valley before him. Valdere was a beautiful land. It was lush and vibrant with gigantic trees, rolling valleys, and vast rivers and lakes. Huge colossal mushrooms, luminescent at night, and painted with bright vibrant colors during the day, contributed to an enchanted-looking land.

Bordered on all sides by the ocean, Valdere was a massive island, a place that many diverse creatures called home. It had rainforests, mountains, plains, and sprawling forests. Although

Scythadon was not far from the ocean, Thadarack had never seen it. He'd wanted to visit the ocean his entire life.

He had heard of the ocean's beauty from those around Scythadon who were lucky enough to see it. He had asked his father numerous times to take him, but the answer always remained no. "It's too dangerous," he always said.

Eastern Valdere was covered by the Great Forest, a vast and dense forest that stretched northeast, beginning just north of the Vlax Pass. It always mystified Thadarack how tall some of the trees were. The trunks were thick with roots that dug deep into the land. *If only they could speak*, he'd think to himself. *I wonder what they'd say?*

And the vegetation, *mmm*, thought Thadarack as he scanned the seemingly never-ending and vast area of plants before him. It was more food than one could eat in a lifetime.

Unfortunately, he only got to taste wild-grown on trips away from the city like these. On any other day, he had to eat from the farm inside the city's walls. *Wild grown tastes better than farm-grown.*

Thadarack quickly caught himself drifting and didn't want to waste this time with his father. "Why was the Carne our enemy?" he asked. "Why couldn't we live together in peace?"

After a lengthy pause and a deep sigh, the King spoke. "The Carne believed us to be inferior—weaker and less intelligent beings. That and their lust for power made us natural enemies. They've tried to kill and subjugate our kin since the dawn of time. They viewed us as nothing more than a food source; the same as the animals that live and crawl in the wild."

Thadarack's heart began to race as he felt a tingle down his spine. He knew there was evil and danger out in the world, but hearing his father speak this way made it all feel too real…and too close to home. "Is there no way that they could eat greens and seeds like us?" he asked. "Why do they have to eat meat?"

"That's how they survive," answered the King. "It would be one thing if they only ate animals and fish, for they are dimwitted and senseless, but the Carne feel we are no better. They need flesh to sustain their being and because of their hate for us, it's natural we're pitted against one another."

"If they are so evil, why did Thrifsaer even bother to build the Wall?" Thadarack asked. "Why didn't he just get rid of them all?"

"He wanted to," King Thax said. "But the death toll was too great for him to carry on. The Southern Peninsula was and always has been a stronghold of the Carne. He viewed invading and trying to take it over as too great a risk. Many more Viridi would have been slain in the process. With their leader dead, he believed that they no longer posed any real threat. Our Wall has proved him correct."

"I guess that makes sense," said Thadarack.

"It does," said King Thax. "We couldn't invade, so the next best thing was to keep them out. But enough talk of the Carne. They aren't a threat any longer. Girozz says they are fighting among one another again and that their world is in chaos."

"But how do we still know that?" Thadarack asked. "Girozz hasn't been there in fifteen years."

"We just do," said King Thax. "But I don't want you to worry about the Carne. Our focus now is on this fruitless war between the Stegokin and Trikin. We should head back to Scythadon anyway. It's getting late."

Thadarack didn't want to leave, but he knew his father had to return. After all, running a kingdom was a full-time job.

"Okay, Father," he said reluctantly.

By now, night had fully set in. The moon shone brightly and together with the starlight, illuminated the valley majestically. After a few more moments of enjoying the serene view, they began their journey home.

CHAPTER TWO

HOMECOMING

The walk back to Scythadon didn't take long. The valley was part of the Eastern Road and only a few miles away, a straightforward enough journey as any. On the way, Thadarack and his father engaged in small talk, but no matter what they discussed, Thadarack couldn't stop thinking about the Great War. He wanted to know more but decided not to ask his father any further questions. *I've had enough excitement for tonight,* he thought.

The two Scythekin saw a shimmer of light as they approached the city. They soon entered the vast Scythadon Glade, a purposeful clearing of dense shrubs, trees, and mushrooms, so the guards had an unobstructed view should the city ever be attacked.

The clearing surrounded the entire city and extended all the way to the banks of the Scythadon River. The river itself almost entirely surrounded the clearing, forming a crescent around it with the only means of access coming from the Eastern Road. The deep river acted like a natural barrier and moat, aiding in the protection of Scythadon.

As the pair got closer, the lit pyres atop the city wall illuminated their way. Thadarack noticed a guard overlooking one of the pyres, and although still somewhat shaken from the discussion with his father, he felt a sense of calmness set in. He was home, the safest place he could be.

The guard greeted them warmly. "Welcome back, my King." She then glanced at Thadarack. "And to you as well, my Prince."

"Anything to report?" King Thax asked.

"No, nothing but a few small rodents scurrying about. Other than that, it's been as beautiful a night as any." The guard turned and looked down behind the wall. "Open the gate! The King and the Prince have returned!"

Thadarack watched as the front boulder gate slowly rolled aside. It was so massive that it took a minimum of four guards to move. While he waited, he looked at the walls of the city and immediately felt a sense of pride. The work of great minds and hard-working claws, the walls were a true testament to the abilities of the Scythekin.

Like the Wall at the Vlax Pass, the city walls were made of great oaks, fallen and layered on top of one another horizontally. Mud and straw were mixed, dried to make cob, and then applied to the gaps between the oaks to keep them secure. Too many thick logs to count were fastened together this way, creating the marvelous structure that protected Scythadon from the outside world.

The same process was completed on the inside of the city wall, but with fewer logs. Smaller platforms were created this way, allowing the guards to climb atop them and peer out over the main wall.

Thadarack shifted his gaze to the pyres. Built upon the flat surfaces of large-weathered boulders, the pyres were placed in carved out portions of the top log on the wall. Certain guards were specifically tasked with caring for the pyres, ensuring they didn't burn out.

Thadarack became hypnotized by the heat light, amazed at how it fluttered uncontrollably, desperately trying to escape up into the sky with the bats and birds. *Incredible*, he thought. It was just one more feat that set his species apart from the non-sentient animals.

He'd heard stories about how his ancestors captured the heat light, subduing and harnessing its power for themselves following a great storm. Keeping it fed and bright took work, but it was well worth it. The heat light's only enemies were hunger and rain, both of which were avoidable with proper care.

Thadarack tilted his head slightly and looked at the transplanted mushrooms, a spectacle in their own right. Replanted just inside the walls, the mushrooms towered over each pyre to shield the heat light from rain.

Nighttime was Thadarack's favorite time to visit the walls. He loved how the heat light roared underneath the luminescent blue and pink glow of the mushrooms. The sight was mesmerizing, captivating the gazes of all those who witnessed it for the first time.

The Prince's trance-like state was abruptly broken when his father spoke loudly to the guard atop the wall. "Where is Septirius? I need to speak with him."

Septirius was the captain of the city guard. Although a little smaller than the typical Scythekin, he was an exceptional fighter, distinguished by his strength and discipline. He had been the captain for as long as Thadarack could remember, maybe even before he was born. As the captain, he was also in charge of the defense of the Wall at the Vlax Pass.

"He's still recovering in the Mending House," said the guard. "I believe he is to be discharged soon."

Thadarack grew concerned and turned toward his father. "Is Septirius okay? What happened?"

Although worried about Septirius' well-being, Thadarack found some solace in knowing that his kin were great healers. The ability to utilize their forelimbs allowed them to do things other Viridi weren't capable of. From sophisticated building to the application of healing ointments, there really wasn't much that the Scythekin couldn't do.

Depending on the specific job a Scythekin had, their claws were adjusted appropriately, allowing them to efficiently carry out the task they needed to perform. In the case of the healers, their claws were trimmed and filed down to create smooth-rounded ends. This ensured they could apply the healing ointment effectively.

King Thax turned and met his son's glance. "Septirius is fine. He's just recovering from some wounds he got while fighting a few Carne at the Vlax Pass. It's nothing for you to worry about."

Thadarack was relieved. He felt safe whenever Septirius was around, knowing the captain put his all into protecting Scythadon. He had just returned from a month-long trip to the Wall, an exceptionally long time compared to the rotations required of the guards. Although they only spent a week there, the guards couldn't wait to come home to see their families. As sad as it was, Septirius didn't have a family. His job was his family, and the care he took regarding it was evident to all those he did his utmost to protect.

"I'm glad he's okay," said Thadarack.

"Me too," said King Thax. "I can't imagine what it would do to the morale of our guards if..." The King's voice trailed off. "I'm just glad he's home."

Once the gate was moved aside, the pair walked into the city. The King nodded toward the guards as he and Thadarack passed by.

Just inside the walls and before any homes, Thadarack looked upon the vast farm before him. All kinds of vegetation were grown and cared for by the city cultivators here. Cycads were his favorite, delicious leaves and seeds alike, plentiful and abundant around the farm.

The farm was so filled with vegetation that the rest of the city was hidden. For someone who visited for the first time, they would surely wonder where all the Scythekin lived and slept. The city itself looked like a forest when walking in through the front gate.

As they made their way through the farm, Thadarack caught his first glimpse of the Scythekin homes. They were constructed similarly to the city wall but made with smaller logs. The roofs were lined with many branches, progressively getting thinner from one end to the other. This natural slant was topped off with a mixture of brush, needles, and cob to ensure a rainproof enclosure.

Pyres and transplanted mushrooms lined the home front in

an orderly fashion, illuminating the city for great distances in all directions. As they walked by, Thadarack once again watched the heat light flicker in the breeze. *It never gets old,* he thought.

After passing the last of the homes, they came upon the city hub. The place where Scythadonians gathered to eat, talk, and spend quality time together, the city hub was always sprawling with activity during the day. But at this time of the night, there were very few Scythekin present. Those that saw Thadarack and his father donned warm smiles, and nodded toward them as they walked through.

After the city hub, they headed for the Scythadon Palace, located at the back of the city. As Scythadon's crown jewel, the palace was so magnificent that all who came to the city, whether it was for trade or rest, admired its beauty and complexity.

At its center stood the Sacred Oak, a massive tree from which the rest of the palace was built. Although the process of using logs, branches, and cob was the same, it was the largest structure in the entire city.

The palace had four wooden spires that jetted up toward the sky along with beautiful carvings that adorned its facade. Thadarack's favorite was the intricate carving of the Hallowed Lumina, a colossal luminescent mushroom in the center of Valdere, said to have given life to all living things. He glanced at it for a moment before shifting his eyes toward the carving of Thrifsaer. *There he is,* he thought, with a smile on his face. *Our hero.*

To the right of the palace was the Sacred Grove, the place where the King and his council met to discuss important matters. Grown from scratch, it was made with over a dozen weeping willows, creating a secluded and quiet place for council meetings. Hundreds of dogwood shrubs were grown around the willows, forming a dense thicket that provided even more privacy for the council. The only way into the Sacred Grove was via a long path carved straight through the thicket. Two guards stood at the front and two guards stood at the rear, ensuring nobody but the King and the council entered.

To the left of the palace, the Royal Garden flourished with beautiful flowers such as cosmos, tulips and gardenia. The aroma emitted by the garden made the entire city smell pleasant. Although ordinary Scythadonians weren't allowed in the palace or Sacred Grove, they were welcome to walk the Royal Gardens whenever they pleased.

Now in front of the palace, King Thax turned toward Thadarack. "You should go get some rest," he said. "Don't forget, you start your combat training in the morning."

Thadarack had entirely forgotten about his combat training. Once a Scythekin turned fifteen, it was required that they learned how to fight. Even though they hadn't been in a war for a thousand years, it was deemed prudent to be ready. The looming war with the Trikin proved this true.

A typical fifteen-year-old Scythekin would learn how to fight at the garrison, not too far from the Royal Gardens. However, as the Scythekin Prince, Thadarack would have private training lessons in a small, secluded area just behind the palace. His father wanted to ensure that he had uninterrupted time to train and focus.

Just when Thadarack opened his mouth to speak, he heard a feminine voice call to him from behind. "Thadarack!" the voice shouted. He turned around and saw his mother, Queen Consort Luxren, approaching.

"Well, I'm off to the Mending House," said King Thax. "I need to speak with Septirius before we leave for Stegodor in the morning."

Thadarack turned back to his father. "Isn't he coming with you?" he asked.

"No," said the King. "He's to stay behind to ensure we are prepared, just in case."

"Prepared for what?" Queen Luxren asked, now standing right beside them. "I hope you're not referring to going to war with the Trikin."

"We must be prepared," said the King. "We don't know what will come of this meeting. I hate to say it, but it could lead to war."

The Queen rolled her eyes and glanced at Thadarack. "We aren't going to war with the Trikin," she said. "I'm sure of it."

"I'm not," challenged the King. "We'll try our best to avoid war, but I'm not sure either side will agree to peace. I'm hopeful but not certain."

"I'll make them agree," said Queen Luxren. "They will listen to reason."

The King shot the Queen a glance, conveying he wasn't entirely convinced. "That's what I love about you," he said. "You're always so convinced that others will do the right thing."

He turned and looked at Thadarack. "And you, don't stay up too late. You'll need a good night's rest. Tomorrow will be a long day. Remember, becoming an effective fighter takes time, hard work, and patience. You won't master everything right away.

Take it slow, listen, focus, and execute. I have faith in you, my son. You will do well."

The young Prince was glad his father spoke in such a way. He rarely had faith in himself. He wanted to do well and succeed just like his father...just like Thrifsaer. But he was nervous for tomorrow and wasn't sure whether it would go well.

He had been excited about his combat training for a long while, but now that it was finally here, he was afraid he would let his father down. Worst of all, he was scared he wouldn't look ready to ascend to the throne one day. He wanted to be king, he really did. But Thadarack knew he wasn't ready, and if he was being honest with himself, he hoped he wouldn't become king for a long time.

"Thank you, father," he said. "I'll do my best."

King Thax smiled. "I know you will."

The King leaned over and rubbed his beak alongside the Queen's. "I'll see you in a little while." He leaned back. "I love you both."

Thadarack's father headed toward the Mending House, the Scythadon hospital located at the back of the city. Strategically built far from the hectic bustle of everyday life, the Mending House was where the wounded and sick went to recover.

The Scythekin healers were exceptionally skilled, completing a rigorous two-year-long training program that was overseen by the Healing Elder, Medicus. Besides joining the army or city guard, which had been voluntary since the Great War, there was no nobler profession. Anyone could enroll in the program, but only a few could pass the difficult training curriculum.

"My son," said the Queen warmly, stealing Thadarack's gaze.

"You are growing up. I can't believe you start your combat training in the morning."

Thadarack was the Queen's only child, and as such, he was the most precious thing in her life. She loved him dearly and wasn't shy about showing it. She often hugged and embarrassed him in front of his friends. Deep down, however, he was content, happy that his mother loved him so.

The Queen was also incredibly smart and King Thax's rock, helping him through times of sorrow and stress. She was a beautiful Scythekin, and whenever she entered a room or public space, everything around her became hazy.

Although stunning during the daytime, nighttime is what really captured the Queen's beauty. Her silvery metallic feathers gleamed under the moonlight, and her matching eyes had the power to stop others dead in their tracks.

Thadarack wished he got his mother's looks but was instead a spitting image of his father. A boring mixture of gray and tan feathers covered his body, and his eyes were the typical golden yellow that most Scythekin had.

In every way, Queen Luxren was a glorious queen and loved by all those she touched. Her subjects admired her, for her kindness and aura were second to none. But to Thadarack, she was his mother. And he loved her very much.

"I know," said Thadarack. "I've been waiting for this forever."

The Queen moved in closer to her son and wrapped her warm arms around him, squeezing him tight. Two Scythekin hugging was quite the spectacle. Although an action to show compassion, it sometimes left a scratch or two on the backs of those partaking.

If one wasn't careful where their claws ended up, the other was in for a real treat. The Queen, however, had mastered the hug, having hugged her son so many times before. Amid the affection, she spoke once more. "Don't grow up too fast," she whispered in his ear. "Enjoy your childhood for as long as you can." She then leaned away.

"Mother," said Thadarack. "How are you so confident that we won't go to war?"

"I just am," said the Queen. "I will do everything in my power to make both King Sturklan and Queen Cerathorn agree to peace."

Although unsure how she could be so confident, Thadarack was relieved. *She must know something*, he thought. *Even if she won't tell me.* He decided he'd rather leave it at that and trusted his mother could convince them to do what was right. Besides, his mind was still stuck on the discussion he had with his father. "How much do you know about the Great War?" he asked. "The Great War of Extinction?"

The Queen glared at her son. "Why do you ask?"

"Father told me all about it," said Thadarack. "He told me everything that happened between the Carne and us. He told me about the Steg—"

"Stop," the Queen interrupted sternly. "He told you...everything?"

Thadarack was about to answer his mother when it dawned on him. Did his father tell him everything? He wasn't entirely sure. "Well, I think so," he said. "He told me about how the Trikin abandoned the Stegokin and how the Scythekin saved them. He told me why the Carne don't like us and about Orzligorn the—"

"That's enough!" the Queen shouted, clearly upset that her mate told such things to her son. "There was no need to tell you all that, at least not yet."

"But Mother, I am to rule Scythadon one day. Shouldn't I know?"

"You just turned fifteen!" The Queen relaxed a bit. "You're still only a child...my child. And besides, the Carne are but a nuisance...all but forgotten beasts that we claw away from time to time. We mustn't concern ourselves with them."

Thadarack opened his beak in disbelief. "What about Gwon?" he asked. "He's one of my best friends. He's not a beast."

The Queen shot Thadarack an apologetic look. "I'm sorry," she said. "You're right. Gwon is not a beast, nor is his father. I'm just a little annoyed. The King shouldn't have told you all that."

Thadarack wanted to push back, but he could tell his mother was distraught. Whenever she referred to his father as "the King," it meant she was mad. She didn't get mad often, but when she did, it made him feel uncomfortable. She was usually the calm one, always pleasant to be around...and rarely ever yelled. He decided he wouldn't irritate her further.

"Why don't we learn about it in school, though?" he asked. "We aren't taught anything about the Great War or the Carne."

"Why scare everyone?" said the Queen promptly. "There's no point. The Carne are nothing. They're not even worth talking about."

I suppose that makes sense, Thadarack thought.

"But you should go," the Queen continued. "Get some rest

for tomorrow. I'm going for a walk around the city before I turn in. I love you, my son."

"I love you, too," said Thadarack.

With a gentle scratch of her right index claw against his beak, Thadarack's mother turned and headed away from the palace, disappearing behind homes in the distance. He then made his way into the palace.

It had four rooms in total, the biggest of which was the greens room, the first room upon entering. This was where the royal family entertained company, ate, and relaxed after a long day.

To the left was the royal chamber, the place where the King and Queen slept. To the right was Thadarack's chamber. As he made his way to it, he stopped and looked toward the fourth room against the far wall. For a moment, he thought about what it would have been like if his sister had survived. His parents never talked about what happened to her egg. All he knew was that it cracked prematurely.

With a newfound sadness, he made his way into his chamber and over to his bed, a comfortable combination of straw and leaves. He laid down with his head on his forearms and his tail wrapped around his torso. It was not long before he was sound asleep.

CHAPTER THREE

COMING OF AGE

Thadarack awoke the next morning just as the sun rose, casting its rays in-between the small cracks of cob in his chamber walls. He got up and headed for the greens room, expecting to see his mother and father eating their breakfast just like every other morning.

This morning, however, the greens room was empty. There was nobody in sight. He walked across the large room and stopped just short of the royal chamber. "Are you two awake?" he called gently. "Mother? Father?"

There wasn't any answer.

He turned and walked over to the table, a large, weathered boulder placed in the back of the room. There were some greens and seeds on top of it. He assumed his parents had left them there for him and ate his fill.

Usually, Thadarack didn't eat breakfast in the palace. He preferred the company of his friends and ate with them in the city hub. Today was different, though. He remembered his training, and as soon as he was full, he made his way out of the palace.

"Prince Thadarack," said a voice approaching from his right. "Are you ready?"

Thadarack turned and saw Arkonius. A big fellow, Arkonius was one of the best fighters in all of Scythadon, and as such, he was one of the best trainers. Although he was getting on in age, he could still hold his own in a fight.

"The King has asked me to train you," Arkonius continued. "I trust you already ate breakfast?"

"Yes, I have," said Thadarack.

Arkonius smirked. "I hope you didn't eat too much. A full stomach and battle training don't go claw in claw."

"I'll be okay. Have you seen my mother and father?"

It wasn't like his parents not to greet him in the morning. They usually stuck to a specific schedule, and were always in the middle of breakfast when Thadarack woke up.

Arkonius shook his head. "No, but the guards said they left well before sunrise this morning. It appeared they were in a rush."

"I'm surprised they didn't wake me to say goodbye."

"They probably didn't want to bother you, considering your training starts today. Being well rested is the first step to success."

"But why do you think they left so early?" Thadarack asked.

"I'm sure they just wanted to get to Stegodor without delay," said Arkonius. "Everyone's on edge lately at the possibility of joining the war."

"What do you think? Do you think we'll join the war? Or do you think they will arrive at a peaceful agreement?"

"The Stegokin and Trikin arrive at a peaceful agreement?"

Thadarack sensed the sarcasm in Arkonius' voice. "Never. I think they've only agreed to this so-called peace talk to make it *look* like they're considering peace. I don't think either will actually consider it."

"My mother thinks they will," said Thadarack. "She's convinced that they'll stop fighting."

Arkonius smiled. "The Queen is very optimistic. That's one reason she's so highly thought of. But I don't see an end to this war anytime soon."

Thadarack shivered as uneasiness set in. Arkonius seemed so confident that the war would rage on. Thadarack hoped he was wrong, but Arkonius was very wise and well-respected around the city. It troubled the young Prince how sure he seemed that there wouldn't be peace.

"But enough talk of the war," Arkonius continued. "Let's begin with your training. Follow me."

Arkonius was a talented fighter, spending most of his time training others. Thadarack hoped he would be able to fight like him, but his anxiety quickly overwhelmed him. His body tensed, and he had a slightly difficult time breathing. On top of that, Arkonius was known to be tough. Almost too tough, always intimidating those he taught.

Although a great trainer, Thadarack had seen how he trained others. They didn't need to catch on right away, but Arkonius would push them until they did…sometimes all day and without a break.

The pair walked to a small clearing behind the palace. When they got there, Thadarack saw a large stump right in the center of it. It had about fifteen or so black lines painted on it in groups of three.

"Okay, your first lesson includes mastering agility and precision," said Arkonius. "In a fight, the placement of a slash could mean the difference between life and death. If you miss, you might not have a second chance."

Thadarack's heart sank. This was all starting to feel too real to him. He looked at Arkonius and could tell he was as serious as he could be. *This is it*, he thought. *I've finally grown up.*

"You see these markings on the stump?" Arkonius gestured toward them with his right claws. "These resemble claw slashes. In relation to this lesson, they're the weak spots on a Carne."

Arkonius paused for a moment and glanced at the markings. "I suppose we could say they're weak spots on Trikin too."

He paused again and opened his mouth, looking as if he was going to say something else but sighed and closed it instead. Was he going to make a comment about the current war? Thadarack was curious, but before he could ask anything, Arkonius spoke.

"We won't focus on what those weak spots are just yet. But the marks will become your marks, your very slashes. The goal in this first lesson is to perform the duck, dodge, and strike attack. Although it appears simple, this one move can save your life. Your objective is to strike the marks at exactly the same place."

Thadarack listened as Arkonius continued explaining the lesson. It sounded fairly straightforward, and the more Arkonius talked, the more Thadarack felt he'd be able to do it.

Duck, dodge, and strike, he thought. *How hard can that be?* His anxiety about the training slowly began to wane. He thought about how he was related to Thrifsaer and grew confident that he'd be able to pass this first lesson. A smile passed over his face as he listened to Arkonius intently.

"Now, let me demonstrate. You're right clawed, correct?" Thadarack nodded.

"Okay, you will master this move with both claws, but let's first practice with your dominant one. Study the mark and focus on how you need to move to strike it successfully."

Thadarack watched Arkonius get into position. He bent his legs, raised his arms, and then slightly bent his elbows as well. In an instant, almost too fast for Thadarack to even see, he ducked to the right, rolled on his back, jumped in the air, and slashed with such strength that he shook the stump almost to the point of tipping it over.

Roll! Thadarack thought. *He didn't say anything about rolling!* He looked at the black mark Arkonius aimed for but didn't see it. He could have sworn there was a black mark where Arkonius' deep claw gashes were on the stump. Then it dawned on him, Arkonius had hit it so perfectly, that the black mark was now gone.

"Now, it's your turn," said Arkonius. "You don't always have to jump. Depending on how the Carne…or Trikin…are charging you, keeping your feet planted might make more sense. For the sake of this training, we'll begin with your feet planted. Once you successfully complete your right claw, we will practice with your left. At first, your left will feel very unnatural, but the more you practice, the more it will come to you. Now stand here and strike this mark."

Arkonius gestured to a low mark on the stump. "Keep your feet planted after you roll."

Thadarack walked toward the stump and stopped just before

it. Although Arkonius was now behind him, he could feel his gaze upon his back. *There's no way I'm going to get this*, he thought with a bout of panic. *How can I stall?*

After a few moments of trying to think of something to say or do, he finally came to terms with the fact that he wasn't getting out of this. He decided it wouldn't be the end of the world if he failed…at least not at first. That gave him some solace. *What's the worst that could happen?*

"Oh, and one more thing," said Arkonius. "I put a lot of strength behind my strike, but I am a seasoned veteran. Strength will come with time. For now, just focus on hitting the mark, even if it's not that hard."

Thadarack looked at the black mark that Arkonius had pointed to. It looked easy enough to hit, didn't it? He got in the same position as Arkonius, took a deep breath, ducked, and rolled…or so he thought. With a tremendous thud, Thadarack crashed to the ground so hard that he saw stars.

He was in pain…already. He didn't even get to strike, never mind hit the mark. After a brief moment of him lying there on the ground with his eyes closed, Thadarack heard Arkonius' voice. "Well, young Prince. That was surely a sight. Rise to your feet and allow me to show you again."

Thadarack heard both surprise and disappointment in his trainer's voice. He had never rolled before; he never had any reason to. Arkonius made it look so easy.

He slowly rose to his feet and blinked his eyes many times, trying to clear the stars and dizziness from his vision. Once he came to, he watched Arkonius follow through with the attack seamlessly, almost as fast as the blink of an eye.

"Now, try again," said Arkonius. "Remember, focus on form and accuracy. All else will come with practice."

Try again? Thadarack was in pain. His back ached and he now had a throbbing headache. He didn't want to try again, but he wouldn't dare say that to Arkonius. He got into position, ducked, and rolled…and same as before, hit the ground with a thud. This time, though, he at least rolled around to his front side.

Thadarack didn't move. He was sprawled out on the ground, too ashamed to roll over and look Arkonius in the eye. Instead, he lay there motionless, woefully waiting for his trainer to speak.

Arkonius let out a lengthy sigh. "I suppose we need to first focus on our rolling. Get back up. Try to focus on simply rolling this time. I'll show you once more."

Although subtle, he could once again sense the disappointment in Arkonius' tone of voice. Thadarack was so embarrassed. All he wanted to do was return to his chamber. The one silver lining was that nobody else was here to witness his failures. His training had barely begun, and he already felt like a letdown.

It didn't feel natural to roll, not at all. Was his body even made for rolling? He tried to tuck his long neck down like Arkonius, but it just didn't feel right. He pulled several muscles in it, and his claws also hurt from jamming into the ground awkwardly. And his tail…he had never felt so much pain in his entire life.

Despite his failures, however, Thadarack could tell that Arkonius was going easy on him; the only logical explanation was that he was the King's son, and in turn, his prince. Thadarack heard Arkonius during his training sessions at the garrison. He was never this gentle, even on the young Scythekin that caught on quickly. That made Thadarack feel even worse. Or did it? Not only was he failing, but he was receiving special treatment. He slowly rose to his feet and turned toward his trainer.

"Watch," said Arkonius sternly. "This is how you roll."

Arkonius slowly demonstrated the motion from start to finish. Thadarack then tried again and was met with similar results. He tried again, again, and again. For all the failed rolls, though, there was one thing that Thadarack wasn't failing at. One thing that was actually growing within him the more and more he tried.

At the time, he didn't realize it because he was in serious pain. But it was his motivation. His motivation to improve is what drove him. Well, that coupled with the intimidating stares from Arkonius, who was clearly beginning to lose his patience.

He practiced his roll all through the morning and into midday. Finally, after countless hours of practice, Arkonius had him begin the original lesson again.

Thadarack stood in position in front of the stump. He ducked, rolled, and swung his right claws as hard as he could. He hit the stump before him, but he missed the black mark that Arkonius had singled out earlier.

After a few more attempts and for the first time since the lesson began, Thadarack noticed how hungry and thirsty he was. He turned around and hoped that he could take a break but was only met with two dissatisfied eyes gazing right back at him.

"Again!" Arkonius yelled.

By now, the tough and demanding side of Arkonius had begun to show. He was no longer babying the young Prince. He was being himself, which was evident in the way he started to yell and act. He probably didn't even realize that his usual training approach was bubbling to the surface.

Although Thadarack's instincts told him to turn around and try again, his pain, hunger, and thirst forced open his mouth. "I think it's past lunchtime," he said to the menacing glare of Arkonius. "Can I just get some water an—"

"Of course not!" Arkonius thundered. "Do you think the Carne or Trikin will allow you to 'just get some water'?"

Thadarack didn't know what to do. He had never been scolded like this before, and if he was being honest, he didn't particularly like it. There wasn't anything that he was going to say, though. He was too afraid of what Arkonius' reaction would've been.

"Again! Go again until you hit the mark! You cannot stop until you get this right!"

Exhausted, Thadarack turned around and got into position with his eyes dead set on the mark. *I'll get it this time,* he thought, lining up his strike.

Just as he was about to duck and roll, Arkonius suddenly bellowed from behind, startling the young Prince so much that he became disoriented. Similarly to earlier this morning, he fell to the ground with a thud, completely taken by surprise.

"Do you think in the heat of battle you have that much time to line up your strike?" Arkonius yelled.

Thadarack desperately tried to rise to his feet as quickly as he could. "I—,"

"You don't! The enemy will throw you to the ground and kill you before you even know what happened!"

Thadarack rose to his feet, embarrassed by his shortcomings.

He wanted to succeed more than anything. He longed to be a good fighter, just like his father. But all of this made him feel weak, and he questioned whether he'd succeed after all.

He wasn't a quick learner, and if his grades in school were any indication, he wasn't the brightest Scythekin that ever lived. He didn't have any specific skills, and he was only an average size for his age.

His motivation was the only thing he had. A quality that he hoped might be enough to end up setting him apart from those around him. But even that seemed like a stretch.

"I'm not trying to be tough on you," said Arkonius, in a much calmer voice. "I'm trying to prepare you for what's out there. The danger that you'll come across. And you will come across danger."

Thadarack snickered inside. "Tough" didn't even begin to describe how this day was going. It was the hardest and most painful day of his life. He performed the same attack over and over, desperately trying to hit the mark. He got close once or twice, and those times, Arkonius was surprisingly encouraging. But most of the time, he just yelled.

Before Thadarack knew it, late afternoon was approaching. He had been training for the better part of the day, trying as hard as he could to perfect the attack. He finally got really close to the mark, becoming excited and more motivated to do it again.

"That's it!" Arkonius shouted. "It's all about repetition. Your enemy will attack from all different angles. Knowing the right way to move and the best placement for your strike is paramount. Repeat that exact move, and then we will begin training with your left claws."

Determined, Thadarack stared at the stump, sizing up the black mark for what felt like the millionth time. He got back into position, ducked, rolled, and...just as he was about to strike, he was rammed from behind, slashing his claws in no particular direction out of sheer desperation. He fell to the ground with a bang, missing both the mark and stump.

"You must always be aware of your surroundings," said Arkonius, in an unexpectedly gentle voice. "The enemy won't *let* you strike them, especially if you're fighting more than one."

Excruciating pain shot through Thadarack's whole body. This time, he made no attempt at getting up, hoping that the sharp pain he felt in his back and thighs would subside. He was more than embarrassed now; he was devastated and angry. "You could have warned me," he said frustratedly.

Arkonius scoffed. "Ha! Do you think your enemy will warn you before they attack you from behind? This is all supposed to prepare you for battle. You must be cognizant of everything around you."

"But I wasn't even expecting you—"

"It doesn't matter! You must always be ready! Even your friends, those you think you can trust, can turn on you when you least expect it. Never let your guard down, not even for a minute."

Arkonius then paused. He must have realized the young Prince was in serious pain. As he turned his head slightly, Thadarack saw him gesture to a nearby waterhole. "Go ahead now, take a drink. You have earned it."

Thadarack slowly rose to his feet, wincing as he did so. He hobbled to the waterhole, submerged his beak, and began to drink. *My friends will never betray me,* he thought. *No chance at all.*

"We'll wrap up here for today," said Arkonius. "You seem like you've had enough."

That's an understatement, Thadarack thought as he continued drinking. To think the young Scythekin was ever looking forward to his battle training was laughable now. He drastically improved as the day went on, but he was ready to get some food and wanted to go straight to sleep.

"Take a day to rest and regain your strength," continued Arkonius. "We'll pick back up at sunrise the day after tomorrow."

Thadarack had never felt so relieved. He had no idea how he'd be able to do this again tomorrow. He was even concerned about his ability to do this again in two days. He considered asking for an additional day or two of rest but quickly put that thought out of his mind. He had been scolded enough for today as it was.

"You need to take this seriously. I know it's hard work, but you need to focus and learn. It's not an option. Do you understand?"

Thadarack nodded while continuing to drink.

"Do you understand?" Arkonius yelled. "Look me in the eye and say it!"

Startled, Thadarack stopped drinking and looked at his trainer. "Yes, I understand."

"Good," said Arkonius. "Learning to fight is the most important thing you will learn in your entire life. I would argue it's even more essential than learning how to lead a kingdom. One move, or lack thereof, could mean your life coming to an end. In an abrupt instant, you could be dead. Worse, you could be a Carne's dinner."

Arkonius' words shook the young Prince. *Dinner?* That was the most revolting thing he had ever heard. Arkonius must have seen his disturbed reaction because he didn't stop there.

"Upsetting, isn't it?" he said. "Imagine being picked apart by a Carne. Not a great thought, is it? That's why I've been so hard on you all day. I know I can be tough at times, but I need to get across how critical it is that you learn how to defend yourself. Especially you, Prince Thadarack. One day you will be the most important Scythekin, one of the most indispensable Viridi leaders in all of Valdere. All of us will look up to you."

Thadarack was stuck on "being picked apart," having lost his appetite entirely. He dry-heaved as he quickly tried to think about something else. That something else, though, quickly found *him*. Every time he moved, the pain he felt in his back shot through his body like the piercing of a claw.

Even though he was relieved the day was over and he had a break tomorrow, he was still upset with how he performed on his first day of training. But at least he had another day or two to improve before his parents returned from Stegodor. By the time they got back, he hoped he'd be much better.

"The King mentioned he wants to bring you to the Wall soon," said Arkonius. "I'm not sure when, but I want to make sure you're ready. The Wall is a dangerous place."

"Have you ever been there?" Thadarack asked.

"Yes. I did many rotations at the Wall before you were born and had my fair share of engagements with the Carne. They're vile beasts and to survive against them, you have to be a flawless fighter. They are used to fighting as they do so against one another constantly. One mistake could mean death. I saw it happen firstclaw. Way too often..."

Thadarack could tell Arkonius was reliving some awful things that happened to him. His somber expression and heavy eyes said it all. "It's definitely not a place for the faint of heart. I've had many friends who fell by the jaws of the Carne."

"I'm sorry to hear that," said Thadarack.

"That's why it's so important that you learn how to fight effectively," said Arkonius. "There are many who think they are ready to face the Carne when they are anything but. I guess it's hard to know for certain if you're ready until it's too late. At least for the guards at the Wall."

"How many guards are usually there?"

"There are about two hundred or so. But with the looming war between us and the Trikin, many of the seasoned guards have been replaced with newer recruits. Septirius has brought many of the battle-hardened warriors back home, just in case they're needed here. I personally think it's a mistake, but Septirius is doing his best and what he thinks is right to keep Scythadon safe."

"Why do you think it's a mistake?"

Arkonius sighed. "We rely too much on Girozz's intel. I know your father trusts him, but I heard this last attack on the Wall was aggressive. The Carne seem to be growing bolder."

Arkonius paused and looked at the ground. "We lost four guards in the fight. I knew them...I trained them all."

He met Thadarack's eyes. "They had families back here in the city. They were taken well before their time."

"What did you mean by intel?" Thadarack asked. "You said we rely too much on Girozz's intel."

A ghastly expression passed over Arkonius' face. Thadarack realized that he may have said something he wasn't supposed to. "I was referring to what he told the King when he came here fifteen years ago. But let's not discuss this further. You need rest. We'll pick up where we left off in two days."

Thadarack could tell Arkonius was hiding something. Then it dawned on him. *Is that why my father is so certain the Carne aren't a threat? Does Girozz return to the Southern Peninsula to spy on the Carne?* The thought sent shivers down his spine. He thought about Gwon and how he must have no idea. If he had, he would have surely told him by now. Wouldn't he? They were best friends after all.

Before Thadarack had a chance to press him for more information, Arkonius had quickly gone. Thadarack's aching body didn't dare try to go after him. He was now alone, desperately trying to move in a way that resulted in the least amount of pain. He slowly made his way back into the palace and didn't even consider having dinner in the city hub with his friends like he usually did.

The Prince didn't want his friends to see him in such pain, nor did he want to talk about how his training went. As a matter of fact, he wasn't sure he'd even be able to make it to the city hub. He knew Gwon would be curious and would probably already be waiting for him.

Instead, Thadarack hobbled into the palace and ate his fill of the greens and seeds that the cultivators dropped off earlier in the day. He then headed straight for his chamber and laid down on his bed. Within a few moments, he was sound asleep.

The sun hadn't fully set yet and his room was still bright, but that didn't stop him. He was out; his body desperately trying to repair the damage it had taken throughout the difficult day. Little did he know that the next day would change his life. Not just in the near future or for a short while but forever. In a matter of hours, this life that he had known would be turned upside down.

CHAPTER FOUR

COMPANIONSHIP

Thadarack woke up the next morning well after sunrise and tried to rise to his feet but was met with sore and achy muscles. To his surprise, he had slept soundly through the night, having been so tired that not even his pain woke him up.

After it took a while to get up, he stood and stretched his arms and legs as best he could, fighting through the soreness and discomfort. He then made his way out of the palace and toward the city hub for breakfast. Some Scythadonians greeted him as he made his way to an empty boulder table.

As soon as he got to the table, a nearby Scythekin quickly approached him. "Good morning, Prince Thadarack," he said warmly. "Same order as always? We missed you yesterday."

"Yes," said Thadarack. "With some extra cycad seeds. I'm starving."

"Coming right up, my Prince."

As Thadarack waited for his food, he looked around and saw his fellow Scythadonians talking and smiling. Just seeing them so happy made the young Prince feel good. He loved it here and enjoyed the company much more so than the loneliness he often felt back in the palace, especially now that his parents were gone.

A few moments later, the Scythekin returned and placed Thadarack's food on the table. "Enjoy," he said.

The Scythekin departed and headed in the direction of a family of four that had just entered the city hub.

Just as Thadarack was about to eat, he saw his friend Gwon approaching. "So, how did it go?" he asked animatedly. "I was hoping you would come tell me last night. I've been dying to know how your training went! You must be very sore."

That's an understatement, Thadarack thought. He contemplated telling Gwon the truth about how bad his training went, but quickly decided against it. After all, who wants to look weak in front of their friends?

"It went pretty well," he said instead, placing the cycad leaf he had pinned to his right index claw down. "I'm very sore, though. Arkonius had me training for the better part of the day. I was exhausted and went straight to bed after."

"Arkonius, huh?" Gwon asked. "That must have been interesting. I'm glad that my father trains me."

"Eh, he wasn't too bad. I'm just glad to be training finally." Thadarack lied. But what does a little white lie hurt? Besides, he really thought he was going to improve.

"Good for you," said Gwon. "My father says I've improved drastically since we began. I feel much more confident in my skills now."

"That's great. I hope to get to where you are soon."

"You will, I'm sure of it. What attack move did you start with? I know the way Scythekin fight is different from how my father and I fight."

Thadarack didn't want to talk about his training anymore, but he could tell how excited his friend was for him. Learning to fight was a big deal, almost like a rite of passage to adulthood. He decided he'd entertain his friend but hoped only for a bit longer.

"He taught me the duck, dodge, and slash attack," said Thadarack. *Or was it strike?* he thought. He wasn't entirely sure what the name of the move was. All he really remembered was that 'roll' should most definitely be included in it.

"That's awesome," said Gwon. "You have to show me. Well, when you're feeling better."

"I will," Thadarack answered, hoping that wouldn't happen for a long time.

"My father says that fighting Trikin isn't all that different from fighting Carne," said Gwon. "If you can fight one, you can learn to fight the other."

"Well, I hope we don't have to fight either," said Thadarack. "At least not for a while."

"Speaking of fighting, when do you think they'll be back? They left extremely early yesterday morning. If my father hadn't woken me up by accident, he wouldn't have even said goodbye."

"I'm not sure," said Thadarack. "Probably not until tomorrow at the earliest. It's about a day and a half walk to Stegodor from here."

"I'm dying to know what's going to happen," said Gwon. "Half of us think we're going to war with the Trikin and the other half think there will be peace."

"Did your father say anything to you?" Thadarack asked. "About what he thinks will happen?"

"He thinks they'll agree to peace. But he was acting kind of strange before he left. I asked him if something was wrong, but he insisted nothing was."

"Acting strange? That's weird. I wonder why."

"I don't know," said Gwon. "I hope everything's okay. He's been going out on hunts a lot more lately. I want to go with him again, but he keeps insisting on being alone. I think he's scared that I'll frighten the Greatdeer away, but I've been practicing my hunting skills. I don't know. He's just been acting kind of weird lately."

Thadarack recalled his conversation with Arkonius about Girozz's intel. Based on what Gwon was saying, it was obvious he had no idea where his father actually went.

Thadarack knew of Girozz's hunts but now understood why he was gone so much. He'd be hunting for days sometimes, and this last time, he was gone for an entire week. When he returned, he told Gwon that the Greatdeer were getting scarcer. His excuse for being gone so long was that it was getting more difficult to find food.

This always seemed a little strange to Thadarack. How could the Greatdeer be getting scarcer when their only predators around these parts were Girozz and Gwon? Something didn't seem to add up. But now, it all made more sense. *Girozz must be spying on the Carne,* he thought. *That's what he does when he leaves for long periods of time.*

Thadarack debated telling his friend his thoughts but decided not to. Maybe he was wrong? Regardless, he didn't want to agitate Gwon, nor did he want to hinder their friendship. Maybe one day he would tell him, but that day wasn't going to be today.

"He's probably just stressed," Thadarack said. "I know my father is. My mother is somehow very confident that there will be peace."

"What do you think about the possibility of us having to join the war?" Gwon asked. "Did the King tell you anything interesting the other day on your walk to the valley?"

"He's concerned that if the war doesn't end soon, we will have to intervene. He's going to try his best to get them to agree to peace, but he's not very convinced they will."

"Well, I think peace is definitely the best way to go. But if it comes to it, I'm ready to fight the Trikin. I'd be more than willing to do my part."

Hearing his friend talk this way made Thadarack even more bothered that he had such a rough training lesson yesterday. He didn't want to fight the Trikin, and he knew he wasn't ready to fight anybody.

Gwon seemed so content with fighting; almost as though it came as second nature to him. He was always confident, no matter what it was about. Thadarack longed for that confidence.

"Me too," said Thadarack, now hoping he wouldn't have to tell a third white lie. "But hopefully it doesn't come to that."

"Well, I'm ready if it does," said Gwon. "But it is sad how Viridi are killing one another."

"I know. My father told me all about how the Viridi helped each other during the Great War. Has Girozz ever told you what happened?"

"Unfortunately," said Gwon. "I never wanted to talk about it because it's so awful. I'm ashamed of what the Carne did. I'm proud of who I am, but I'm not proud of what my kin are like.

Sometimes I wish I was a Viridi like you. I've even tried eating greens, but..." Gwon smirked. "I found them revolting...needless to say, they came back up as soon as they went down."

They both laughed, a pleasant sight to all those who witnessed it. A Scythekin prince and a Gigakin, the most unlikely of friends, talking peacefully to one another. It might have been said that they knew no differently, having grown up together ever since they could remember.

If not for the actions of their ancestors, the thought of strife occurring between their kinds wouldn't even be a thought. They'd live peacefully together, side by side, laughing and joking as best friends would.

"I guess I just wish that Viridi and Carne could get along," Gwon continued. "I don't understand why all Carne can't just eat animals like my father and I. The thought of eating Carne or Viridi is disturbing to me. And in a twisted way, it'd be kind of like eating myself..."

Thadarack saw Gwon's expression of befuddlement, assuming his friend had never thought about it that way before. "That's unsettling," he said disgustedly. "I can't believe Carne actually eat each other."

Gwon rolled his eyes and trilled his lips as his serrated teeth glistened in the sunlight.

"They do," he said, shaking his head. "It's embarrassing. You would think that after thousands of years, my kind would move past their savage ways. But nope, my father tells me Carne still don't get along among themselves. He says they have no problem killing, maiming, and eating one another. It's one of the main reasons he left. Well, along with…" Gwon paused for a moment. "I've never told you about my mother, have I?"

"No, you haven't," Thadarack said.

Gwon looked up at the sky as his eyes began to water. He opened his mouth a few times, but nothing came out. After another lengthy pause, Thadarack spoke instead. "You don't have to tell me. Let's talk about something else."

Gwon looked back at his friend. "It's not me," he said, clearly fighting back tears. "It's my father. He never talks about her, but when he does, he breaks down."

Gwon turned and looked out over the city hub. "My father and mother traveled with a group of Carne. They roamed all around the Southern Peninsula looking for a safe place to go. They didn't have a home, nor did they want one. Carne settlements are awful places. They wanted to live free and do as they pleased, not be subjected to the strife of typical Carne life. One day, fellow Carne attacked them, brigands whose sole purpose was to wreak havoc on anyone they came across. They didn't care that they were attacking their own kind."

Gwon looked down at the ground as a few tears rolled off his snout. He then looked back up at Thadarack. "I had just been born. I wasn't but one month old at the time. My mother hid me in the brush while the fighting ensued. One of the Carne saw me and charged my way. I remember nothing about her."

Gwon looked back down at the ground. "My mother gave her life to protect me. My father was the only one who made it back to me alive. He vowed to do everything he could to keep me safe. Not only because I'm his son but also in honor of my mother. He then renounced his Carne ways and brought me to the Wall, hoping to find asylum."

Gwon looked back up at his friend. "He never told me why your father accepted him, but I know he is beyond grateful. My father would do anything for his king and so would I. I would do anything for you too."

Thadarack smiled. "You know I'm going to name you my Right Claw when I'm crowned king." He took a deep breath. *When I'm crowned king*, he thought. He had never said those words out loud before and felt a rush of anxiety pour over him.

The thought of his father being gone and the fact that it would be *his* responsibility to ensure the safety of Scythadon made him nauseous. Everyone in Scythadon would look to him for guidance. They'd look to him for protection. They'd look to him for safety.

He realized he looked shaken and quickly tried to suppress his feelings, hoping his friend wouldn't notice.

"It'd be an honor," said Gwon in a serious tone. "I'll do everything I can to aid you in protecting this great city. I've been learning all I can from my father regarding warfare."

Thadarack knew Girozz was a great fighter, as strong as he was smart. He didn't know how he learned to fight so well, but he had heard he'd proven his abilities time and time again against other Carne at the Vlax Pass Wall.

"You should also talk to Dassius, my father's military advisor," said Thadarack. "Both of us could learn a lot about warfare from him. My father believes him to be a brilliant tactician. That's why he named him his Right Claw."

"I definitely will," replied Gwon. "I'm looking forward to engaging in my first fight. My father says I'm still not ready, but

I think I am."

Here we go again, Thadarack thought. *More talk about fighting.* He wasn't looking forward to his first fight...not in the slightest. The thought of fighting a Carne, or even a Trikin, sent chills down his spine. "I'm sure you are," he said.

"Who are you going to name your Left Claw?" Gwon asked. "Thexis?"

"Of course," said Thadarack in a way that conveyed it was an obvious fact. "She is so crafty and convincing. She will make an excellent Left Claw."

"I would be hurt if it was not so," said an approaching feminine voice.

Thadarack and Gwon looked to the side and saw their friend, Thexis, carrying a plentiful pile of leafy greens and seeds. She was slender for a Scythekin and even though this was common for the females, Thexis had an exceptionally petite figure.

Also rather pretty, she drew the attention of many. Her beak was shorter than average and her belly was slim, but her long neck and beautiful feathers protruding down her back espoused golden bronze and chestnut hues that shimmered in the daytime sun.

Thexis was gorgeous, and she knew it.

"Can you repeat that?" she asked, looking over at Thadarack with a grin. "That part about how I am...how did you put it...crafty?"

Thadarack and Gwon laughed as Thexis placed her lunch on the table.

"In all seriousness, though," continued Thexis. "I am honored that you would put me in charge of diplomacy. I will

61

not let you down and will always do what's best for Scythadon."

"You get that craftiness from your grandfather," said Gwon.

"My father told me that Paxtorr is a diplomatic genius."

"I think you're right," said Thexis. "He was the one who finally convinced King Sturklan and Queen Cerathorn to sit down to discuss peace."

"Well, that doesn't surprise me," said Gwon.

"Yeah, I really hope he's still on the council when I'm king," said Thadarack.

There he went again. *When I'm king.* The thought of becoming king was really getting to him. He had never said those words until today, and now he'd said them twice. He decided it wouldn't happen a third time.

"Speaking of the council, I'm still not really sure how it works," said Gwon. "Since I'm to be part of it, I should probably know."

Thadarack looked at Thexis, hoping she'd chime in. He should know how the council functioned, but he didn't. He immediately regretted not paying attention during his studies, but his sharp feeling of anxiety was quickly put at ease when Thexis began speaking.

"The council is currently made up of five members: the King, the Queen, the current Right and Left Claws of the King, and all other past Claws that are still alive. The number of members on the council can vary because of this. Sometimes there may be four, and other times there could be more. It depends on when a king dies and which Claws still draw breath. The King, of course, chooses his Right and Left Claws on coronation day. It's strongly believed, and rightfully so, that the wisdom of past

Claws is invaluable. Hence, they remain on the council for life when selected. That's why my grandfather is still part of it...even though he's ancient."

The three friends started laughing again.

"He sure is," said Gwon, smirking. "How old is he?"

"Honestly, I'm not sure," said Thexis. "I think we've lost count."

"Well, I'm glad we live longer than we used to," said Gwon. "My father said we would have been lucky to hit thirty years old back in the day."

"We have modern medicine to thank for that," said Thexis. "But I believe that's how old King Thaidrik was when he died."

"Paxtorr was his Left Claw, right?" Gwon asked.

Thadarack had always wished he knew his grandfather, King Thaidrik. His father, as well as the elders around the city, spoke very highly of him. He wasn't king for very long, but peace and prosperity marked his short reign. If not for him, Ceragorre and Stegodor may have gone to war much sooner. When he died at thirty from unknown natural causes, Thadarack had not been born yet.

"Yes," said Thexis. "I do feel bad for Sentrisia, but at least she gets to learn from the best."

"I'm not sure who that is," said Gwon.

"She's King Thax's Left Claw," said Thexis. "But since my grandfather is still alive, he remains the head diplomat. She's a little irrelevant right now, but she gets a lot of insight from him."

"What about my father?" Gwon asked with a puzzled expression on his face. "He isn't the Right or Left Claw. Nor was he ever one. He always attends the council meetings, though.

Why?"

"He's not officially part of the council," answered Thexis. "But he attends at the request of King Thax because he's a Carne."

Gwon looked even more perplexed. "What do you mean?"

"Oh, Gwon," said Thexis playfully. "The King feels like having a Carne attend the meetings is insightful. He can contribute a different point of view than the others on the council, especially when the matters involve your kin."

"Oh, that makes sense," said Gwon, nodding his head. "He never tells me anything about the council meetings."

"That's because it's forbidden," said Thexis. "Whatever is discussed in the meeting is between the council members and the King, nobody else. Only the King can decide if it is to be shared with all of us."

"Oh, I see," said Gwon. "So, who went to Stegodor? Did they all go?"

"Yes," said Thexis. "The King, the Queen, and the council, plus about twenty guards or so. Hoping to come across as non-threatening, my grandfather insisted no guards accompany them, but Dassius said it would be foolish to not bring any. He's afraid Queen Cerathorn might try something, considering her army will be there."

"Her army?" Thadarack asked. "What do you mean?"

"Your father didn't tell you? Queen Cerathorn's army will be camped not but a mile from Stegodor during the peace talks. Supposedly, that's the only reason she agreed to go."

"Wow," said Gwon. "I'm surprised King Sturklan would agree to that."

"Well, I doubt Queen Cerathorn would agree to meet in Stegodor without her army close by," said Thexis.

"That makes sense," said Gwon.

"Why wouldn't they just meet in a neutral place?" Thadarack asked. "Then none of that would be necessary."

"I don't know all the details," said Thexis. "I just know what Paxtorr told me."

"It does seem strange," said Gwon. "I guess the only logical explanation is because Stegodor is in between Scythadon and Ceragorre. And maybe King Sturklan refused to go anywhere else."

"Who knows," said Thadarack. "I just hope they stop fighting."

"Me too," said Thexis, looking over at Thadarack's food. "Are you going to eat that? Your cycad leaves look like they're drying out."

Thadarack had been so distracted from the conversation with his friends that he forgot he even had breakfast in front of him. As soon as Thexis pointed it out, his stomach began to rumble. "Yes," he said, stabbing a cycad leaf with his right index claw.

"Let's eat," said Thexis, scooping up a few confider seeds and putting them in her mouth.

The three friends were no longer a surprising sight, especially not in the city hub. It wasn't always so. Surrounding parties used to stare, whisper even, as Gwon stood at their table. Seeing them together was a spectacle for many years.

Girozz and Gwon, even to this day, were the only Carne ever to set foot in Scythadon. Seeing a Carne inside the city walls was new and something everybody had to get used to.

At first, many were reluctant to accept them. However, they did so at King Thax's behest. They were truly outliers in the city, a kin that Thadarack's kin feared even a simple mention of.

Gigakin were known to be one of the most vicious enemies during the Great War, and aside from Girozz and Gwon, they still were. Luckily, the Scythekin had grown accustomed to seeing the pair and now respected them both. Well, that's what Thadarack hoped, at least.

"I don't know how you two eat that," said Gwon as he watched the two Scythekin chow down on their leaves and seeds with a disgusted look on his face. "I told Thadarack earlier…I tried greens once, and I'll never try them again."

"They're delicious," said Thexis as she tossed some cycad leaves into her mouth. "Here, have another." She stabbed her left claws through a bundle of cycad leaves and held them up close to Gwon's face.

"Get those atrocious things away from me!" Gwon howled, leaning away from her. "Unless you want me to hurl all over you." He then leaned toward Thexis and pretended to eat them.

"Gross!" Thexis cried as she pulled them away from his face.

"I'd have to agree with Thexis on this one," said Thadarack. "Greens are delicious."

"Let me run back home and grab a Greatdeer thigh," said Gwon as he smacked his lips. "If you want something delicious, that's what you ought to have. My father brought them back fresh last night, still steaming and dripping with—"

"Now you're going to make me throw up on you!" Thexis interrupted with a disgusted look on her face.

Thadarack was also disgusted. He was glad he never had to

see Gwon and Girozz eat, an act that they did in private so the others in Scythadon wouldn't get dismayed. When it was time to eat, Gwon and Girozz would return to their home near the back of the city. Girozz did his best to sneak the Greatdeer in, but every once in a while Thadarack would see them. Just thinking about it made him queasy. "That's so gross," he chimed in.

The three friends continued joking and talking all through breakfast, their voices echoing among the others all throughout the city hub. It was a beautiful sunny day and there wasn't a cloud in the sky.

Thadarack looked up and saw some birds flying high overhead, appearing as if they hadn't a care in the world. Despite all the stories he'd heard of the Carne south of the Wall and the current war raging to the north, Thadarack felt grateful. He was thankful that he lived in such a place as this, with his friends by his side and fellow Scythadonians enjoying themselves close by.

He scanned the never-ending blue sky and breathed in the fresh air as it lightly blew through his feathers. He closed his eyes and savored that moment, hoping the peace and happiness he felt wouldn't leave him.

He abruptly opened his eyes to the sound of someone yelling a good distance away. "Prince Thadarack! Come to the front gate, quickly!" He turned his head and saw Septirius quickly disappear into the farm.

"Well, that was strange," said Thexis.

"What do you think is going on?" asked Gwon.

"I don't know," said Thadarack. "But we should probably find out. He seemed unsettled."

The three friends headed in the direction of the front gate.

Septirius' yell silenced many around them while others quietly murmured to one another. Everyone in the city hub watched them as they walked away.

Thadarack's heart sunk in his chest. He had no idea what to expect. He didn't think Septirius would have yelled like that unless something terrible had happened. His pace quickened with each stride he took. He pulled ahead of Gwon and Thexis, and continued on his way...curious, anxious, and concerned.

CHAPTER FIVE

THE RECKONING

Gwon and Thexis tried to keep up with Thadarack as he rushed through the farm. When the front gate became visible, Thadarack saw more than a dozen guards grouped around it. Many of them were desperately trying to roll the large boulder gate to the side.

Although Thadarack couldn't yet piece together their words, he could hear the muffled yells of the guards, both on the ground and atop the wall. When he got closer, he could see frightened and solemn expressions on their faces.

By the time the trio made it to the gate, other Scythadonians within earshot had already gathered around. The sounds of whispers permeated through the air, and the tension was so thick it could be sliced with the slash of a warrior's claw.

"Excuse me," said Thexis to one of the guards. "Can you tell us what's going on?"

The guard didn't respond to her. As a matter of fact, he acted as if she wasn't even there. Not seemingly because he was ignoring her, but because he was hard at work trying to move the gate.

Although four guards could usually make do and move the boulder gate, it sometimes took more due to its massive size, especially if time was of the essence. In this case, there were six guards trying to move it. Many more huddled around waiting for it to open.

Thadarack saw countless other guards atop the ramparts looking out across the clearing with ghastly looks in their eyes. They were talking to one another; although, what they were saying was inaudible to him down below.

"What could be out there that has everyone so spooked?" Thexis asked.

"I don't know," said Thadarack. "But whatever it is, it can't be good."

"Prince Thadarack!" Septirius yelled from up above. "Get up here! It's King Thax!"

Thadarack's heart dropped even further into his chest, bouncing off his rib cage so hard he felt the thud in his ears. *My father?* he thought. *What's going on?*

Thadarack, Thexis, and Gwon began ascending the ramparts while the guards below continued to push the gate aside, almost far enough now for one guard to squeeze through. When he got to the top and looked out across the clearing, Thadarack saw his father, accompanied by Girozz and one other warrior, approaching the city.

They were moving slowly, and only about halfway between the tree line and the city wall. The warrior was helping the King walk, while Girozz gently used his snout to push him upright each time he began to fall to the side. King Thax was hunched over, putting most of his weight on his right leg.

As they got closer, Thadarack saw blood on his father's neck and abdomen. His left leg was mangled and bloodied from his thigh to his four broad toes. He had dried blood on his beak and a deep gash down the right side of his face.

Girozz had dried blood from his jawline down his neck along with what looked like numerous bite marks on his torso and left thigh. The warrior had blood-soaked claws and a few minor wounds—the worst of which looked like an arch of teeth marks on his neck. It was as though something had begun to bite him and stopped mid-clench.

Thadarack froze as sheer terror befell him, a feeling so raw it consumed every inch of his body. His father limped in apparent agony, closer and closer to the city. At one point, the King fell to the ground, the warrior beside him desperately trying to help him back to his feet.

Everyone on the ramparts watched as King Thax gasped for breath and ever so slowly, made his way toward them.

"Get that gate open, forthwith!" Septirius shouted from atop the ramparts to the guards down below. "My King! We'll be right there!"

Septirius descended the ramparts just as the guards were able to open the gate enough for a body to slip through. He, along with a few others, hurried through the gate and quickly reached King Thax. Septirius and a guard swapped places with the warrior and Girozz, and continued to help the King make his way toward the city.

Girozz and the warrior pulled ahead toward the front gate. As they got closer, Gwon and Thexis descended the ramparts.

Thadarack heard Septirius shouting something to Girozz but couldn't make out what it was from this far away. A few guards ran past the King, looking cautiously toward the tree line.

Thadarack couldn't take his eyes off his father. Never had he seen him so helpless...so incapable that others had to help him walk. He was so upset that his mind hadn't even allowed him to think about anything else. If he had, he would have surely thought about what the guard next to him shouted before she shouted it.

"Where's the Queen?" she yelled. "Where's everyone else?"

Full on panic set in as Thadarack dissected the guard's words. Where was his mother? What had happened? A million questions flooded the young Prince's mind. He froze with his gaze glued to his father. *This can't be happening,* he thought. *This must be a dream.*

Surrounding noises began to fade while everything around his father transitioned into a blur. The tightness in his chest grew more intense the closer his father got to the city wall, and the more he thought about what might have happened to his mother.

He wanted to go to him, but he couldn't move a muscle. He felt limp like his body had been paralyzed from a nasty fall from the ramparts. His blank stare was abruptly broken when he heard Girozz, now just inside the gate below, collapse into the wall with a loud bang.

The warrior followed closely behind Girozz, falling to the ground just as she entered the city. They were both gasping for breath, unable to answer all the questions they were being bombarded with.

"Fetch the healers!" Septirius yelled, now only about ten paces

72

from the gate. One of the guards below ran at full speed in the direction of the Mending House.

Thadarack, still watching his father, was able to hear Gwon when he spoke from below him. "Father, what happened?"

By this time, there were dozens of Scythadonians huddled all around, watching and waiting for some kind of explanation. Girozz looked terrifying, his bloodied body and jaws most likely frightening all those around him.

A few of the guards tried to help him get up, but it was to no avail. He continued to lean against the wall, using it to support his enormous weight. "We were…" Girozz paused, panting as he desperately tried to catch his breath. "…ambushed by Carne."

Thadarack began to tremble as did all those who were close enough to hear. His heart fluttered around in his chest, and for the time being, he had difficulty breathing.

There was silence as everyone waited for Girozz to continue. It was obvious he was trying to speak, but his exhaustion seemed to overwhelm him, turning a few seconds into what felt like an eternity.

This isn't real, thought Thadarack as he closed his eyes, hoping to drift off to the calmness and tranquil comfort of his chamber. Instead, he was only met with ominous darkness and the ever-increasing pounding echoes of his heart that he could now feel in the back of his throat.

He hoped when he opened his eyes, he would wake up and these feelings that antagonized him would dissipate. He suspected, however, that this was not a dream, for it felt way too real. No nightmare his subconscious could conjure up would make him feel this level of fear, a fear he wanted more than anything to go away.

Girozz's next words confirmed his suspicion. "We were about halfway to Stegodor when the Carne attacked us," he said while fighting for the breath to continue. "We were caught by surprise…they were upon us before we even knew what was happening."

Thadarack finally turned around and looked at Girozz down below, locking eyes with him. "Once they realized the King was among us, they went after him relentlessly. If he wasn't such an exceptional fighter, he surely would have been slain."

"But where's the Queen?" yelled a guard on the ramparts. She kept shifting her gaze back and forth between Girozz and the clearing.

It wasn't long before Scythadonian voices piled on top of one another, everyone yelling questions simultaneously.

"How are there Carne this far north?"

"What happened to the Vlax Pass Wall?"

"Are we in danger?"

"Give him some space!" a guard howled, quieting down some onlookers while others continued to press for answers.

Girozz looked up at the sky and then closed his eyes. His constant wincing and shallow breathing were clear signs he was still in pain. "We were able to beat them back," he said. "But I'm afraid that we're the only ones that survived."

He looked back at Thadarack, his eyes heavy and conveying remorse. He didn't have to say anything else…

Thadarack felt like he had been pummeled by twenty claws all at once. He was so distraught that he was actually emotionless, not fully comprehending reality. His mind couldn't register everything that was happening, not all at once.

The awful feeling in Thadarack's chest and the pounding of his heart had not subsided at all. If anything, they'd grown worse each time Girozz opened his mouth. Thadarack had so many questions, but he couldn't bring himself to ask any. He just stared at Girozz, waiting for him to continue.

Thadarack then caught a glimpse of movement from the corner of his eye just as Medicus and another healer arrived. He turned and saw his father limp through the gate, still being assisted by Septirius and a guard. His eyes were closed, and he was barely moving his legs.

Thadarack descended the wall, but before he could address his father, Medicus spoke sternly.

"My King, we need to get you to the Mending House as soon as possible. I'm afraid we cannot delay." He then turned to the crowd. "Out of the way! Make way for the King to pass!"

"King Thax, what happened?" an onlooker shouted.

"Where's the Queen?" another yelled.

"Move aside!" Medicus howled as he swapped places with Septirius.

Additional guards came to help clear the way, and Thadarack watched in horror as his father, bloodied from head to toe, hobbled past him. He then finally found his voice.

"Father!" he shouted in dismay as a tear began to roll down his beak. The gravity of the situation had finally caught up to him as ten emotions flooded him all at once.

Slow to react, King Thax's eyes eventually met his son's. The weariness within them was only surpassed in caliber by the brutal bite marks and scrapes that covered his entire body.

Thadarack had never seen so much blood, nor had he seen so many scrapes and bite marks. He had seen wounds from time to time on warriors from the Vlax Pass Wall who returned home for healing treatment, but nothing like this. His father looked as if he had gone for a swim in blood. His entire body was a burgundy red.

Thadarack turned to Medicus. "Is he going to be okay?" he asked, trying hard to fight back his tears.

"We need to get him to the healing chamber immediately," said Medicus, motioning the guards toward the Mending House. "I know you want to speak with him, but it's best if I have uninterrupted focus to tend to his wounds. Give me adequate time to look after him."

"Tha…Thada," said the King in a light, barely audible whisper. "I need to sp…speak…with you."

"My King, I need to treat you as soon as possible," said Medicus. He then looked toward the young Prince. "Come by later. He needs his wounds cleaned and treated. He's also severely dehydrated."

"But will he be alright?" Thadarack asked.

Medicus hesitated before answering. "I don't know. Give me the time I need to care for him."

Thadarack turned back toward his father. "I'll come see you soon." His father, Medicus, and the guards slowly walked away.

He wanted more than anything to go with his father, but he also wanted to heed and respect Medicus' wishes, especially if doing so would aid in his father's recovery. He turned and saw the other healer tending to Girozz's wounds, who was still resting near the wall where he had fallen.

The healer held up a leaf and poured water into Girozz's mouth. Fortunately, he was already beginning to look livelier. The healer had applied some healing ointment to his wounds, and once Girozz finished drinking, he made his way over to the warrior that had the teeth marks on his neck.

Thadarack watched as the healer dipped his index claw into the ointment and began gently applying it to the warrior's wounds. Nobody besides the healers knew what was in the ointment, but nobody cared because it was so effective. The only ingredient commonly known within was Marigold, a beautiful yellow, red, and orange plant widely known for its medicinal properties.

The healer carried the ointment in a large tree stump, hollowed out with three holes on each side, close to the bottom. That's how all containers were built, perfect for the Scythekin to slide their claws in and out, allowing them to carry various items when needed.

Thadarack looked back at Girozz and saw him talking to Septirius; although, he couldn't quite hear what was being said. He walked closer and could tell Girozz was feeling better. His voice was clearer and his expressions were more animated.

"We didn't come across any other Carne on our way back," Girozz said. "If there were others close by, I'm sure they would have attacked. We were moving very slowly."

"But how did the Carne get that far north to begin with?" Septirius asked. "We haven't seen any around Scythadon, nor have I gotten any news from the Wall. Surely if the Wall fell, someone would have made it back to warn us."

"Could they have swam across one of the bays?" a guard asked. "Carne can swim, can't they?"

"There's no way they would make that swim from the peninsula to the mainland," said Septirius. "I don't know how they got here, but we're going to find out. How many were there?"

"About twenty or so," said Girozz.

"What tribe?" Septirius asked.

Girozz didn't answer right away, and to Thadarack, it looked like it was because he was tired and hurt. That theory came crashing down just as soon as he spoke. "It was a few tribes."

Septirius froze, as did all the others who heard. At first, Thadarack was unsure why Septirius seemed so distraught, not fully grasping what Girozz had said. Then it dawned on him. Something that, if it could have made him feel worse than he already did, it would have.

"What do you mean?" asked Septirius. "All at once? Together?"

"Yes," said Girozz. "Tarbokin, Carnokin, and Allokin."

"But didn't you tell us they were still fighting among one another?" Septirius asked, his voice cold and angry. "You just returned from the peninsula and told us that they don't pose any threat…that they still kill one another every single day! You said you saw it with your very eyes!

Thadarack looked at Gwon and saw a perplexed expression on his face. "What does that mean, Father?" Gwon interjected. "You returned from the peninsula? Why were you there?"

Girozz looked at his son before turning back toward Septirius. "The Southern Peninsula is huge. I do my best to provide

accurate intel. I didn't see any signs of the Carne tribes together."
He choked a bit on his words as he continued. "If I—"

"I trusted you!" Septirius shouted. His voice sounded even colder than before. "They've broken through the Wall, haven't they?"

"I honestly don't know," said Girozz, still fighting his fatigue. "They might have swam across—"

"No way!" Septirius howled. "They would never make that swim! You know that! They must have broken through the Wall!"

He turned and looked at a Scythekin beside him. "Clarrius, take a few scouts with you and head toward the Wall! At the first sign of any Carne activity, I want you to come straight back here as fast as you can! Do not engage!"

Clarrius nodded, signaled to a few others nearby, and took off through the front gate.

"Farglius!" Septirius shouted toward a guard still atop the ramparts. "Fan out your company in all directions around the city!" His voice grew sterner and more aggressive. "Do not let your guard down! Go now! Assume the Carne have broken through the Wall!"

"Yes, sir!" Farglius descended the ramparts while signaling to a large group of nearby guards. "Move out!"

"City company, retrieve the scythes and ensure the slingers are combat-ready!"

With a bunch of nods at Septirius, other nearby guards took off in various directions. Some ascended the ramparts while others ran through the farm.

"Arkonius! Go warn Beroyn and Rhinn! Tell them to muster

the army!" Thadarack looked over and saw Arkonius take off in the direction of the garrison.

Septirius turned back toward Girozz. "I am to assume that the Wall has fallen," he said in a much quieter tone. "That's the only explanation for what has happened."

A moment later, a few guards returned clutching many scythes, one of Scythadon's finest defenses. The scythes were the claws of deceased Scythekin, surgically removed from their arms, as dangerous in this state as they were when commanded by their masters.

The Scythekin's claws were naturally curved, so to create straight projectiles, they were carved and filed down. From each claw, two symmetrical scythes that measured just over a foot long each were produced. One end was left dull and flat, so a notch could be carved into it, resembling that of a hook.

Thadarack watched as the guards loaded the slingers, magnificent devices created by his kin during the Great War. Two crossed oak limbs made up the frame, the bottom one larger, heavier, and longer than the one that lay on top. The bottom limb pointed toward the target, and had a slot carved into its center so the smaller limb could rest on it.

Two scythes were inserted into bored holes on each end of the smaller limb, and a length of sinew was fastened across. One scythe, by its notch, was then placed in the center of the sinew, drawn back, and fired.

It took three guards to shoot. Two held each end of the top limb so it remained lifted, and they adjusted it to aim at a specific target. The third drew back the scythe and let loose. It was an honorable way for deceased Scythekin to aid their brothers and sisters from the afterlife.

The shouting of questions by hysterical Scythadonians grew louder, and soon, the guards couldn't even hear one another. Pandemonium had broken out, attracting even more Scythekin to the front gate with each passing moment.

Septirius ascended the ramparts and turned to address the large crowd, now numbering over a couple of hundred. "My fellow Scythadonians!" he shouted as loud as he could. "Please! Calm down! We must stay calm!"

"But what's going on?" one onlooker shouted.

"Are the Carne on their way here?" another yelled.

"What happened to the Queen?" a third cried.

The crowd was out of control, shouting over one another frantically, drowning out their own questions until they had become completely inaudible. A few guards tried to calm them down, but it was to no avail.

Amidst the chaos, Girozz finally rose to his feet. He turned toward the mob and opened his mouth, letting out a roar that was so ferocious it shook not only the surrounding walls but also the very ground on which they stood.

Everyone froze, and once he stopped, there was silence. Septirius nodded at Girozz before looking back out toward the crowd.

"Everyone!" he shouted. "We don't yet know what the extent of this threat is! We've sent scouts out in every direction, and we'll update everyone once we know more! For now, return to your homes! Spend some time with your loved ones!"

A few Scythadonians began to yell more questions but stopped after noticing Girozz had opened his mouth again.

Septirius continued to yell as loud as he could. "You all know me! I will do everything I can to keep our city safe! Please, let me do my job!"

Although still on edge, the Scythadonians began to disperse, heading in the direction of their homes and the city hub. Septirius descended the ramparts and approached Girozz, Thadarack, Thexis, and Gwon.

"Father, why were you south of the Wall?" asked Gwon.

Girozz looked at his son with sorrowful eyes.

"He's supposed to provide us with accurate information about what the Carne are up to," said Septirius. "He's been doing it for years."

Gwon looked horrified. "Why didn't you tell me?" he asked.

"I didn't want to worry you," said Girozz. "I—"

"You can talk about this later," interrupted Septirius. "I need to know more about the skirmish. From which direction did the Carne attack?"

"From the south," said Girozz. "We had just made camp for the night."

Septirius was silent for a moment, staring back at Girozz deep in thought. To Thadarack, he looked defeated and no longer seemed angry.

"What are you thinking?" Girozz asked.

"I've failed," said Septirius. "It was my charge to defend the Wall. I let this happen."

"This isn't your fault," said Girozz. "And if anyone can protect Scythadon, it's you. You're not alone. We're all in this together. But I do think it'd be prudent to send notice to Stegodor and Ceragorre as soon as possible. As well as the other

Eastern kingdoms."

"Not yet," said Septirius. "My focus is solely on Scythadon's safety. I will not risk sending one scout or warrior that far from the city until I know more about the Carne's whereabouts."

"What's going on?" a voice of a rapidly approaching Scythekin yelled. "Are there Carne on their way to Scythadon?"

Thadarack looked over and saw Beroyn, the First Commander of the Army. A masterful tactician, Beroyn came from a very prestigious family. He could trace his lineage back to some of Thrifsaer's most trusted lieutenants during the Great War. He was a rather large fellow, rivaling even Girozz in height.

Rhinn accompanied him as his second in command. Where Beroyn had muscle and strength, Rhinn was nimble and stealthy. They complimented one another perfectly in battle. She was just as cunning as Beroyn and together, the pair managed a well-trained and disciplined fighting force, having seen quite a bit of action at the Vlax Pass Wall.

"We're not sure yet," said Septirius. "I've sent scouts out, but all we know is that the King was ambushed less than a day's walk north along the Eastern Road."

"Arkonius said they have broken through the Wall," said Rhinn. "How can that be?"

"We haven't confirmed they have," said Septirius. "But I don't see how else this could have happened. Your guess is as good as mine."

"We have more than two hundred guards at the Wall," said Beroyn. "No more than twenty Carne at once have ever assaulted it. How could they have broken through?"

Septirius turned toward Girozz. "Tell them what you told me

about the Carne that attacked you."

After an exceptionally long pause, Girozz spoke. "Three different tribes attacked us," he eventually said.

"That means that they've…" Beroyn's voice trailed off.

"That they've stopped fighting among one another," said Rhinn.

"What does that mean?" Beroyn asked as he looked Girozz right in the eye. He spoke in a way that conveyed he already knew what the answer was.

Although many bystanders had cleared out, there were still a couple dozen or so Scythekin watching and listening intently. Most had gone to find and warn their families of what had happened. Everyone present turned and looked at the Gigakin. "We don't know anything for certain," Girozz said. "It could be just a rogue—"

"Just say it," said Septirius. "You know better than any of us. If the Carne stopped fighting among themselves, that could only mean one thing."

"There's a new High King," said Beroyn. "Isn't there?"

Thadarack saw the look on Girozz's face, a mixture of fear and anguish. His own fear was getting the best of him, and although he wanted to know what was happening, he almost didn't want Girozz to speak. When he did, Thadarack shut his eyes in terror.

"Most likely," he said.

Everyone around him gasped.

CHAPTER SIX

THE KING'S ORDER

Thadarack stared at the doorway to the Mending House, contemplating whether to just walk in. After all, he was a prince, wasn't he? What were the healers inside going to do? Hurt him? Turn him away?

He decided against it, though, wanting to respect Medicus' wishes. Especially if that meant that his father had a better chance of surviving. If anyone could help keep him alive, it was Medicus.

Medicus had only come outside one time since King Thax was brought to the Mending House. He let Thadarack know he was alive. But if it weren't for his words, the blood on his claws and arms might have indicated otherwise.

"When are they going to let you see him?" Thexis asked. "We've been waiting out here for hours."

"I don't know," said Thadarack. "I just hope he's going to be okay."

"He will be," said Gwon. "Your father is as tough as claws. It will take a lot more to bring him down."

Bring him down, thought Thadarack. It seemed like he was

already down. He looked absolutely awful when he returned to the city. Although he didn't want to, Thadarack had reimagined it a hundred times. Each time he did, his feathers crawled.

"I still don't understand how they got that far north," said Gwon. "It just doesn't make sense."

"You heard Septirius," said Thexis. "He thinks they broke through the Wall."

"But even if they did, how didn't we know?" asked Gwon. "Surely some guards would have been able to get back to Scythadon to warn us."

"Maybe the Carne that ambushed the King and company were faster than our guards," said Thexis. "If they did overtake the Wall, there's a chance that some of them caught up to the guards who may have been trying to retreat back to the city."

Thadarack had been so upset about his mother and father that he hadn't even thought about all the other Scythekin that had most likely died. The thought that they may have been chased down and killed really got to him.

"That's troubling," said Gwon. "We should have had a better system in place to ensure this kind of thing couldn't happen."

"While I do agree with you, the Carne haven't caused any significant problems for over a thousand years," said Thexis. "It caught us all off guard."

"Arkonius did mention to me that he thought the Carne were growing bolder," said Thadarack. "He said he was concerned."

"Well, what's in the past is in the past," said Thexis. "We have to focus on the future now."

"And what does the future hold?" Gwon asked snarkily. "We don't even know what's going on yet, and the King almost died.

Many have already died."

"I don't know," said Thexis. "Getting frustrated isn't going to fix anything, though."

"But I am frustrated," said Gwon aggressively. "I just don't understand why my kind are so evil. It makes me so mad."

Evil, Thadarack thought. *That sums it up well.* He also thought it was very cowardly for the Carne to attack unsuspecting Scythekin. Per Girozz's explanation, they had just set up camp when the Carne ambushed them.

"I can't imagine they are all evil," said Thexis. "I mean, look at you and your father. You're about as far from evil as can be."

Gwon's frustrated demeanor transitioned into a look of sadness. "They're all so angry with my father," he said. "Everyone hates us now. Just like they did before."

Gwon tried to get more information out of his father when he returned to the city, but Girozz quickly volunteered to go out scouting. Nobody questioned or stopped him. As a matter of fact, nobody even acknowledged him.

Shortly after Beroyn, Rhinn, and Septirius got the information they needed, they began to shun him. It was clear who they blamed for what had happened. But was that blame accurately placed? Most seemed to think so, even his own son.

Had it not been for the pleading of his two best friends to stay, Gwon would have surely followed after his father. Thadarack felt bad for his friend. He felt like he was also being blamed, even though he had nothing to do with what had happened. Guilt by association, it seemed.

"No, they don't," said Thexis. "Everyone's just scared, that's all."

"I don't hate you," said Thadarack. "You've done nothing wrong. And neither has Girozz."

"He was giving them inaccurate information," said Gwon. "You heard Septirius. He said he trusted my father. It's because of him that we let our guard down."

"Did you also hear what your father said?" asked Thexis. "The Southern Peninsula is a huge place. How is he supposed to know everything that happens there? If you ask me, this is more our fault. I think Septirius is mad at himself, but he wants to put the blame elsewhere to make himself feel better."

Gwon sighed. "I guess you could be right. I know he wouldn't give them false information on purpose."

"No, he wouldn't," said Thadarack. "And who knows, maybe the Wall didn't fall. Maybe the Carne that ambushed them swam…or they have been hiding out somewhere on the mainland already."

"For a thousand years?" Thexis quipped. "No way. And there's no way they swam."

"How do you know that?" Thadarack asked. "Can't Carne swim?" He glanced at Gwon.

"How should I know? I've never tried."

"Ah, you two," said Thexis. "It has nothing to do with them being able to swim or not. It has to do with what lurks in the water."

For a moment, Thadarack's mind was full of confusion. *Lurks in the water?* Then it dawned on him. "The Seaborne!" he said animatedly. "I forgot about them."

Thadarack knew of the Seaborne Carne but only from stories that he'd heard—stories that weren't told very often. Whenever anyone talked about the Carne, they were more often than not referencing the Landborne Carne. As a matter of fact, when someone mentioned "Carne", the word itself was synonymous with Landborne.

He didn't know of any specific Seaborne kin, but he knew they lived in the sea, and according to the few stories he'd heard, they weren't very fond of their Landborne counterparts. He didn't know why, nor had he ever really cared. Well, not until now.

Gwon smirked. "And that would be the main reason I've never tried to swim. The thought of the Seaborne lurking in the depths below me would be enough to give me a heart attack."

"Well, I don't really blame you," said Thexis. "It's believed that they helped us Viridi during the Great War."

"Why?" Thadarack asked. "Why would they help us?"

"You really don't know?" Thexis asked.

"I'm not sure I want to know," Gwon said, while Thadarack shook his head.

"Have you ever heard of the Spinekin?" Thexis asked.

"No," said Thadarack. "Who are they?"

"Well, the Spinekin were adept swimmers and competed with the Seaborne for dominance in the water," said Thexis. "The Spinekin became natural enemies of the Seaborne for two reasons. First, they competed with them for food. Since both preferred fish, Spinekin were invading their space and taking their food. Second, Spinekin would prey upon the Seaborne themselves."

Gwon rolled his eyes and shook his head. "Wow, us Landborne really are awful."

"But how did they help us?" Thadarack asked. "They can't leave the sea, can they?"

"The name Seaborne is actually misleading," said Thexis. "Many Seaborne can live in freshwater. During the Great War, there was an understanding between Seaborne and Viridi. I'm not sure how we communicated with them, but the Seaborne would allow the Viridi to travel across rivers and lakes, but would attack Landborne if they followed. It helped the Viridi tremendously because they could travel across bodies of water for safety."

"But if the Spinekin were so comfortable in the water, why haven't they tried to swim to the mainland?" Thadarack asked.

"It is believed that they died out during the Great War," said Thexis. "They haven't been seen since, not even at the Wall."

"That doesn't mean they are extinct," said Thadarack. "Couldn't they just be hiding out?"

"Hiding out?" Thexis asked sarcastically. "For a thousand years? I don't think so. Besides, Girozz even said as much." She turned toward Gwon. "Surely you must know."

"He never tells me anything," said Gwon, rolling his eyes again. "He told you all of this?"

"No, not quite. Paxtorr loves to…" Thexis paused and frowned. "Paxtorr *used* to love to tell me stories. He was happiest when he had someone to talk to. That's probably one of the reasons he was so good at his job."

"That makes sense then," said Thadarack. "That must be why the other Carne never tried to cross one of the bays."

"Exactly," said Thexis. "If the Carne really have broken through the Wall, I just hope that they will help us once again when we need them."

"Are there any Seaborne in the Scythadon River?" Gwon asked.

"I don't know," said Thexis. "If there are, I've never seen them."

The prospect sent chills down Thadarack's spine. He loved looking out across the river, but not once thought about how there could be Seaborne in the water. His thoughts suddenly came to a halt when he heard someone leaving the Mending House. Medicus emerged and walked toward them.

"We've been waiting for hours," said Thexis. "When can Thadarack see King Thax?"

"He can go see him now," said Medicus.

"Is he going to be okay?" Thadarack asked.

Medicus shot glances at both Gwon and Thexis before returning his eyes to the young Prince. "I can't say for certain. But I'm hopeful he will pull through."

"So, there's a chance he'll live?" Gwon asked.

Medicus hesitated. "Yes. There's a chance."

Although many hours had passed since the King had returned to Scythadon, Thadarack was still in shock. He hadn't fully processed what had transpired, nor had he fully come to terms with the fact that his mother might be…dead. He did everything he could to block it out of his mind, and for a time, it seemed to work.

He was too afraid to ask Girozz earlier, but the look on the Gigakin's face as others asked him all but confirmed his greatest fear. Was the Queen dead? Was his mother really gone? Deep down, he hoped she and the others made it to Stegodor and that Girozz was wrong. He hoped that they were safe and sound there, waiting to be rescued. At least, that's what his subconscious kept telling him.

Thexis handled Paxtorr's death surprisingly well. Thadarack wished he could be brave like her, but had been in denial since his father returned. Thexis and Gwon tried to comfort him, but he changed the conversation when they mentioned his mother. After a while, it appeared they got the picture, and they decided it was better to avoid talking about her altogether.

"I wanted to warn you, though, he is in rough shape," continued Medicus. "He's doing better than before, but he's in a lot of pain. He lost a lot of blood."

"Did he say anything else to you about what happened?" Thexis asked.

Medicus shook his head. "No. He's stable now, but he was very weak and dehydrated when he returned. He was incoherent." The healer turned toward Thadarack. "That's one of the reasons I didn't allow you in until now. Please accept my apologies, but I wanted to do everything I could for him. He's been asking for you for a while, but I didn't think it would be good for him to speak too much or get too excited."

"You don't need to apologize," said Thadarack. "I was happy to wait. I know you were doing everything you could to help him."

Medicus smiled. "King Thax...your father is so important to us all. I don't know what..." Medicus paused as it appeared he was trying to quell the tears that began to form behind his eyes. "I will do everything I can for him. But go, go see him. I don't know how long he'll be awake. He is very weak and tired."

Thexis gave Thadarack a comforting smile. "We'll be right out here."

"Give the King our best," said Gwon. "Let him know we're here for him."

Thadarack entered the Mending House and saw a healer standing at the far corner of the room.

To his immediate right, he saw the studies parlor, the area where the healers would broaden their knowledge and improve their techniques. To his left, he saw the apothecary station, the place the ointment was made and new concoctions were developed.

"He's back here," said the healer as she gestured to the farthest room in the back.

Thadarack walked toward her and caught his first glimpse of his father lying down. Both of his eyes were closed, and he wasn't moving a muscle. The young Prince turned to the healer.

"Is he awake?" he whispered.

"Yes." The healer approached the King and began speaking quietly. "My King, your son is here. Prince Thadarack is here."

King Thax slowly opened his eyes and stared straight ahead. After a few moments, he turned his head ever so slowly toward Thadarack, groaning while he did so. His left eye was open more than his right due to a small but seemingly painful scratch that crossed over it.

"I'll give you two some privacy," said the healer. "I will be right outside if you need me."

Thadarack watched as she walked over to one of the stone tables and picked up a container of nearby ointment. She walked over to the apothecary station, placing it among various other containers of healing compounds. She then approached the exit and turned around, giving Thadarack a slight smile before leaving.

Thadarack turned back toward his father, who still hadn't found his bearings yet. Although it was apparent the healers had cleaned him up, he still had dried blood all over his body.

There were countless burn marks, too many to even count. Thadarack knew of cauterization, a technique his kin had discovered to quickly thwart bleeding but had never seen its effects. He did now, and it made him queasy.

Thadarack hadn't noticed when he saw him earlier, but his father's left arm had dozens of teeth marks all over it. As he looked closer, its disfiguration made him uneasy, causing a flutter in the pit of his stomach.

"I can't," King Thax paused. His pain was evident as he tried to speak. "I can't move it anymore."

Thadarack didn't say anything. He looked at his father's arm, trying as hard as he could to keep it together. He wanted to collapse to the ground. The sheer enormity of the situation was quickly becoming too much for him to bear.

As he fought tooth and claw to keep himself from crying, his father spoke to his pain. "I'll…," The King let out a hacking cough. "I'll be okay," he finally said once he stopped.

"You don't look okay, Father," said Thadarack. "I'm so sorry this happened to you. I wish I could have been there to help."

"I don't," said King Thax. "It was a massacre. We had no idea until they were upon us."

Thadarack wanted to ask about his mother but couldn't bring himself to do so. As he began to think about her, he closed his eyes and did everything he could to keep from sobbing.

The King must have known what his son was thinking because he tried to put him at ease. "She's in a better place," he said gently. "She loved you very much."

Thadarack couldn't help it any longer. He broke down and started to cry. Although deep down he knew it to be true, he hadn't heard anyone say it yet. To hear his father confirm his mother had died pushed him over the edge. Ashamed, he turned his head to the side in an effort to hide his tears.

"My son," said the King softly, reaching out his right arm and gently wiping a few tears from Thadarack's beak. "There is a time to weep for those we love that have died..." his voice trailed off as he lowered his arm and tried to catch his breath. "And there is a time to be brave for those we love that still live. You may weep for your mother. But do not weep for me..."

Thadarack tried desperately to heed his father's words, but it proved too difficult. He couldn't stop thinking about his mother, and the fact he'd never see her again was unbearable.

"For me...be brave," continued the King hoarsely. "Make our kin proud. Make your mother, Thrifsaer, and all those that came before us...proud."

His father's words finally struck a chord. Thadarack slowly stopped crying and wiped away his tears with his index claws. After a few moments, he found his courage and met his father's eyes. "What should I do?"

"I need you to be a beacon of hope for our kin in my stead. You must convey that no matter what happens next, we will prevail if we're strong. They have to believe that."

"I will do my best," said Thadarack. "But what do you think is going to happen?"

"I don't know," said King Thax. "But my gut is telling me that this ambush was just the beginning."

Thadarack didn't want to ask, but his curiosity got the best of him. "You think the Wall has fallen?"

King Thax closed his eyes and sighed. "I do," he said, reopening his eyes and looking back at Thadarack. "It's the only way this could have happened."

"But how did they get so far north?" Thadarack asked. "I just don't understand."

"I don't have all the answers," said King Thax. "But I'm hoping we will know soon enough what they're planning."

"The three of you are really the only ones that survived?" Thadarack asked.

"Yes," said King Thax lightly.

Thadarack heard some commotion coming from outside the door. There was some muffled yelling, but he couldn't quite make it out. When he turned, he saw Beroyn, Septirius, Arkonius, Clarrius, and a few other guards storm into the Mending House.

"My King!" Septirius shouted. "Pardon us for intruding, but Clarrius just returned, as did a few of the other scouts." He turned toward Clarrius. "Tell the King what you just told us."

"King Thax," Clarrius said raspily. "There are Carne in just about every direction. Many of us engaged in small skirmishes all over the place. I barely…" He knelt down and desperately tried to catch his breath. "I barely made it back to the city."

Thadarack's heart dropped. He noticed Clarrius' claws were bloody, and he had several small scratches on his tail and torso. He had a bite mark on his right shoulder that was still bleeding, although not profusely.

"How far from the city?" King Thax asked.

"Most of the skirmishes have occurred about ten to fifteen miles away," said Clarrius as he looked down at the ground. "We've already lost many good scouts."

"Sound the horn," said the King, turning toward one of the guards. "Pull everyone back to the city immediately."

"Yes, my King," said the guard as he took off out of the Mending House.

"How many Carne attacked you?" the King asked.

"There were about five Carne in the group we came across," said Clarrius. "The other scouts said they came across groups of about the same size."

"How could this have happened?" Beroyn asked as he shot Septirius a glance. "How have your guards not seen anything? You let this happen!"

Septirius was silent, and Thadarack could see the distraught look on his face. Just as Septirius opened his mouth, King Thax spoke and cut him off. "This isn't Septirius' fault," he said while looking at him. "We have all been so focused on the Stegokin and Trikin war that we lost sight of the Carne."

He turned his head slowly and locked eyes with Beroyn. "You have even been training your warriors on how to effectively fight the Trikin. We have all been focusing elsewhere. If this is anybody's fault it's mine."

"No, my King," said Septirius. "It's—"

"Stop," interrupted King Thax. "I'm the king, nobody else. I should have seen this coming."

"But I still don't understand how they could have gotten past the city," said Beroyn.

"The Carne are natural hunters," said Arkonius. "The smaller Carne can stalk and sneak up on you without you even noticing them. They can be totally silent due to their size and mastery of stealth."

"They must have circumvented Scythadon without us knowing," said Septirius.

Thadarack then heard the Horn of Scythadon sound, a loud and massive conch. Anyone within ten miles of the city would have heard it. All Scythekin knew that when the horn was blown, it meant trouble. Wherever they were, they should return to the city immediately. Up until that point, it had never been blown, at least never during Thadarack's lifetime.

"But what's their plan?" Beroyn asked. "We can easily fend off a few Carne. I'd like to see them try to attack Scythadon. I'll stick them like the wild beasts that they are!"

"It's not just a few Carne," said Clarrius, finally rising to his feet. "I haven't told you the worst of what I saw shortly before the Carne were upon us."

It gets worse? Thadarack thought. How could it get worse than this? Carne had surrounded Scythadon, and Scythekin were already being killed. It didn't seem like it could get any worse.

"Before the Carne attacked us, we saw a massive army sprawled across The Clawed Plains," continued Clarrius. "It's on its way to Scythadon."

Everyone in the room went silent and looked at King Thax, seemingly waiting for a response. Thadarack still couldn't believe this was happening. His sadness for his mother temporarily transitioned into fear. To hear that a "massive" Carne army was approaching was the most frightening thing he'd ever heard.

"How many Carne did you see?" asked King Thax.

"It was hard to tell," said Clarrius. "We stayed a good distance away. But I'd estimate at least a couple thousand."

"A couple thousand!" King Thax tried to yell, but instead, he choked and coughed as he spoke. "How far away were they?"

"I believe they'll be here by nightfall," said Clarrius.

A new rush of anxiety poured over Thadarack. *Nightfall,* he thought. *But that's only a few hours away. Thousands of Carne are on their way to Scythadon right now?*

He decided he must be dreaming and closed his eyes again, just like he did when his father first returned. He desperately hoped he would wake up from such a nightmare and hear his mother and father chatting outside his chamber door.

Instead, he heard his father fight with his own throat to speak audibly. "What Carne tribes make up the army?"

"I'm not sure," said Clarrius. "But the Carne we fought were a mixture of Tarbokin, Carnokin, and Allokin."

"The same Carne that ambushed us," said King Thax. "We must assume that's what the army is also made up of." He turned toward Beroyn. "Has the army been raised?"

"Yes," said Beroyn. "Rhinn is currently overseeing the preparations."

"Summon everyone who is able to fight," said King Thax. "We must send the children and elderly to the palace and the surrounding homes for safety. Barricade them inside. Ensure the army is ready and well-fed." He looked at Clarrius. "Are you able to fight?"

"Of course I can fight," said Clarrius. "I'm ready to take down even more Carne."

"Good," said the King. "You and your scouts are now under Beroyn's command. Go, both of you."

Beroyn and Clarrius nodded before quickly heading out of the Mending House.

"What about the slingers?" the King asked while looking at Septirius.

"They're ready," said Septirius. "The guards are already atop the city wall, watching and waiting."

"Good," said the King. "Go, ensure all preparations are taken care of." He turned toward Arkonius. "You stay behind."

Septirius and his accompanying guards ran out of the Mending House. Thadarack then heard Septirius yelling from just outside. "Stay back!"

He guessed there were Scythadonians beginning to crowd outside the Mending House. He didn't blame them. If he were them, he'd want to know more of what was going on too.

"Father, what should I do?" he stammered, shaken to his very core.

"You must go to Stegodor," said King Thax. "You must warn King Sturklan and Queen Cerathorn and ask them...convince them to send aid."

This took Thadarack by complete surprise. Of all the things going through his mind, all the things he thought he might have to do, leaving Scythadon was not among them. He wanted to stay with his friends and fellow Scythekin. He wanted to fight...or at least try. He wanted to help protect his city.

"But Father," he said. "I can't leave Scythadon. My duty is to everyone here. I'm their prince. And what if you..." Thadarack couldn't finish his thought, for it was too painful to even think, never mind say out loud.

"I'm still alive, and I'm still the king. I'm not dead yet."

"But Father—"

"Stop." King Thax tried to raise his voice, but it was difficult for him to do so. "This is more important than anything you could do here."

"Why can't you send someone else?" Thadarack protested. "And besides, you heard Clarrius, there are Carne everywhere."

"It must be you. Only you can convince the King and Queen to do what's necessary. You, my son, the heir to Scythadon and Thrifsaer's kin. I need everybody else to stay and fight to defend the city. I can't part with anyone else, especially not now."

He let out another nasty hacking cough and turned toward Arkonius. "Except you. You must accompany my son to Stegodor and ensure he makes it there. At all costs."

"Of course, my King," said Arkonius. "I will protect him with my life."

"I know you will," said King Thax before turning back toward Thadarack. "You must make it to Stegodor. Our future may depend on it."

"I don't want to leave," said Thadarack.

"This isn't about what you want," said the King sternly. "It's about what our city needs. I'm fearful that unless Stegodor and Ceragorre send aid, Scythadon will fall. We can't stand up to this many Carne alone. Staying in the city is more dangerous than leaving right now." He closed his eyes and clenched his right claws. "I can't believe it's come to this."

Thadarack now understood why his father asked him to carry out this task. He finally realized the magnitude of what he needed to do. He wasn't abandoning his home or turning away from his responsibility as the prince.

It's his job to do what's necessary to protect his kin, no matter the cost. If that meant he had to leave his city to save his city, so be it. Although he finally understood, it didn't make him feel any better.

King Thax opened his eyes and looked at his son. "I know you're scared," he said. "But you need to put your fear aside and be the Scythekin you were meant to be. When I'm gone, you'll be king. You'll be king of Thrifsaer's city. Start by honoring that legacy and by doing what's needed to keep your kin alive."

"But how do we even get to Stegodor?" Thadarack asked. "How are we supposed to get past the Carne?"

"You have to find a way," said the King. "You must make it to Stegodor. Failure isn't an option."

"I don't know the way," said Thadarack worriedly.

"I do," interjected Arkonius. "We'll take the old path through the Great Forest."

"Old path?" Thadarack asked. "What old path?"

"There is an old path that our ancestors used to use, directly north of the city," said Arkonius. "It's overgrown now, but we will have a better chance of going undetected if we use it. It will lead us directly to Stegodor. We might not even come across any Carne on the way."

"You will make it," said King Thax as he reached out his right arm and interlocked his claws with Thadarack's. "When I'm gone and you're king, protect your kin until your last breath. But I also want you to promise me something."

"Anything," said Thadarack.

"Try…try to make the Carne see that their hate for us is misplaced."

The King quickly took his arm back and brought it up to his mouth as he coughed some more. Thadarack could see blood on his claws as he placed his arm back down beside him.

"Show them that Carne and Viridi can live side by side, peacefully. That will be your legacy."

"How?" Thadarack asked.

"This war between Stegodor and Ceragorre has had all my focus," said the King. "If there's one thing I regret not trying harder to do, it's not making more of an effort to reason with the Carne."

"But Father, they only ever *attack* the Wall. How were you supposed to reason with them?"

"Do you reason with Gwon?" the King asked. "Does he ever hurt you? Has he ever hurt anyone?"

Thadarack's father made a good point. As difficult as it was for Thadarack to admit, Gwon was a Carne. But to him, he was a Carne in name only. He never truly associated his friend with the "Carne" south of the Wall. Although he looked different, in Thadarack's eyes, Gwon was a Viridi.

"I could have tried to reach out to them," continued his father. "I've just been so distracted by other things."

Thadarack could tell his father was upset. He wanted more than anything to comfort him but didn't know what to say. "I will try," he said instead.

"You must. It's too late for me but not for you. Make sure you keep Gwon close. Although the safety of Scythadon must always be your top priority, try everything you can to obtain peace with the Carne. Fight only if you have no other choice."

"But I heard Septirius and Beroyn say there is a new High King of the Carne," said Thadarack. "I doubt he'll just let me talk to him."

"You'll figure something out. I know you will. Please promise me."

It comforted Thadarack that his father thought so highly of him. He had no idea how he would carry out his father's wish, but he decided right then and there that he was going to try. "I promise."

"Now go," said King Thax. "And hurry. The sooner you get there the sooner we can get reinforcements."

"But how do I convince them?" Thadarack asked. "They're both technically still at war with one another. What am I to even say?"

"My son, you must have more faith in yourself. You'll know what to say and when to say it when the time comes."

"Come on Prince Thadarack," said Arkonius. "We must go."

"I love you, Father," said Thadarack.

"I love you, too," said King Thax.

Thadarack and Arkonius turned and walked toward the exit. Before Thadarack left, he turned back around.

"I won't let you down," he said in a determined voice. "And I *will* see you again."

"I know you will, my boy. Be safe but travel with haste. A lot rests on your shoulders."

With one final glance, Thadarack turned around and exited the Mending House with Arkonius by his side.

CHAPTER SEVEN

COMMENCEMENT

As Thadarack exited the Mending House, he saw Thexis and Gwon turn toward him immediately. He also saw Medicus talking to the healer from the Mending House earlier when he went in to see his father.

"How's King Thax?" Thexis asked.

"He's doing alright," said Thadarack. "He's in pretty rough shape, but he's doing okay."

"Good," said Thexis.

"I'm glad to hear that," said Gwon.

"Have you heard about what's happening with the Carne?" Thadarack asked.

"Beroyn and Septirius told us," said Thexis. "They said they'll be here by nightfall."

"My Prince," interjected Arkonius. "We must go. We can't delay any longer."

"Go where?" Thexis asked.

"Arkonius and I are going to Stegodor," said Thadarack. "We are to warn King Sturklan and Queen Cerathorn and ask them to send aid."

Thexis and Gwon shot each other glances before turning back toward Thadarack.

"And we're leaving right now?" Thexis asked.

Thadarack hesitated. "Well, *we* are," he said.

"Yeah, and we're coming with you," said Thexis.

"No, you're not," said Arkonius. "Only the Prince and I are going. You two are staying here."

"Over my dead body," said Gwon. "Because you're literally going to have to kill me to keep me from coming."

Thadarack smiled, a welcome action despite everything that was happening. He was thankful for his friends and realized how lucky he was to have them. They were so willing to have his back, even in the face of such a dangerous journey.

"What do you think the Stegokin will say when they see you?" Arkonius asked. "Did you even think about that?"

"I honestly don't care what they think of me," Gwon said. "I'm going with the Prince regardless."

"No," said Arkonius. "I forbid it. The King made it very clear that it is to be just the Prince and me."

"What are you going to do?" Thexis asked. "Kill us? Forget about it. We're coming."

Arkonius rolled his eyes, sighed, and shook his head. It was evident from his reaction that he knew nothing he said was going to change their minds.

"Okay," he said eventually. "But I'm only responsible for getting Thadarack to Stegodor safely. I cannot be responsible for your lives as well."

Thexis smirked. "Right back at you."

"My Prince!" Medicus shouted from a good distance away. "Come here. I must speak with you alone."

Thadarack began walking toward Medicus just as Arkonius addressed him. "Please make it quick, Prince Thadarack. We need to leave right away."

As Thadarack approached Medicus, he could hear distant talking from atop the city walls. When he looked far in the distance, he saw the many outlines of guards on the ramparts peering over the edge, keenly watching in case any Carne arrived.

There were a lot more guards up there than there were when Thadarack had first gone into the Mending House. From one end of the ramparts to the other, they stood ready, eagerly waiting to shoot the fifty plus slingers should they need to.

When he got closer, the Prince heard a bit of Medicus' and the healer's conversation. "I don't know, Haelicus," Medicus said. "It's a very risky procedure."

"But don't you think it must be done?" Haelicus asked. "You're the one that taught me everything I know. Can't an infection…"

Haelicus paused, turning toward Thadarack and smiling. "Prince Thadarack," she said warmly. "I'm so very glad the King has returned home."

Procedure? Thadarack thought nervously. *My father has an infection?* Thadarack heard Haelicus continue speaking to him but was stuck on what he overheard.

Just when he was about to ask about the procedure and infection, Medicus spoke. "Haelicus, please give us some time to chat alone. Go check on King Thax."

Haelicus nodded and shot Thadarack another quick

smile. Then, she walked in the direction of the Mending House.

Medicus stepped closer and began to whisper, checking his surroundings as he did so. "Prince Thadarack, I'm concerned for your father," he said. "As you know, I was able to stop his external bleeding, but due to his description of pain, I think he may have internal bleeding as well. I'm afraid I have no way to heal him."

Medicus paused and cleared his throat. "I gave him something for the pain, but that is all I can do."

Thadarack's heart dropped in his chest. That terrible feeling he had when he first saw his father overcame him once again. He hadn't even had a proper chance to grieve for his mother, and now he learned that his father was also going to die.

He longed for the feelings he had when he was in the valley with his father and for the warmth of his mother's hug not but two days ago. The Prince wished more than anything that he could go back in time. Now, he realized he took all those moments for granted. "There's nothing...nothing you can do?" he stammered.

"I'm sorry, I'm afraid not. I would do anything I could to save King Thax, but internal wounds can't be cured." Medicus sighed deeply. "And that's not all."

Not all, thought Thadarack. What else could there be? Medicus had just said that he thought Thadarack's father was going to die. What else was there to say?

"We may have to amputate his left arm," Medicus continued. "That's what Haelicus and I were discussing."

"Because he has an infection?" Thadarack asked.

"Yes, and the blood flow has been cut off from it. We're afraid that if it's left untreated, he'll become afflicted with greenskin. That alone might kill him sooner."

Thadarack was on the verge of breaking down again, but he did his best to hide it. His father's words played over and over in his head. "Do not weep for me…do not weep for me."

He took a deep breath and tried to appear collected, then raised his head slightly and spoke as clearly as his voice allowed. "How much time do you think he has?"

"It's hard to say, but it depends on how he's feeling and if we are successful in the surgery. If he goes downhill fast, it may be only a matter of days."

"Does he know?" Thadarack asked.

"No," said Medicus. "Although the King is very smart. He might suspect it. I didn't know how to tell him, nor did I think it was the right thing to do at the time."

Thadarack decided he wanted to go see his father again. He turned around and took one step toward the Mending House just as Haelicus came out. "The King is asleep, my Prince," she said.

Thadarack paused, deciding whether to go wake his father. He stood there for a few moments before Medicus addressed him. "I know you want to go to him, but it's probably best that he sleeps. We'll stay by his side and perform the surgery when he wakes up. I will send for you as soon as he does."

"We'll look after him as best we can," said Haelicus.

Thadarack stared at the entrance to the Mending House, deciding whether to go in. He wanted to go see his father one last time but didn't want to risk waking him. Besides, Medicus could be wrong, couldn't he? Maybe his father would get better and all he needed was rest. *I should let him sleep,* he thought.

Thadarack turned back toward Medicus, but something crossed his mind in a moment of realization. He had to make a decision. A decision that, to him, was not simple.

Would he carry out his father's command and go to Stegodor? Or would he stay in Scythadon and try to fight alongside his friends and fellow Scythadonians?

The King didn't know he was about to die. Would he want Scythadon leaderless? Thadarack thought to himself for a few moments before recognizing something that convinced him that leaving was the right choice.

He was only one Scythekin, not even a battle-hardened warrior. *What can I really do behind these walls for my kin? I can hopefully do more for them by bringing back reinforcements.* "You needn't send for me when he wakes up," he said.

"Why not?" asked Haelicus who was now standing next to him.

"I won't be here. I'm leaving for Stegodor to ask for help."

Thadarack saw worry pass over Haelicus' face. "But you must know there are Carne everywhere," she said. "It's way too dangerous."

"But he has to do it," interjected Medicus. "We'll need help in the battle that is to come."

"But why him?" Haelicus asked, turning toward Medicus. "Why must it be Prince Thadarack?"

"Because he is Thrifsaer's blood," said Medicus. "And the Stegokin revere Thrifsaer. Even the Trikin honor his memory."

Thadarack was surprised. Why was Haelicus so concerned? Was it because he was her prince? Or was it something else? He

wasn't sure, but he did like how much she cared about his safety.
He smiled at her, but just when he opened his mouth to let her
know he'd be okay, he heard Arkonius yell from behind. "Prince
Thadarack! We must get going!"

"Go," said Medicus. "We'll look after your father."

Haelicus gave Thadarack another worried look. "Stay safe,"
she said.

"I will," said Thadarack. "I didn't have a chance to say this
earlier, but thank you for caring for my father."

Haelicus' worried expression lightened up a bit. "Of course,
my Prince. It's the least I can do."

Thadarack approached Arkonius and his friends. Just when
he reached them, Gwon shouted. "Father!"

The Prince turned and saw Girozz. Although it was apparent
he tried to wash it off, the Gigakin had dried blood on his jaws,
a sure sign he had been in some kind of struggle.

"What happened?" Gwon asked as he ran to his father. "Are
you okay?"

"Yes, I'm fine," said Girozz, turning toward Thadarack.
"How's the King?"

At first, Thadarack didn't know what to say. He wanted
to tell Girozz what Medicus had told him, considering how close
he was with his father, but he didn't want to upset everyone else.

Then again, what if Medicus *was* wrong? What if his father
would live after all? The young Prince tried to think
optimistically. "He's doing alright. I spoke with him for a long
while, but he's sleeping now."

Girozz looked distraught. "I'm sorry I let this happen. I
let everyone down."

"It's not your fault," challenged Thadarack.

Girozz looked down at the ground just as his eyes began to water. "But it is," he said quietly. "I told them not to worry about the Carne...that they posed no threat. Septirius and...the King...both trusted me. It's because of me that the Carne were able to destroy the Wall so easily. It's because of me everyone let their guard down."

"It's not your fault," repeated Thadarack. "It's not right they blame you."

Girozz met Thadarack's eyes. "Just promise me...promise me that you will always look out for Gwon, no matter what happens. No matter what happens to me."

"Of course," said Thadarack. "You know I will."

Girozz smiled slightly.

"The King tasked Prince Thadarack and Arkonius with going to Stegodor," said Gwon. "Thexis and I are going with them. Come with us, Father."

Girozz shot his son a surprised look. "No," he said. "My place is here, by King Thax's side. Are you sure you want to do this?"

"There's no doubt in my mind," said Gwon. "I know it's going to be dangerous, but I'm not letting him go without me."

"It will be dangerous," said Girozz. "It's also going to be tough on you. I'm not going to say you can't go because I know I won't be able to stop you. I just want you to understand what you're getting yourself into."

"What do you mean?" Gwon asked. "Tough for me?"

"You don't remember because you were too young," said Girozz. "There was a time when we weren't welcome here. We were...despised. I can only imagine what the Stegokin and Trikin will think when they see you, especially after learning what has happened."

"I don't care," said Gwon. "I'm going."

"I know," said Girozz. "Just be ready and stay safe. That's all."

"Don't worry about us," said Thadarack. "We're going to do everything we can to keep out of sight from the Carne. We're using an old path through the Great Forest."

"Well, still be careful," said Girozz. "It appears their plan is to block us from reaching Stegodor. They've created a perimeter around Scythadon, so although you'll be in the forest, they may be there too. Just don't let your guard down, no matter what you do or where you are."

"We won't," said Thadarack.

"We must leave," Arkonius cut in sternly.

"You said the King was asleep?" asked Girozz.

"Yes," said Thadarack.

"I will wait by his side until he awakens," said Girozz. "There's something I need to discuss with him. Go. Fulfill this critical mission. With faith and resolve, Scythadon shall be here waiting for your return, hopefully with armies at your back."

"I want you to know I don't blame you," said Thadarack. "This isn't your fault."

Girozz gave Thadarack a warm smile. "You are your father's son," he said. "There's a good in you that I wish was in everyone. Now go, don't delay any longer." He glanced at Gwon. "Stay safe, my son."

Girozz turned toward the Mending House as the group of four went through the city hub. When they made it to the farm, one of the cultivators who was gathering food for the warriors noticed Thadarack.

"My Prince," she said as she quickly approached. "We know very little of what is happening. All we know is that there is a Carne army on its way here. Is there anything more you can tell us?"

Thadarack could see the fear in her eyes. Out of the corner of his eye, he also saw a few other cultivators within earshot turn their heads toward him. Although he wasn't looking at them, he felt their gaze, sharp as a claw scraping against his back.

He wished he had something to tell them, something that could improve their spirits. Like them, however, he didn't know very much either. What he did know about the King's condition was not something he was going to share.

"Unfortunately, I don't have any further information," he said. "What I do know is that our kin are very brave and will be ready once the Carne arrive."

He tried to say more but could feel a lump forming in the back of his throat. He felt as if he was about to choke on his own words. Many Scythadonians, from young children to the elderly, gathered around and stared back at the young Prince, waiting for him to speak.

It wasn't long before they grew a bit rowdy and started raising their voices. "How could King Thax let this happen?" one yelled.

"Yeah! How could he let the Wall fall?" another shouted.

"Our leaders have let us down!" a third howled.

Frozen in place, Thadarack looked back at all those around him, unable to open his mouth. His muscles locked and he was unable to speak, unsure of what he would've even said. He desperately wanted to defend his father, but couldn't find the courage or the words to do so.

Arkonius tried to calm the crowd down, but it was to no avail. Many more crowded around the group, heckling and growing more unruly with each passing moment.

Just when Thadarack thought he might run and hide, a stern and confident voice echoed from just behind him. It was so loud and commanding that everyone abruptly stopped and listened.

"Blame should not be laid upon King Thax's feet alone!" Thexis shouted. "We have all grown too comfortable and too complacent. We have worried and bickered about petty things, things that shouldn't even matter!"

Thexis looked down at the ground for a moment before returning her attention to the silent crowd. "I know I have…We have been so wrapped up in our daily lives that we have forgotten what happened all those years ago. We've forgotten about all those Scythekin that gave their lives, so we could live safe and free!"

She gave Thadarack a quick glance before looking back out at the crowd once more. "Instead of placing blame on a king who has always had our best interests in mind, how about we ask what we can do in return to help him? Help him keep our city safe, our families safe, and protect our way of life!"

After a brief pause, one by one, the Scythekin began to clink their claws together, a sure sign they agreed. Even those who yelled at Thadarack joined in. This moment of solidarity was followed by another in the crowd shouting, "What can we do to help?"

"All those able to fight should report to Beroyn at the garrison immediately!" Thexis yelled. "Everyone else should seek shelter in their homes!"

The crowd dispersed, heading in their appropriate directions. Thadarack could see the fear in the eyes of the children as they parted ways with their parents, sobbing and weeping as they said their heartfelt goodbyes. They cried as their parents tried to comfort them, albeit in vain.

"Thank you, Thexis," said Thadarack quietly. "If you hadn't done that, I…"

"You don't need to thank me. I am to be your Left Claw. When you need me to speak, I will. When you can't find your words, I will find them for you. I was only doing my duty to the future king of our great city…and to my friend."

"That was very impressive," said Arkonius. "You'll make a fine Left Claw."

The young Prince smiled. He was still anxious but felt a little better knowing that his friends were by his side. He knew that as long as he had the two of them, he'd be able to get through almost anything.

"Nice job, Thexis," said Gwon. "I wouldn't have been able to do that."

"Of course you wouldn't have," quipped Thexis.

The three friends laughed, and for that split moment, it seemed like things were back to normal. Thadarack wished more than anything that they were, but reality set back in just when Arkonius scolded them that they needed to leave…again.

They made their way through the farm and arrived at the front gate. Once there, they saw hundreds of warriors preparing and sharpening their claws on whetstones.

"My Prince!" Rhinn shouted, making her way through a few warriors toward Thadarack. "I heard the King lives. How was he when you spoke to him?"

The warriors that overheard Rhinn grew silent, eagerly awaiting the Prince's response. Many of the guards atop the city wall also turned toward him.

Thadarack couldn't tell them the truth. He didn't want to distress them, especially not before the battle that was to come. They needed hope, hope that their King would recover and lead them through this difficult time.

Just prior to opening his mouth, Thadarack remembered what his father had told him. *Be a beacon of hope,* he thought. That's exactly what he decided he was going to be. "He was doing well," he said. "I spoke with him for quite some time. I'm hopeful he will recover."

Almost immediately, guilt started to set in, having first believed he had lied. Then Thadarack realized he didn't lie at all. He *was* hopeful his father would recover, even despite what Medicus had told him.

"That's welcome news," said Rhinn. "The exact thing that our warriors need to hear." She turned around and approached the warriors. By now, many others had noticed the pair talking and had turned in their direction. "King Thax lives!" she yelled as she held up her right claws.

Thadarack couldn't help but notice how sharp Rhinn's claws were. There was a fine balance between making them sharp and making them too brittle. The Scythekin had truly mastered the ideal thickness. The warriors' claws became sharper than a Gigakin's tooth, but stronger than a mountain.

The claws could slice into flesh so easily, that when not patrolling outside the city or guarding the Vlax Pass Wall, the warriors had to wear a protective covering made from plant fibers over them. This ensured they didn't cut themselves, or those around them by accident.

"We rejoice at this news, and at this hour, we look to the healing and protection of our great King for inspiration and motivation to hold back the enemy!" Rhinn continued. "These Carne wounded our King and brought him close to the darkened doors of death! They murdered our Queen, Dassius, Paxtorr, and so many others in cold blood! We will fight for vengeance! We will fight for our home! We will fight to protect our King, protect our families, and protect our way of life!"

The warriors let out a unified roar, as Rhinn's speech seemed to inspire them. Some vigorously scraped their claws together while others raised theirs high into the air. Seeing his kin so eager and ready to protect his home made Thadarack hopeful that they'd achieve victory.

After Arkonius signaled to the trio for what seemed like the tenth time to be on their way, the group continued making their way toward the gate. They exited the city and headed north, moving at a steady, quickened pace.

"Come on," said Arkonius, waving his left arm forward. "We're almost there. If we hurry, we will make good time before sundown."

Thadarack looked toward the treeline, but only saw dense forest. *I don't see any path*, he thought as they approached.

"Are you sure there's a path this way?" Thexis asked.

"Yes," said Arkonius. "It's overgrown, but it's there."

Thadarack turned around and looked back at his city. It looked so small from this far away. He thought about his father and wondered how he was doing now. He wondered if he was awake and if Medicus and Haelicus were performing the surgery.

After a few more moments, they reached the outskirts of the Great Forest. The three friends followed Arkonius as he walked alongside it, peering into the dense thicket as they went. Thadarack tried to find a path but didn't see anything that resembled one at all. The only thing he saw was dense foliage, almost too dense to even walk through.

"Here it is," said Arkonius.

"That's the path?" Gwon asked, gesturing toward it with his snout. "That's where we're going?"

"Yes," said Arkonius. "Unless you'd rather take your chances along the Eastern Road."

Gwon's silence was a clear indication of his choice.

Thadarack thought about the valley he and his father had visited not but two days ago. He wondered if it was now full of Carne, making their way to Scythadon. The thought sent shivers down his spine.

"Let's go," said Arkonius as he took his first step into the woods.

The three friends followed closely behind. The forest grew thicker the further they went. The path was barely visible as it had not been used for a very long time. If not for the rest of the forest being so dense, it would have been impossible to tell where the path was.

It continued along like a maze, going left, going right, and going left again. At times, they had to veer a little off the overgrown path, when pushing through was not an option. They walked for a long while, only stopping to take brief breaks. They moved quickly, but quietly, hoping to go unnoticed should they not be alone. Thadarack heard a few noises that at times gave him pause, but the noises turned out to be none other than a few rodents scurrying about.

"How long is this going to take us?" Gwon asked.

"We should reach Stegodor by midday tomorrow if we keep pushing at this pace," said Arkonius. "It's about a half day quicker than the Eastern Road, for it's a straight shot to the city."

"Why did we stop using it?" Gwon asked.

Arkonius stopped walking and turned back toward Gwon. "Look around," he said. "Would you like to be here if it weren't necessary?"

"That's fair," Gwon conceded.

"How did you know of this path?" Thexis asked when they began walking again.

"All guards, scouts, and warriors are required to know of its existence," Arkonius said. "I suppose a crisis such as this is why."

"That makes sense," said Thadarack. "I'm thankful it's here, even if it is awful."

As they kept on their way, Thadarack grew to hate the forest. He was no longer thankful for it and pretty soon, he didn't hear any noises. There were no rodents scurrying about nor birds flying overhead. The only other living things in the forest were the bugs. Flies, spiders, mosquitoes, and gnats were plentiful, tormenting the group as they pushed onward.

Thadarack realized why his ancestors stopped using the path. It was the equivalent of torture. The lifelessness within the forest grew more pronounced the deeper they went in.

The way became darker, and the trees got closer together. Tangled vines and thick leaves blocked the now-setting sun from lighting their way. Small glimmers of light, a light that was slowly giving way to darkness, helped them on their way, but that too was slowly fading away.

Without heat light, navigating the dense forest proved difficult. To make matters worse, Thadarack began to hear thunder and saw sharp flashes of lightning pierce the thick canopy above.

Before long, it started to rain. Although he hated it, Thadarack conceded that the one bonus to being in such a dense forest was that the foliage overhead shielded them from most of the direct rainfall. The rain clouds, coupled with the setting sun, made it almost impossible to see.

"This is terrible," Thexis complained. "I need to get out of this forest before I lose my mind."

"Me too," said Gwon. "I'm also getting very hungry."

Thadarack hadn't seen any signs of wildlife for hours, apart from the bugs, of course. It was evident that nothing lived in this part of the forest, a place that seemed more dead than alive.

Arkonius smirked. "Happy you two came?"

Gwon rolled his eyes and Thexis exhaled deeply, but neither of them said anything.

With darkness setting in, Thadarack was starting to feel claustrophobic. It looked like the surrounding trees were closing in all around him. It wasn't long before the light had disappeared, almost immediately becoming pitch black.

"We must stop," said Arkonius. "If we don't, we will surely

lose the path."

It was cold, dark, wet, and damp. Thadarack was beyond uncomfortable. His feathers were soaked, and his feet were tired and achy. He shivered, longing for the warmth of his chamber and his cozy bed.

The only light came from the occasional lightning that shot through the forest in the blink of an eye. It was truly bone-chilling when they decided to lay down, somewhat close to one another. They interlocked their tails for warmth.

"Do you think they're there yet?" Gwon asked quietly.

"I'm not sure," said Arkonius. "But let's not think about Scythadon right now. Our focus must be on getting some rest. Tomorrow is going to be another long day."

Thadarack curled his head around under his left arm and chest, trying to use them as shields from the rain. He closed his eyes and thought about his father and everyone else back home in Scythadon. He didn't think he'd get any sleep, but to his surprise, his exhaustion from the last few days overcame him. With his mother and father on his mind, he slowly drifted off to sleep.

CHAPTER EIGHT

AN UNLIKELY JOURNEY

Thadarack felt something nudge his leg. "Wake up." He slowly opened his eyes and saw Arkonius standing over him. "We must be on our way."

"How'd you sleep, Thadarack?" Thexis asked.

"Surprisingly well," said Thadarack. He rose to his feet and stretched.

"You were probably still tired from your training the other day," said Gwon.

"And it didn't help that yesterday was such an awful day," said Thexis. "I slept terribly."

"Me too," said Gwon.

"Let's eat quickly and be on our way," said Arkonius. "We're lucky the rain has stopped."

Thadarack looked around for something to eat, passing many plants he wasn't familiar with. Although he could technically eat anything around him, he recognized a few plants he knew tasted horrendous. He wanted to find something tasty…especially considering his current circumstances.

"We can't be picky," said Arkonius, chowing down on the first plant he saw.

"What is that?" Thexis asked.

Arkonius stabbed another leaf of the plant with his left index claw and brought it close to his face, examining it. It was a large blue leaf with green edges and orange veins. "I have no idea," he eventually said before taking another big bite.

Thadarack decided it might be worthwhile to eat the same thing. It didn't appear that Arkonius minded the taste at all. Both he and Thexis stabbed some of the anonymous plant's leaves and at the same time, bit them.

"Disgusting!" Thexis cried as she and Thadarack spit them out simultaneously. "These leaves taste like dirty claws!"

"I didn't say they tasted good," said Arkonius. "I said we can't be picky."

"I'll pass," said Thexis, scraping her tongue clean of any remaining leaf remnants.

"Me too," said Thadarack as he did the same. "Maybe we'll come across some cycads or something further down the path."

"I'm so hungry," said Gwon as he watched Arkonius eat. "Even that looks yummy right now."

It hadn't dawned on Thadarack when they left Scythadon, but Gwon couldn't eat anything he saw unlike they could. The Prince immediately started looking around for any signs of animals. "We'll try to find you some food," he said.

"Where?" Thexis asked. "We haven't seen any wildlife since we first entered the forest."

"I don't think there is any," said Arkonius.

"Well, we know it eventually ends," said Thadarack

optimistically. "We just have to keep pushing on and hopefully we'll come across something Gwon can eat."

"Are we sure it ends?" asked Gwon. "What if we lost our way and we're not heading in the right direction?" He gestured with his snout to the surrounding woods. "This doesn't even look like a path to me."

Thadarack grew concerned, having not even contemplated that there was a chance they would lose their way. He trusted Arkonius and followed blindly, relying on him to lead them in the right direction.

Now that he looked too, where they were didn't look like a path. What if they had gotten lost? What if they wouldn't ever make it to Stegodor? What would happen to those he cared about back in Scythadon? He began to panic as he scanned the surrounding forest.

"We're still on the path," said Arkonius. "We must get going."

"We might be on *a* path," said Gwon. "But what if it's not the right path?"

Arkonius rolled his eyes and shrugged, then glared at Gwon. "Will you just trust me?" he said. "I'll get us to Stegodor."

"Shh," whispered Thexis as she crouched. "I think I just heard something."

"Stay behind me," whispered Arkonius sternly, now crouching as well. He extended his claws forward and slowly started making his way further down the path. Thadarack and Gwon joined Thexis behind him.

After a few hesitant strides, the way ahead had grown brighter, a sign that the dense forest was breaking up. The wind picked up and the leaves on the trees began to rustle. Thadarack's anxiety

125

started to fade. He grew excited about the prospect that the forest was ending. But was it? Did they really make it through that fast?

The path wound to the right alongside a tall ridge, while the left opened up into a clearing. With a sigh of relief, Thadarack emerged from the forest into a glade where the morning sun shone effortlessly.

This joyous sight was beyond welcome due to the forest's suffocation. Tall, lush grasses and vegetation made up the glade's interior, while a small brook bubbled a good distance to the left.

Crouched, they slowly made their way, trying hard not to make sudden movements or loud noises in an effort to go undetected should they not be alone. A calm, fresh breeze combed through the tall grass, swaying it in a rhythmic motion from side to side.

"Stay quiet," whispered Arkonius. "Let's head for the brook."

After only a few steps, Thadarack saw Gwon freeze, staring off into the distance. "Stop," his friend whispered shortly after.

"What is it?" asked Arkonius. "What do you see?"

Gwon peered through the tall grass in the distance, squinting his eyes. Thadarack tried to look in the same direction but couldn't see anything. His anxiety came back with a vengeance. He hoped that what his friend saw wouldn't want to make a meal out of them. When Gwon spoke, he quickly put Thadarack's mind at ease.

"It's a Greatdeer," he said quietly. "I'll take it from here."

"I don't think it's a good idea for us to split up," said Arkonius in a low voice. When Gwon didn't turn back, Arkonius raised his voice a little louder. "Gwon!"

Gwon slowly crept forward. Arkonius' words appeared to

have gone in one ear and out the other. Thadarack could tell his friend was completely gone. Gwon's gaze was locked in on the Greatdeer. The Gigakin's hunting instincts had seemed to fully kick in, and nothing else around him appeared to matter.

"You two, stay here," said Arkonius as he slowly started to follow Gwon.

Thadarack and Thexis knelt behind a tall bush as Gwon methodically and stealthily pushed on further into the center of the glade. Both he and Arkonius were crouched, moving at a very slow but steady pace.

Thadarack had seen many Greatdeer in the valley, and he knew them to be fast and nimble. One swift movement or sound could make the difference between Gwon eating his fill or continuing the journey hungry and tired. Gwon, not but a hundred paces from the Greatdeer, suddenly stopped moving.

"What's he doing?" Thexis whispered.

Gwon turned his head to the right toward the forest, away from the Greatdeer.

"I'm not sure," Thadarack said.

"He's looking at something," said Thexis. "I don't see anything, though."

Thadarack and Thexis looked to the tree line in the same direction as Gwon, trying hard to see what their friend was looking at. The trees and bushes then began to rustle, and a large animal leaped from them straight toward the Greatdeer, locking its jaws around its neck.

The animal, not but a streak of light, was so quick that Thadarack couldn't make out what it was. He then saw Arkonius quickly scramble behind a nearby tree trunk as Gwon stayed still, crouched down low to the ground.

After a few moments of painful wailing from the Greatdeer, the sounds abruptly ceased. Thadarack heard the dead Greatdeer's body fall to the ground with a loud thud, sending chills down his spine.

"This is mine," roared the creature that attacked the Greatdeer in an accent so thick, that it was almost too difficult to understand.

A moment later, Thadarack felt sheer terror as he watched what he thought was some kind of animal stand up not far in front of Gwon, much taller and bigger than his not-yet-fully-grown friend. It turned its head slowly at Gwon and looked at him menacingly.

"It's…it's a Carne," stammered Thexis. She and Thadarack lowered themselves even closer to the ground.

Thadarack was stricken with dread as he looked at the Carne. He desperately wanted to turn away, but he couldn't. His eyes were glued to the Carne's every move. It clenched its bloody teeth together and snarled at his friend.

He couldn't help but notice that it was different from Girozz and Gwon. Its jaws were broader, and its snout was a bit shorter. Its teeth were conical, and although thicker, they were shorter than Girozz's. Even though this Carne was smaller than Girozz, he still towered over Gwon, looking more fearsome than anything Thadarack had ever set his eyes upon.

He had countless gashes across his dark green, scaly body and a long scar that ran down the right side of his jawline. For a moment, Thadarack forgot to breathe, anxiously waiting to see what was going to happen.

"Who are you?" the Carne asked, his voice deep and gruff.

Thadarack was scared clawless for his friend, fully expecting the Carne to lunge at Gwon at any moment. But he then remembered Gwon was a Carne himself, and he had a newfound hope that his friend would be able to trick the Carne into thinking he was one of them.

"I asked you a question!" the Carne bellowed. "Who are you? You're not in my unit!" The Carne cocked his head slowly and squinted eerily at Gwon. "You're a Gigakin. And a young one at that. What are you doing all the way over here?"

"Can you see Arkonius?" Thexis whispered. "I can't see him."

Thadarack looked for Arkonius but didn't see him anywhere. "No," he said.

"I'm...I..." Gwon stammered over his words. "I've lost my way."

The Carne scoffed. "Lost your way? You're going to lose your hide once Galzore gets ahold of you. And your voice sounds...strange."

The Carne then looked past Gwon in the direction Thadarack and Thexis were hiding. "Where did you come from?"

Thadarack thought about how scared Gwon must have been, considering the Carne before him was almost twice his size. The Carne not only looked different but acted differently, too. He assumed it had to do with where they originated from...the Carne from the Southern Peninsula and Gwon from Scythadon.

"Speak!" the Carne roared, taking a step closer to Gwon.

Gwon took a step back and leaned a bit on his left leg, giving the impression he might run.

"I'm not the one you have to be afraid of," the Carne snapped as he stepped back and bent his head down toward the Greatdeer. A moment later, he tore into its flesh, ripping it apart gruesomely and eating his fill.

Although Thadarack couldn't see the Greatdeer, he could hear squelching sounds and see blood spraying through the air. He became nauseous while the Carne devoured the animal in a matter of seconds.

"I got turned around in the forest," said Gwon. "I'll head back now."

Gwon turned around and started heading back toward Thadarack and Thexis. After only a few steps, the Carne lifted his head and looked at Gwon. His entire face was covered in blood, and flesh was hanging from his jaws and teeth.

"Turned around in the forest?" he asked. "You shouldn't even be anywhere near this forest."

Gwon stopped dead in his tracks, and Thadarack could see the fear in his eyes.

"Come here," growled the Carne as he started walking toward Gwon. A short moment later, he stopped approaching. Thadarack glanced from Gwon back to the Carne and saw the Carne's cold eyes dead set on him. Thadarack ducked lower into the grass, but the Carne's words proved it was too little, too late. "What is that?" he roared as he began charging toward Thadarack and Thexis.

Just as Gwon turned around to face the Carne, Thadarack saw Arkonius fly through the air so fast that he wasn't but a blur. He struck the Carne's left shoulder with a slash of his right claws and impaled him straight through his bottom jaw with his left.

Right when Arkonius was about to thrust his right claws into the Carne's gut, the Carne ferociously wriggled his jaw free and whipped his tail at Arkonius, knocking him a few steps back. The Carne let out such a ferocious roar that the ground they stood upon shook.

The Carne, sinisterly grinning, lunged at Arkonius with his mouth wide open. Thadarack watched in horror as the Carne charged at his protector. It didn't appear as if the puncture wounds through his jaw had even hurt him; although, they were bleeding profusely.

Just before the Carne reached Arkonius, he ducked to his right side, rolled, and jumped high into the air. The Carne tried to adjust his jaws to his left but missed. He snapped his mouth shut with such strength that the sound of his teeth clashing against one another echoed throughout the forest.

Arkonius drove his right claws straight into the back of the Carne's head, jamming them down as hard as he could. The Carne twitched for a few seconds before finally tumbling to the ground with a loud thud.

Arkonius glanced at Gwon. "Run!" he yelled at the top of his voice. "Thadarack! Run!"

In an instant, before Thadarack could move, the ground shook. The sounds of stampeding feet grew closer and closer. In the heat of the moment, they sounded like they were coming from every direction.

"Look out!" Thexis yelled as a Carne emerged from the forest not far from Arkonius.

Arkonius whirled around to face it just as two more emerged from the tree line a little further up the glade. Although a little bigger, the Carne closest to Arkonius looked similar to the one that lay lifeless on the ground behind him.

The other two Carne were significantly smaller, and they had what looked like two horns on the top of their heads. In a flash, they viciously charged and roared at Arkonius, approaching from his left.

Arkonius leaped to the right as the larger Carne pounced at him, snapping its jaws shut, barely missing his left arm. Arkonius swiped at the Carne's neck with his right claws but just grazed it. He tried to uppercut the Carne's jaw with his left claws, but it swiftly dodged his strike.

"We have to go help!" Gwon yelled, who had retreated near Thadarack and Thexis. "He'll be torn apart three to one!"

The two other Carne were about the same size as the trio of friends, smaller than Arkonius and the Carne he was fighting. They were now about the same distance from Arkonius as the friends were but were on the opposite side of the glade.

Thadarack's angst was unbearable, and he was unsure of what to do. On one claw, he knew Gwon was right. Arkonius did need help. There was no way he could fend off three Carne by himself. At least, Thadarack didn't think so.

But on another claw, he wasn't even sure if the Carne knew the three of them were there. Sure, Thexis and Gwon had yelled, but the noise of the Carne's stampeding charge may have drowned out their voices. Besides, Thadarack knew his mission was more important. Or was it?

Could he really turn away and let Arkonius die? He risked his life to save all three of them. He was a great fighter, but surely three against one were odds that not even his skill could overcome.

"Come on!" Gwon thundered as he ran full speed into the fray.

Thadarack watched as Thexis took off too, not far behind Gwon. In a panic, he looked at Arkonius and saw him try to slash the Carne's jaw. The Carne was fast for his size and dodged out of the way with ease, instead lunging toward Arkonius. It latched onto his left arm and clenched its teeth hard.

Arkonius let out a yelp and swiped at the Carne's abdomen with his right claws, scraping a deep gash across its belly. The Carne released Arkonius' arm and wailed in pain.

Arkonius swiftly turned around just in time to see Gwon and Thexis run past him. "No!" he yelled. "Go!" But it was too late.

Gwon was running at full speed, straight toward the other two approaching Carne. Thexis quickly followed only two strides behind him.

In a violent clash, Gwon and one of the horned Carne smashed into one another, both biting their jaws down on each other's shoulders. They viciously shook their heads and growled with menacing ferocity.

The other Carne launched itself at Thexis, but at the last second, she jumped out of the way and slashed its hip with her left claws. It roared in anger as it turned back toward her. The two slowly circled, staring at one another dead in the eyes.

Arkonius turned back toward Thadarack, who had not moved at all. "Thadarack!" He screamed as loud as he could, but it was almost drowned out by the deafening roars of the Carne. "Run!"

In an instant, the larger Carne leaped toward Arkonius and snapped its jaws down on the Scythekin's neck. Arkonius shrieked in agony.

He tried to push the Carne away with his left arm, but it refused to let go, shaking its head violently. Arkonius struck the Carne's underbelly with his right claws, but due to the painful struggle he was in, he didn't have the strength to thrust his claws in all the way like he did against the first Carne he fought. But to Thadarack's relief, the Carne released Arkonius' neck and took a step back.

Meanwhile, a little further in the distance, Thadarack saw Gwon still toe-to-toe with the horned Carne he was fighting. Evenly matched and of similar size, the two Carne bit at one another, each landing blows and missing from time to time.

Thadarack turned toward Thexis and saw the horned Carne she was fighting charge at her, lowering its head and leading with its sharp horns. "Thexis!" he yelled as he took his first steps toward his friend.

He ran as fast as he could, but right before he got there, the Carne reached her, knocking Thexis back and causing her to stumble to the ground.

As Thadarack approached, he was beyond relieved when Thexis pushed the Carne aside, having sunk her claws deep into each side of the Carne's head. The Carne lay limp on the ground with its lifeless eyes staring forward.

"Are you okay?" Thadarack asked.

"Yes, I'm fine," said Thexis. She then spun around and ran toward Gwon.

Just as Thexis neared, Gwon wrapped his jaws around the Carne's neck and pushed it backward, right in the direction she was coming from. In the ultimate display of teamwork, Thexis stuck her claws forward just as Gwon rammed the Carne into them.

It wailed and cried as it slowly became limp. It tried to break away, but it was too late. Gwon dug his teeth deeper and deeper into the Carne's neck, while Thexis' claws were fully injected into its side. When the Carne became motionless, they both let go, causing its body to smash to the ground.

Thadarack, Thexis, and Gwon turned and saw Arkonius still heroically battling the larger Carne. "Behind you!" They yelled simultaneously just as two more horned Carne emerged from the woods.

The three friends stood helplessly as the two Carne charged straight into Arkonius' back, propelling him forward into the larger Carne's wide-open jaws. He desperately tried to get away, but their horns were dug deep into his back. In a flash, the bigger Carnes' jaws wrapped around Arkonius' neck once more. Thadarack watched in terror as Arkonius shrieked, unable to do anything to aid him.

A moment later, the three friends heard more footsteps coming from behind them. "They're surrounding us!" Thexis yelled. "Thadarack, you must go! Gwon and I will try to hold them off!"

Thadarack watched as Arkonius' life began to fade. He was being thrown around by the larger Carne with such ease—like a feather blowing in the wind. The two-horned Carne kept their horns lodged in his back, rendering it impossible for him to break free.

"Thadarack!" Gwon screamed. "Go!"

Thadarack didn't know what to do. The approaching Carne sounded far enough in the woods behind him that he might have been able to sneak away. But he knew that he had to leave at that very moment if he was going to have a chance.

Then, it dawned on him. If the roles were reversed, would his friends leave him? Would they abandon him when it was clear that he needed help? He didn't think so. *I can't*, he thought. *I won't leave them.*

He turned back to look at the tree line, the direction the footsteps were coming from. He then looked back toward Arkonius, who by this time, seemed very near to death. *Duck, dodge, and strike,* he thought. "I can't leave you," he said. "I'm sorry, I just can't do it."

Thexis and Gwon most likely heard him but didn't say anything. They both looked toward the tree line and got ready to fight.

Gwon growled and clenched his bloody jaws, lowering his body closer to the ground. Thexis stretched her arms forward, flexing her claws back and forth. The blood from the dead Carne was still freshly dripping from them.

Thadarack got in his ready stance, the same position that Arkonius had taught him not but two days ago. *Duck, dodge, and strike!* he thought just as the attackers emerged from the forest.

Gwon let out a mighty roar and took one step forward before coming to a halt. Thadarack and Thexis did the same, but all three stayed in combat-ready positions, waiting and watching.

"Charge!" one of the attackers yelled as it leaped out of the trees.

More than fifteen or so of the creatures before them ran right past the three friends as they stood there, shoulder to shoulder, unsure of what to do.

Thadarack turned around as they went by and saw the Carne finally drop Arkonius. Within an instant, the creatures rammed into the three Carne, one after another. They headbutted them and stabbed them with short, sharp spikes that ran down the backside of their heads.

The larger Carne snapped his jaws at one of them but missed. The creatures were quick, about the same height as the horned Carne, but not as bulky. Their smaller frames allowed them to avoid the Carne's attacks nimbly.

Severely outnumbered and suffering small, but seemingly painful wounds, the three Carne turned and fled into the woods. The creatures circled about and then slowly approached the trio with their heads down and eyes fixated on them.

Unable to register what had happened, Thadarack heard Thexis speak beside him. "They're Pachykin."

Thadarack looked at the approaching Pachykin intently. "Don't Pachykin live in Western Valdere?" he asked.

"Yes," said Thexis. "They—"

"Not anymore," said the Pachykin that had shouted the order to "charge." Now, not but five paces from one another, the Pachykin began to ease their aggressive stance and halted their advance. "We need to get out of here," the Pachykin continued. "There are Carne all over. Many more would have heard the fighting."

She then glanced at Gwon menacingly. "You're lucky we saw you helping these two Scythekin."

Thadarack heard Arkonius groan from behind the Pachykin line. "Arkonius!" Thexis shouted as the three friends ran toward the dying Scythekin.

Arkonius lay on the ground in the exact spot the Carne had dropped him. His neck was mangled, and he was bloody from his head down to his shoulders. His back was disfigured, and it looked like his hips were out of place.

Thadarack knelt down beside him with sorrow in his eyes. "Arkonius," he said gently. "I'm so sorry."

Unable to move his neck, Arkonius moved only his eyes in Thadarack's direction.

"D...don't be," he stammered, desperately trying to speak clearly. "I would do it again to keep you safe."

"Can we do anything?" Gwon's voice cracked.

"Go," whispered Arkonius in a barely audible voice. "Leave now for Stegodor."

"I can't just leave you here," said Thadarack as tears dripped down his beak.

"We need to leave," said the Pachykin leader, looking at the tree line. "Now! We know a safe place! Follow us!"

The Pachykin started running toward the forest just as Thadarack heard roars from not that far away.

"Get to Stegodor," choked Arkonius. "Save Scythadon."

With great reluctance and the fear that more Carne were on their way, Thadarack said goodbye to Arkonius and took off after the Pachykin. Thexis and Gwon followed closely behind. Just before he made it to the tree line, he turned back and looked at Arkonius one last time. *I'll make it to Stegodor,* Thadarack thought. *I'll get there for you.*

CHAPTER NINE

ILL TIDINGS

Thadarack, Thexis, and Gwon were now deep in the woods again but completely off the path. The Pachykin kept running, not having slowed their pace at all. Although difficult to traverse the thick terrain, they followed as closely as they could.

Thadarack began to hear a loud sound coming from in front of them. At first, his heart dropped as he thought it might be the roaring of more Carne. But the closer they got, he realized it was something else, a sound he had never heard before.

When they emerged from the trees, they were upon a ravine with a raging river down below. Thadarack approached the edge and looked upriver. He saw white rapids and a massive waterfall up ahead. Had it been under better circumstances, the sight would have been beautiful.

The sunlight bounced off the crisp water spray as it poured down over the side of the cliff above. A gorgeous rainbow penetrated through the water, and it glistened as the sun shone down on it.

As they approached the waterfall, Thadarack felt the cool mist of the splashing water upon his face. The waterfall's magnificence calmed him but only for a brief moment.

"Come on!" the Pachykin yelled. "Over here!"

The Prince walked along a small ridge that protruded out into the river, just behind the waterfall. It was barely large enough for Thadarack, Thexis, and Gwon to walk across without falling into the water below. Had they been fully grown, they may not have been able to pass.

Once they got about halfway across the river, the cliff wall behind them opened into an enormous cave hidden out of sight behind the waterfall. The Pachykin walked into the cave, and the trio followed closely behind.

"Gwon, are you alright?" Thexis asked abruptly.

Thadarack looked at his friend and saw his neck was all bloody. There were countless teeth marks across it. He had been so distracted by the attack, Arkonius, and the Pachykin, that he hadn't even realized his friend was hurt.

"I'm okay," said Gwon. "It probably looks worse than it is."

"Well, it looks pretty bad," said Thexis.

"And we don't have any healing ointment," said Thadarack.

"I'll be okay," said Gwon.

"Keep up!" the Pachykin shouted, now quite a bit further along in the cave than they were.

As the trio tried to catch up, the way grew darker. For a few moments, Thadarack could barely see anything. After a bit further, he began to see flickers of what looked like heat light coming from around the next bend. As soon as it grew a bit lighter, the Pachykin turned around.

"You must stay here," she said sternly at Gwon. "We saw you

helping these two Scythekin, but my kin will not tolerate your presence."

"But he's one of us," pleaded Thexis. "He and his father grew up with us. He's our friend."

The Pachykin cocked her head at Gwon, looking him up and down from head to toe. "Even if that's true, he can't go any further." She turned toward a few of the other Pachykin that were among them. "You three, stay here, and keep an eye on him."

"Of course, Kylesia," they said simultaneously.

Thadarack and Thexis turned toward Gwon.

"I'll be okay," Gwon said. "Don't worry about me."

"Come on," said Kylesia. "Let's talk further in the cave."

With a potent feeling of sadness, Thadarack left his friend behind.

As they made their way around the bend, it opened up into a huge cavern lit by many pyres of heat light. There were stalactites hanging from the ceiling for as far as the eye could see, as well as cave crystals that gleamed in the flickering of the heat light. Thadarack gazed around in awe, mesmerized by the cavern's beauty.

He saw many other Pachykin scattered throughout, weaving in and out of the stalagmites on the ground, coming toward them. The ones that were already close enough were staring and watching the unexpected visitors intently.

Kylesia stopped, as did the others who accompanied her, and turned to face Thadarack and Thexis. "We will be safe here," she said. "The Carne haven't been able to find us."

"Why are you here?" Thexis asked. "You're Pachykin, right?

I thought the Pachykin settlement was to the west of here."

Kylesia hesitated. "It used to be," she eventually said. "Until the Carne ran us from our homes."

"The Carne?" Thexis asked.

"Yes," said Kylesia. "They attacked us without warning." She looked down and then angled her head back toward the rest of her kin. "We're the only ones that escaped." She turned back toward the pair of Scythekin. "We traveled east hoping to find asylum with your kin, but when we saw the Carne were here too, we fled into the forest. We came upon this place by chance and were lucky we did so. The Carne have been looking for us but haven't been able to find us."

Thadarack looked at the Pachykin woefully. *All that's left?* he thought. He tilted his head to look past her and saw what looked like only a couple hundred Pachykin.

"I'm so sorry to hear that," said Thexis.

Kylesia nodded. "Has Scythadon fallen to the Carne too?" she asked. "Are you seeking refuge in the forest?"

Thadarack and Thexis looked at one another. Thadarack realized he didn't know what the current status of Scythadon was. He assumed Thexis was thinking the same thing. Had the Carne army attacked yet? Clarrius said it would arrive by nightfall yesterday, but did it?

"We don't actually know," said Thadarack, turning back toward Kylesia. "There was an army on its way, but we left before it got there."

"That's probably for the best," said Kylesia. "We encountered Carne in every direction while trying to find the Scythekin settlement. We eventually gave up and searched for a place to hide."

Find the Scythekin settlement, thought Thadarack. Then it dawned on him. He remembered that his father told him a few years back that the Pachykin and Scythekin hadn't spoken with one another in hundreds of years.

He recalled learning that, after the end of the Great War, all the Viridi tribe leaders would gather at the Hallowed Lumina annually. They'd catch up on happenings in their part of the world as well as discuss efforts to ensure all Viridi tribes continued to live peacefully together. Most importantly, they would discuss happenings at the Vlax Pass Wall and if the Carne were posing any threat.

As is the way of time, and with the waning threat of the Carne and growing strife at home, fewer and fewer Viridi tribe leaders would attend the gathering each year. It was only a couple hundred years after the Great War that the gatherings ceased to happen altogether.

Although depressing, it made sense to Thadarack that the Pachykin didn't know the exact location of Scythadon. The Pachykin, just like all other Viridi tribes of the West, had lost communication with the Scythekin. As a matter of fact, they lost communication with all the tribes of the East.

"The Carne have entirely surrounded Scythadon," said Thadarack. "We are on our way to Stegodor to warn King Sturklan and Queen Cerathorn. We need their help."

Kylesia cocked her head at Thadarack in confusion. "Forgive me. But we aren't familiar with these parts. I'm not sure of where or who you're talking about."

"Scythadon is the name of our home," interjected Thexis.

"Stegodor is the Stegokin city. The Stegokin king is King Sturklan. Queen Cerathorn is queen of Ceragorre, the Trikin city."

"Ah, much better," said Kylesia. "We knew that they also lived somewhere in the East, but we don't know anything about them."

"They're unfortunately at war with one another right now," said Thexis. "The Carne ambushed…" Thexis paused, looked at Thadarack, and then back to Kylesia. "They ambushed our king while on his way to Stegodor to mediate peace talks. As he never made it, we're on our way there now."

"Well, I'm sorry to hear about your king," said Kylesia. "Did he survive?"

"Yes," said Thexis. "This is his son, Prince Thadarack." Thexis gestured toward her friend with her left claws.

Kylesia's eyes widened as she glanced at the young Prince. "Has your family ruled Scythadon from its founding?"

"Yes," said Thadarack.

"So you're Thrifsaer's heir?" Kylesia asked.

"I am. And my father is King Thax of Scythadon."

The Pachykin around them gasped and began murmuring among one another. At first, Thadarack didn't know how to take it. It almost seemed like they were displeased. Did they not know what Thrifsaer did?

It had been a thousand years since the Great War. Maybe the stories about Thrifsaer had become tainted when passed down from one generation to the next.

Then, to his surprise, Kylesia knelt in front of him, bowing her head slightly. Shortly after, one by one, every Pachykin around her, as well as all the Pachykin within sight, knelt and bowed.

Thadarack looked on with astonishment, unsure of what to say or do. He looked out at the couple hundred Pachykin in front of him, all of which were showing the greatest sign of respect possible.

All the anxiety, pain, and despair that he had felt for the last day vanished. The fear that had haunted him and the sadness that had overtaken him were replaced entirely. He was proud. To see a Viridi tribe that he had never seen, nor met before, show such respect simply because he was related to Thrifsaer felt incredible.

In all honesty, however, he also felt a little weird. Nobody had ever bowed to him before. He quickly decided he wanted them to rise. To his relief, Kylesia did just that, and the others followed suit.

"It is a great honor to be in the presence of Thrifsaer's heir," she said. "We may not know anything about the East or even about you, but we all know of Thrifsaer and what he did for us all."

Thadarack couldn't help but smile. "I will do everything I can to live up to his reputation."

"I'd say you already have," said Kylesia. "You made it through a group of Carne. That's more than impressive."

The joy that Thadarack had slowly melted away as he thought about Arkonius. Not only that but he realized he did absolutely nothing during the fight. He wanted to blame it on the fact that he needed to carry out his mission, and above all else, make it to Stegodor. But was that the truth? Or was he just scared?

He remembered how he wasn't going to leave his friends,

which gave him a little solace. But the events leading up to that were a little hazy in his mind.

"I don't want to be rude," said Thexis. "But we really must get going. We need to make it to Stegodor as soon as possible. I'm afraid we don't even know the way now. We were on some old path, but it seems we have lost it."

"Of course," said Kylesia. "And fear not, we can help you get to Stegodor."

"You know where it is?" asked Thadarack excitedly.

"Well, not exactly. But yesterday, when we were foraging for food and wood, we saw some Stegokin in the distance. We can take you back to where we saw them."

"If you saw Stegokin, how come you're still here?" Thexis asked. "Why didn't you go ask them for help?"

"It did cross my mind. But we also know the stories of how the Stegokin can be aggressive and stubborn. I didn't want to take any risks, especially considering what we've already been through."

It saddened Thadarack to hear Kylesia speak this way of a fellow Viridi tribe. He didn't understand why they all couldn't just get along. Sure, the Trikin abandoned the Stegokin in the Great War, but is fighting among one another the answer? Thadarack didn't think so.

"I'm sure they'll help you," said Thexis. "Even if they would have had reservations before, we have a good relationship with them. Come with us."

After a short pause, Kylesia spoke. "I will come with you, but I'm going to keep everyone else here until I know for sure that it's safe."

"But Kylesia," said the Pachykin to her right. "It's too risky. What if something happens to you?"

Kylesia turned toward the Pachykin. "I'll be alright, Fulgro. I trust them."

"But you just met them," Fulgro said. "I understand he's Thrifsaer's heir, but we can't risk losing you too...especially not after losing—"

"Please," Kylesia interrupted. "Don't speak of her."

"I'm sorry," said Fulgro. "I will come with you then."

"No, you must stay here. Just in case. I *will* come back. You have my word. In the meantime, you know what to do." Kylesia then turned back toward Thadarack. "Before we go, though, are you sure this Carne you travel with can be trusted?"

"Yes," said Thadarack. "His name is Gwon. He's grown up with us. His father brought him to Scythadon when he was no more than a few months old."

Thadarack recalled the day his father told him he had to befriend Gwon. Just like everyone else in Scythadon, Thadarack wanted nothing to do with the scary-looking Carne. He was mad at his father at first and angry that he would force him to do such a thing.

Remembering this anger really upset him. He thought about how thankful he was to have Gwon as his friend now. Thinking about how others shunned him just because he was different deeply troubled Thadarack.

Sure, he looked scary, especially if one didn't know him. But once they got to know him, it was evident that his heart was just as good as any Viridi's, if not better. For a moment, Thadarack thought about how there must be more Carne like him out there.

But where were they? *I have to find them*, he thought.

"But why did his father come?" Kylesia asked. "And more importantly, why didn't Scythadon turn them away?"

"His mother was killed right in front of him by another Carne," said Thadarack. "His father wanted Gwon to grow up in a place where he would be safe. He showed up at the Wall one day and pleaded with my father to allow them into our city."

"He never told me that before," said Thexis quietly.

"He only told me yesterday," said Thadarack.

"I suppose that makes sense," said Kylesia. "It's just extremely strange to be in the presence of a..." her voice trailed off.

"A peaceful Carne?" Thexis finished her thought for her.

"Yes," said Kylesia.

Thadarack thought about the conversation he had with his father, remembering how he had asked him to only fight the Carne when he had no other choice. "Before we left, my father asked me to promise him something. He asked me to show the Carne that Viridi and Carne can live side by side peacefully."

Kylesia, along with many other Pachykin, laughed mockingly.

"Why is that funny?" Thexis asked. "Gwon proves that it's a possibility. We just need to get through to them."

Fulgro smirked. "Good luck. I'd be surprised if you get a word in before one of them bites your head off."

"This is the problem," said Thexis. "We assume that they are all evil. We—"

"We assume?" Fulgro shouted. "They've just murdered our families, our friends, and our queen!"

He briefly glanced at Kylesia, who had now turned to the

ground. "They enslaved many others and burned our homes to the ground! I will not stand here and listen to you say that I "assume" they are evil and that I am somehow confused or misguided. I *know* they are evil, and I will never stop fighting them for as long as I draw breath!"

All at once, many in the crowd behind Fulgro started to yell similar things. The anger and fear in their eyes was unmistakable.

"Enough!" Kylesia shouted at the top of her voice. Those around her quickly quieted down as she turned toward Fulgro. "I will never forget what the Carne did to us, not only recently but also a thousand years ago. Not today, tomorrow, or any day in the future."

She turned toward Thadarack. "But if Thrifsaer's heir thinks that we can somehow achieve peace, then it's peace we shall strive to achieve. I don't want to fight for the rest of my life, nor do I want to hide. I will never forget what they did. To our families…to our friends…to my mother. But I will also look to the future. A future that I hope is safe and bright for our children and the children that follow them."

"My apologies, Kylesia," said Fulgro. "I spoke out of line."

"No," said Thexis. "I did." She shook her head. "I wasn't thinking about…about…"

"It's okay," said Fulgro. "I understand."

"We only know of the Carne from the stories we've heard and from what they did to us," said Kylesia. "You've clearly been fortunate enough to know a Carne who is good. I will trust your judgment about him."

"Thank you," said Thadarack.

"Let's go," said Kylesia. "You need to get to Stegodor."

Kylesia walked past them in the direction they had come.

"Princess!" Fulgro shouted. Kylesia turned back. "Be safe."

Kylesia gave Fulgro a smile before turning back toward the cavern exit. Thadarack and Thexis nodded at Fulgro before turning to follow her. After a few moments, they came upon Gwon and the Pachykin that had stayed behind with him.

"Everything okay?" Gwon asked.

Thadarack's heart melted in his chest when he looked at his friend. He could understand why some would be frightened of him at first, but all they had to do was get to know him. Then, they would surely understand that he was good. Even if every single other Carne in the world was evil, Thadarack knew that Gwon wasn't.

"Yes," said Kylesia. "I'm going to take you and your friends to the Stegokin."

"That's great news," said Gwon.

"I haven't seen any Carne in the direction we're going yet, but that doesn't mean there aren't any," said Kylesia. "Come on, follow me."

The three friends followed Kylesia and emerged from the cave. Same as before, the waterfall was crashing down right in front of them. They slowly made their way across the small ridge back to the land above the river.

They headed in the opposite direction they had come and entered the forest. Thadarack wasn't happy to be back in the forest, but he knew he had to keep going to fulfill his mission.

The direction the sun shone down told them it was about midday. Thadarack remembered what Arkonius had said. If they kept their quick pace, they would reach Stegodor by midday today. Although they'd taken a detour, Thadarack hoped it wouldn't extend their journey by that much.

The group walked quietly, but with haste in their steps. They continued for a long while, traversing the difficult forest terrain. Just like their earlier experience in the forest, it grew darker and darker the further they went. The light barely penetrated through the thick canopy overhead. Unlike before, however, they could hear sounds of eerie howls coming from various directions.

"What do you think that is?" Thadarack whispered.

"I don't know," said Thexis. "But I think we now know why we didn't hear any animals before."

At first, Thadarack wasn't sure what she meant. Then, it clicked. The Carne were most likely responsible. They must have nearly rid the forest of its wildlife, needing some kind of sustenance to stay alive. Strangely enough, the eerie howls didn't sound so eerie anymore. They put Thadarack's mind at ease. *Maybe this means there aren't any Carne around here,* he thought.

A few hours went by, and Thadarack's disdain for the forest continued to grow with each stride he took. At various times, it opened into pleasant little glades and meadows with babbling brooks and lush green grass. But most of the time, it suffocated him.

"Are we almost—"

"Quiet!" Kylesia whispered sternly, cutting Gwon off. "I just heard something."

It wasn't long before the sounds of leaves, twigs, and branches being crushed by footsteps grew closer and closer to them. The sounds got louder and soon were coming at them from all directions. The denseness of the forest made it difficult to see, but Thadarack thought he saw silhouettes of whatever was approaching in the distance, but he had no idea what they were.

A bout of panic took hold of the Prince as he vigorously turned about, trying to see what was closing in on them. A few moments later, he heard a grim voice call out. "Who goes there? Who enters the realm of Stegodor? Speak quickly!"

The unknown creatures got close enough now that the group could see them. A group of Stegokin emerged from the thicket, surrounding the unlikely companions on all sides. Thadarack discerned the fierce-looking gazes upon them, but he still couldn't help feeling relieved. They had found the Stegokin at last.

Before any of them could answer, though, one of the Stegokin yelled. "It's a Carne!" he howled while smacking his thagomizer into the ground with a massive thud. The other Stegokin among them did the same and started to roar.

"Wait!" Thadarack yelled. "He's with us! He's our friend!"

The Stegokin looked at one another sporting expressions of confusion, and then one of them spoke. "This *beast* is your...friend?"

"Yes," said Thadarack. "His name is Gwon."

Thadarack had just been through this with the Pachykin. It was starting to get old...having to explain to everyone they came across that Gwon was their friend. He could understand their initial reactions but couldn't help but think they were misplaced.

The Stegokin somewhat eased their aggressive-looking posture, but many still appeared on edge at the sight of Gwon. After all, it was the first time that any of them would have ever even seen a Carne.

"What are two Scythekin…" The Stegokin paused and glared directly at Gwon. "A Carne and…" He then looked at Kylesia. "And whatever you are…doing this close to Stegodor?"

"I'm Prince Thadarack of Scythadon, and these are my companions: Gwon, Thexis, and Kylesia of the Pachykin. We've come to seek an audience with your king. We—"

"Pachykin?" interrupted the Stegokin. "I'm more confused now. Why is the Prince of Scythadon traveling with a Carne and a Pachykin? In the woods, nonetheless. And where is King Thax? He was supposed to arrive yesterday."

"That's what we have to discuss with your king," said Thadarack. "My father was ambushed on his way to Stegodor. The—"

"Ambushed!" the Stegokin shouted. "How dare they! I knew the Trikin were planning something! They only agreed to these peace talks so they could finish off your leadership and then attack Stegodor outright!"

"No," said Thadarack quickly. "It wasn't the Trikin, it was Carne. Carne ambushed my father while on his way here."

"Carne!" the Stegokin howled. "You're saying that Carne ambushed King Thax?"

"Yes," said Thadarack. "And a large Carne army is on its way to Scythadon…or it might actually already be there. We're here to ask King Sturklan and Queen Cerathorn to send help as soon as possible."

The Stegokin's eyes widened, and his beak dropped open. Then, in an abrupt instant, his expression changed. He narrowed his eyes. "The Trikin have spies everywhere. How do we know this isn't a ploy to drive us from our city and attack when we're

153

defenseless?"

He then shot Gwon a threatening look. "I wouldn't be surprised if they somehow recruited savages like you to do their dirty work. After all, that's why we're out here patrolling these woods, to catch rotten spies like you!"

"Do we look like spies?" Thexis challenged. "The Carne broke through the Vlax Pass Wall. They've surrounded Scythadon and almost killed our king. They did kill...our queen. As well as my grandfather, Paxtorr."

Thexis gestured toward Kylesia. "They ran the Pachykin from their homes in the West and are attacking our city as we speak. We are not spies. We're here to plead for help!"

"Paxtorr is dead?" a voice from behind them asked.

The group turned around and saw a massive Stegokin approaching. His dark green scales were complimented by dark red plates that ran atop his back. He had a large scar stretching from his right eye all the way to his right shoulder. He also had what looked like three somewhat deep gashes on the left side of his tail. *A Trikin wound,* Thadarack thought.

"Yes," said Thexis.

The Stegokin shook his head remorsefully. "I'm sorry to hear that," he said. "I was very fond of Paxtorr. It's because of him that King Sturklan agreed to the peace talks."

"Are you buying all this?" the Stegokin who accused them of being spies asked. "They're trying—"

"Quiet!" the massive Stegokin bellowed. "Look at them. She's right, they don't look anything like spies." He gestured toward Kylesia with his beak. "Does she look like a spy to you?"

The other Stegokin stammered over his words.

"My name is Riktlan," continued the massive Stegokin. "I am the captain of the Stegodor city guard." He then glanced at Thadarack. "And you're the Prince of Scythadon?"

"Yes," said Thadarack.

"Then you are most welcome here," said Riktlan. "And if you vouch for this Carne, I will take you for your word. But heed my warning. If he causes any trouble, it will be you who must answer for him."

"I won't cause any trouble," said Gwon. "I promise. I'm on your side."

"My side?" Riktlan scoffed. "I may not strike you down where you stand because Prince Thadarack vouches for you, but that doesn't mean we're on the same side."

Gwon turned toward the ground, his shoulders drooping. Thexis put her right claws on Gwon's shoulder and whispered something in his left ear, but it was too faint for Thadarack to hear.

Riktlan looked at Thadarack. "Does King Thax live?"

"Yes, but he was very wounded in the fighting." Thadarack contemplated telling Riktlan that Medicus thought he was going to die, but he still didn't want to believe it was true. He decided he'd be optimistic about the future.

"Well, I'm glad to hear he's alive," said Riktlan. "I take it this means the Wall has fallen?"

Thadarack nodded reluctantly.

Riktlan sighed. "That is most alarming. Come, I will take you to King Sturklan. He will want to know of such things immediately."

They began walking toward a barely visible clearing. The

closer they got, the more the light began to show itself, growing brighter with each passing stride. The fact they almost made it to Stegodor and the hopeful prospect that King Sturklan would send aid to Scythadon made Thadarack rejoice. *We're almost there,* he thought. *I've almost made it, father.*

CHAPTER TEN

STEGODOR

As the group entered the clearing, it was evident they were emerging from the Great Forest. Knowing that Stegodor was located outside the Great Forest, Thadarack was relieved when he caught his first glimpse of the city on the horizon. They had finally made it through.

"We've made it," said Gwon. "We're almost there."

"I couldn't have made it without you two," said Thadarack while turning toward Kylesia. "And you, too. You're the reason we made it here."

Kylesia smiled. "It was my pleasure to help you."

They continued toward the city. Set a good distance from the tree line, Stegodor was preceded by a vast open field on three of its sides. It didn't have a river to its back, but was built on the lower slopes of the Spikedback Mountains.

The city was a beautiful sight to behold. It wasn't as large as Scythadon, but it was nevertheless as marvelous. Having been mostly built by the Scythekin, it mirrored Scythadon quite a bit.

As the group approached, Thadarack saw what he thought

might be a Trikin standing just outside the city gate. Although he had never seen one, he knew what they looked like. There was a time when Trikin visited Scythadon frequently, but those days were long gone. Thadarack had heard of some of their features, the most prevalent being that of their three fearsome horns across their face.

The Trikin was large, almost matching Riktlan in size. She approached once they got close. Thadarack immediately knew why she had a disgruntled look on her face. He turned and looked at Gwon. *Here we go again*, he thought.

When they first set out on their journey, he hadn't fully considered what others might think of Gwon. He was so used to him and desensitized by the fact he was a Carne that it really didn't dawn on him that he would draw so much attention. He didn't regret bringing him along, however. Not one bit.

As the Trikin approached, she was the first to speak. "What is the meaning of this?" she asked rudely. She scanned the group before her, glaring menacingly at Gwon. "What is this abomination doing here?"

Riktlan scowled at her before gesturing his head toward Thadarack. "This is Prince Thadarack of Scythadon, King Thax's son."

The Trikin smirked. "Well, if he's the Prince of Scythadon, of course he's King Thax's son."

Riktlan took a step at the Trikin. "How dare you—"

Seeming to have sensed rising anger, Thexis lunged between the two, facing the Trikin. "Please, we're here on King Thax's behalf," she said. "He was attacked by Carne on his way here. We're here to ask you to send aid. A large Carne army—"

158

"Back up." The Trikin sneered. "You're talking crazy. How did Carne attack King Thax?"

"We don't know yet," said Thexis. "But they did while he was on his way here."

"It's true," interjected Kylesia. "My kin were also attacked by Carne. We fled east hoping to find sanctuary among the Scythekin, but there were Carne everywhere."

"I believe them," Riktlan said. "We both know how important this peace meeting was to King Thax. Something bad must have happened for him not to show up."

"Of course you believe them," said the Trikin snarkily. "Not much reasoning goes on up there." She gestured with her snout toward Riktlan's head.

"I will strike you down where you stand!" Riktlan shouted. The other Stegokin that accompanied him began to slowly circle the Trikin.

"You'd have to catch me first!" yelled the Trikin as she took a few steps back.

"Please!" Thadarack shouted. "Stop! We need to work together if we want to prevail. The Carne are probably attacking Scythadon as we speak! We need to hurry!"

The Trikin gave Thadarack a perplexed look. "We?" she asked. "Even if the Carne are attacking Scythadon, what concern is it of ours?"

"Incredible!" Riktlan yelled. "The Trikin have not changed at all in the last thousand years! You'd forsake us all over again, wouldn't you?"

"Give me one reason why we shouldn't!" the Trikin shouted back.

The two Viridi gave each other such awful and hate-filled looks that Thadarack's stomach turned. He was getting a firstclaw glimpse into the relationship between the two stubborn Viridi tribes. His questions about why the war had started were getting answered right before him. Unfortunately, it was all starting to make sense.

"Can we please go speak with the King and Queen?" Thexis asked. "I'm sure Queen Cerathorn would want to know that the Carne have broken through the Vlax Pass Wall. Just take us to her."

The Trikin stared back at Thexis for a few moments. "I'll go talk to my Queen," she eventually said. "But I can't promise anything." She then glared at Gwon. "And you still haven't told me why there's a Carne in your company."

"We can stand here and ask them questions all day," said Riktlan. "Or you can go fetch your leader, so we can instead decide what we're going to do."

The Trikin shot Riktlan a scornful look. Then, in an abrupt instant, she took off in the opposite direction.

"What was that all about?" Thexis asked. "Why was she standing there in front of the city?"

Riktlan didn't answer. Instead, he turned and began to make his way toward the city gate. "Let's go," he said, having ignored Thexis.

As they got closer to the city, Thadarack saw Stegokin atop the ramparts watching them approach. He heard them talking among one another but couldn't make out what they were saying. Besides, at this point, he pretty much knew what was on their minds. *Gwon.*

Thadarack looked at how the city walls were made in exactly the same way as the walls of Scythadon. *My kind made all of this*, he thought as he walked through the city gate. He once again felt proud of his kin and all their accomplishments.

The Scythekin were pioneers and shared what they developed with the other Viridi tribes of the East. Thadarack often saw the skilled Scythekin builders leave for Stegodor, having been hired by the Stegokin to not only build their city but also maintain it. He wondered if he'd see any of his kin during his visit.

The first thing he saw upon entering the city was a giant sculpture made from what looked like an enormous tree trunk. It was a Stegokin and was easily five times bigger than Riktlan himself.

"What is that?" Gwon whispered.

"I believe that's the Colossus of Stegodor," said Thexis. "It's a sculpture of the legendary founder of the city, Pyklania. Paxtorr had told me all about her. She led the Stegokin in the Great War and was one of the Viridi leaders that fought the Carne."

Riktlan quickly turned around and glanced at Thexis. "Valiantly," he said sternly. "She fought the Carne valiantly."

Riktlan then turned and looked up at the sculpture. "It's magnificent, isn't it?"

Thadarack looked at the sculpture in awe, starstruck by its grandeur. It was such a massive sculpture of a Stegokin that the tail was a marvel to look at in its own right. The spikes were as big as he was, and the level of detail in the sculpture was amazing.

"It is," said Thexis.

"Thrifsaer had it sculpted for us," said Riktlan. "It was a great gesture of friendship and tribute to Pyklania." He turned toward

Thexis. "It astonishes me what you Scythekin can do with your claws. If not for your kin, I'll admit that Stegodor wouldn't be what it is today."

Thadarack smiled. *We really have done a lot of good, haven't we?* he thought. He was also amazed at how well the sculpture had held up, even though it was a thousand years old. He didn't know of any wood preservation techniques but assumed his forebears had figured something out.

He remembered the story his father had told him about how the Stegokin leader had died, and how all hope had seemed lost during the Great War. Well, until Thrifsaer saved the day. His smile broadened just thinking about his ancestor.

"I'm sure King Sturklan will send aid to Scythadon," continued Riktlan. "I can't say for certain what the Trikin will do, however. I really wouldn't be surprised if those cowards attack our city while our army is gone."

"You don't think the Carne invasion will help end the war?" Thexis asked.

"I don't know for certain," said Riktlan. "But I know my King. He wouldn't be too stubborn to agree to peace, especially now knowing that the Scythekin are in danger. The Queen, however…" he paused and shook his head. "She's unpredictable. She wasn't even committed to this meeting until after the last battle. King Sturklan agreed to sit down and discuss peace months ago."

"Last battle?" Thexis asked.

Thadarack wasn't sure he wanted to know what happened in this so-called "last battle." It sounded a bit too ominous for the young Prince's liking.

"You haven't heard?" Riktlan asked. "We routed a much larger Trikin army. We absolutely kicked their tails. We killed at least three Trikin for every brother or sister we lost. It was a glorious day."

Glorious? Thadarack thought. *That doesn't sound glorious at all.* It disgusted him how proud Riktlan seemed at the deaths of fellow Viridi. Fellow Viridi that could have come to Scythadon and helped his kin fight against the Carne.

"Our balladeers will surely tell tales of the Battle of Scattered Hills for centuries to come," continued Riktlan. "It was only after this battle that Queen Cerathorn agreed to the peace talks. But even then, Paxtorr was the only one able to convince her."

"If you ask me, we should be the ones to pull out now!" one of the Stegokin that accompanied them back to Stegodor shouted. "While the momentum is on our side!"

"Eh, they're not worth it," said Riktlan. "No more Stegokin need to die by their filthy horns. That's the only reason I'd be okay with peace."

Thadarack wanted to challenge Riktlan and explain how awful not only the battle sounded but the entire war. However, he had a feeling that such a challenge might not be warmly received, especially considering how hot-tempered it seemed Stegokin could get.

"Let's not delay any longer and keep moving," continued Riktlan. "King Sturklan will want to speak with you as soon as possible. Queen Cerathorn…well, she may or may not show up."

"What do you mean?" Thexis asked. "Why did that Trikin run off toward the woods?"

"Queen Cerathorn refused to stay here while we waited for

King Thax. She's in her camp with her grimy army just over the hill north of the city. She said if King Thax didn't come by the end of the day, the war would resume."

The group started moving again past the Colossus and through the city's farm. Although its layout was similar to Scythadon, Thadarack couldn't help but notice that it was much smaller. It was evident that there weren't nearly as many Stegokin as there were Scythekin.

The only explanations that made any sense made him sad and fearful. Was it a result of what happened long ago during the Great War? Or was it due to the present-day war with the Trikin? Regardless, Thadarack started to worry that there may not be enough Stegokin to help his kin fight off the Carne.

As they made their way, Thadarack noticed the stares and whispers of those around them. Gwon stole the gaze of everyone who saw him, all of whom looked frightened and angry at the same time.

The young Prince assumed it would have been the first time that any of these Stegokin saw a Carne, never mind one leisurely walking through their city. Or was it? Thadarack knew that Girozz had met King Sturklan but wasn't sure he had ever been to Stegodor.

After a few more moments, Riktlan stopped to address the gathering crowd. "It's okay everyone!" he shouted before looking at Thadarack. "This is Thadarack, the Prince of Scythadon!" He looked at Gwon. "The Prince has vouched for this Carne!"

"He doesn't belong here!" one of the bystanders yelled.

"Carne are not welcome amongst our kin!" another weighed in.

"Do not be fearful!" Riktlan pleaded. "I will not let him out of my sight!"

"Please, I'm here as a friend!" Gwon shouted shakenly. "I swear, I do not mean you or your loved ones any harm."

"Liar!" another onlooker screamed. "We know your kind only knows harm! You have wreaked havoc and destruction since the beginning of time! We don't want you here!"

The group tried to press on amid fierce heckling, but the rambunctious crowd made it difficult for them to make it through. It only began to die down once they reached what appeared to be the palace courtyard.

Stegokin guards stood at the entrance and blocked the rowdy crowd from following them in. It was a beautiful courtyard, and it reminded Thadarack of the Royal Gardens back in Scythadon. There were abundant, vibrant-colored flowers and plants alike, all of which looked pristinely kept and cared for.

Thadarack wasn't going to say anything to Riktlan, but he wondered how the Stegokin cared for the vegetation. They definitely seemed resourceful, but there had to be limitations on what they could physically do. *Maybe Scythekin look after them,* Thadarack thought.

Riktlan turned around. "Wait here," he said. "I will brief the King and confirm your audience." He then turned to a few guards. "Make sure they don't go anywhere. Especially him." He gestured toward Gwon with his beak.

The guards nodded as Riktlan made his way toward the palace. Built similarly to the Scythadon Palace, the palace before them was breathtaking. It was a little smaller than the Scythadon Palace, and although the Sacred Oak wasn't at its center, it still looked incredible.

"What do you think the King will say?" Thexis asked.

"I don't know," said Thadarack as he watched Gwon watching the guards around stare at him.

Thadarack couldn't get over how awful the Stegokin were acting toward his friend. Although he did somewhat understand why, the fact he was being treated differently just because of what he was upset the young Prince greatly.

Gwon hadn't been anything but friendly and supportive of the Viridi and their way of life. His father, especially, had given and helped so much. Thadarack thought about how every single time he returned to the Southern Peninsula, he risked not only being discovered but also being killed.

Thadarack recognized that Girozz endangered his life every time he went there, potentially leaving a fatherless son behind. Not only that, but it would have made Gwon the only Carne north of the Wall. *It just isn't fair,* he thought. "It'll be okay, Gwon," he said.

"I know," replied Gwon. "I don't blame them, though. They have a right to hate me."

"No, they don't," said Thexis. "You have done nothing wrong. Just because you're a Carne doesn't make you their enemy."

"They're just scared," said one of the nearby guards. "Everyone's a little on edge because of the war. To top it off, we all know of the meeting called upon by King Thax, a meeting that many of us hoped might have led to peace. Seeing you walk through the gate instead of him, with this Carne by your side, didn't help matters either."

"What do you mean?" Thadarack asked. "Why?"

"King Thax was supposed to be here yesterday," the guard said. "There has been nonstop talk throughout the city about how he hasn't shown up. Many are concerned that the war will continue. Then his son, accompanied by a Carne, walks into the city. They're rightfully apprehensive, and to be honest, I am too."

"But they don't have any right to treat Gwon any differently," said Thexis. "He has done nothing wrong."

"We don't know…Gwon," replied the guard. "We were expecting the King to come, and instead, a Carne shows up. I know you vouch for him, but we only know of Carne from our history. What they did to us. Do you know what they did to us? What they *almost* did to us?"

"I do," said Thexis. "And I don't blame you for hating *those* Carne. But Gwon has shown us that not all Carne are bad. He's proof that there's a possibility, no matter how small, that we might one day live together in peace."

"Ha!" The guard scoffed. "Live together in peace? With Carne? Are you crazy? If you haven't noticed, we can't even live together in peace with other Viridi." He glanced at Gwon. "There's no way we will ever live in peace with these atrocious and vile beasts."

"He is not a beast," said Thexis. "Show him some respect!"

"Watch your tone!" the guard yelled. "You are soon to be hosted by King Sturklan of Stegodor. You will not command such an attitude in his presence! We might yet be able to accomplish peace with the Trikin, but Carne and Viridi are not meant to coexist! Look at him, even now he's in our midst with blood on his jaws. He's nothing but a flesh-eater through and through. How can we coexist with the very beast that wants to devour us?"

Thadarack saw Gwon quickly try to lick the blood from the fight off his mouth.

"But that's the problem," said Thexis. "I don't believe that every Carne is evil, nor do I think that every Carne wants to kill or eat us. Gwon is good. We have seen it since the day we met him. When no one else gave him a chance, Prince Thadarack and I befriended him and opened everyone's eyes. Now, he is respected around Scythadon. His father has even been a close friend and advisor to—"

"Stop!" the guard interrupted. "I have heard enough! Just because the Scythekin have been fooled doesn't mean the Stegokin will be! I couldn't care less what you think! My kin were slain by the Carne in the Great War and were almost..."

He paused for a brief moment, calmed himself, cleared his throat, and continued. "...almost destroyed. I do not want to hear another word about good Carne. There aren't any. Now, be quiet before I decide you have overstayed your welcome."

Thexis didn't say another word. Thadarack could tell she was trying hard to stay silent. He didn't think there was anything she could have said that would have changed his mind anyway. It was evident how the Stegokin felt about the Carne, and even though there may be some good Carne in the world, he didn't care.

Thadarack knew the Stegokin were set in their ways and very stubborn. He was now witnessing firstclaw how unwilling they were to see other points of view. There wasn't any room for negotiation, nor the slightest chance that they'd be persuaded otherwise.

After a few silent, awkward moments, Gwon whispered quietly. "When do you think Riktlan will be back?"

"I hope soon," said Thadarack. "We need King Sturklan to send help as soon as possible."

"I don't think it's King Sturklan we have to worry about," said Thexis. "Paxtorr told me that he and King Thax have a great relationship. I have no doubt that he will send reinforcements. I think it's Queen Cerathorn we have to convince."

"But maybe the Stegokin will be enough," said Gwon. "Maybe we won't need the Trikin."

"You heard what Clarrius told Beroyn," said Thexis. "The Carne army he saw was massive, numbering at least a few thousand. We're going to need all the help we can get."

Thadarack thought about how scary it must be for everyone still in Scythadon, especially the young children. He remembered how fearful they looked when they parted ways with their parents and loved ones. He wanted to return as soon as possible, hopefully with armies at his back. "Well, we'll just have to convince the Queen then," he said. "She has to understand that this threat is real."

"Not only that, I doubt the Carne will stop at Scythadon," said Thexis. "I mean, they've already invaded the West too." Thexis looked at Kylesia. "If you don't mind me asking, how big was the army that attacked your home?"

Kylesia shrugged. "It's hard to say. It all happened so fast. But there had to be at least a few thousand Carne, if not more."

The three friends gasped. It terrified Thadarack to hear that there were so many Carne on mainland Valdere. A week ago, the Carne were an afterthought, nothing more than the antagonists of a few old tales told around the city from time to time. Now, they were a great threat, wreaking chaos wherever they went.

"What I don't understand, though, is why the Carne split up," said Gwon. "Wouldn't it make more sense to stick together instead of fighting on various fronts?"

"Maybe they didn't want to give us a chance to join forces," said Kylesia. "After all, that's what happened during the Great War, right?"

"Yes, once the Scythekin helped the Stegokin, the various Viridi tribes all joined together," said Thexis.

"I think I know why the Carne went west," said Kylesia. "At first, I didn't understand why they came after us. But now knowing that they are targeting Scythadon as well, it's obvious."

"What's obvious?" Gwon asked.

"They're trying to finish off who they perceive as the greatest threats first," said Kylesia. "And doing so in a way that won't give us time to join forces."

Thadarack was confused. In large numbers like in the forest, it looked like the Pachykin could fend off a few Carne but not an army. They didn't seem like they posed much of a threat to the Carne, if at all.

Thadarack didn't want to be rude, but what was Kylesia saying? *The Pachykin don't look very strong*, he thought. Maybe they had some secret weapon he didn't know about? Or maybe they were more dangerous than they appeared?

"So, that's why you think they attacked you?" Thadarack tried to ask in a way that didn't convey he was skeptical.

"No," answered Kylesia. "Well, sort of. Our settlement is…was located between the Serrated Marshes and the Crescent

Mountains."

"We're not familiar with Western Valdere," said Thexis. "We don't know where those are or why they're significant."

"To reach the Far West, the Carne had to pass through our settlement first," said Kylesia. "Or, they would have had to travel for miles around the marshes in order to get there."

"The Far West?" asked Thexis. "Why would they..." she paused for a moment, and then her eyes widened in a moment of realization. "They're going after the Longnecks!"

"That would be my assumption," said Kylesia. "They went through us to get to them."

"How many Longneck kingdoms are there?" asked Thexis. "I know *of* them, but not much about them."

"Four," said Kylesia. "Well, at least there used to be. I'm actually not sure now. A few of them have been at war, and last I heard, one was on the brink of defeat. We haven't traveled there in a few years to avoid hostilities."

Thexis shook her head. "Wow. There are wars happening between the Western Viridi kingdoms too? That's despicable."

"I know," said Kylesia. "Without a common enemy, everyone's been at each other's throats since the Great War."

"Here he comes," said Gwon, gesturing with his snout toward the palace.

Thadarack saw Riktlan approach with two additional guards. "Prince Thadarack," he said. "Follow me. King Sturklan has agreed to host you."

"What about my friends?" Thadarack asked, making his way toward Riktlan.

"The Scythekin and Pachykin can accompany you but not the

Carne." Riktlan looked at Gwon. "The King said you can't go in." He then turned to the guards. "Take him some place out of sight."

Thadarack glanced at Gwon. "I'll be okay," Gwon said. "Go, convince King Sturklan to help us. That's the most important thing right now."

"Are you sure?" Thexis asked. "I can stay with you."

"No," replied Gwon. "You need to be with Thadarack. You're much better with words than he is." He turned to Thadarack. "No offense."

Thadarack agreed, as it was most certainly true. He didn't realize it when Thexis offered to stay behind, but now that Gwon had said it, he was relieved she would be coming with him.

He knew there was a high chance that Thexis would have to chime in. Knowing the importance of the matter, however, he was determined to give it his best shot at convincing the King and the Queen. Well, should the Queen come, that is.

"He'll be alright," said Riktlan. "The guards have orders to keep him safe."

"Good luck," said Gwon.

"We'll be back soon," said Thadarack as he, Thexis, and Kylesia began following Riktlan toward the palace.

CHAPTER ELEVEN

ALLEGIANCE AND BETRAYAL

Like the Scythadon Palace, the palace before them was adorned with countless carvings above the arched entrance. One in particular caught Thadarack's eye. It was a carving of a Scythekin and Stegokin standing side by side. It made Thadarack optimistic that King Sturklan would help his kin.

As they entered the palace, they walked down a long corridor that was illuminated with small heat light pyres. Thadarack glanced into the first room they passed, and he saw a few young Stegokin eating greens. *King Sturklan's children?* he thought. He wondered which one was the heir to the throne and hoped that their relationship would mirror his father's and King Sturklan's.

They walked past two more empty rooms before finally reaching a large circular room at the end of the corridor. As they walked in, Thadarack saw five Stegokin present. He immediately knew which one was King Sturklan. He'd never met him before, but had heard countless stories about him from his father and others around Scythadon.

The King was massive, much bigger than any of the Stegokin

that Thadarack had encountered so far. Taller and burlier than those around him, his stature matched that of even Beroyn and Girozz. It was no surprise that he was the leader of the Stegokin.

Thadarack recalled his father telling him how a Stegokin became king or queen. It was much different from the dynastic rulers of Scythadon. The Stegokin partook in the Duellum, a fight to the death between the two strongest Stegokin from among those on the Stegodor council. It was an honorable death for the one that died, but even more of an honor to live and become the king or queen of all Stegokin.

While recalling this story, Thadarack realized that he didn't know how the Stegokin selected their council. He assumed the king or queen selected them but then again maybe not. The Duellum seemed barbaric to the young Prince, so he wouldn't be surprised if there was some other strange process for selecting council members.

"My King," said Riktlan upon entering. "I present to you, King Thax's Heir and future ruler of all Valderian Scythekin, the tyrant slayer and Viridi hero Thifsaer's very blood and kin, Prince Thadarack of the Kingdom of Scythadon." Riktlan glanced at Thexis and Kylesia. "And his companions, Thexis of Scythadon and Kylesia of...the Pachykin."

Thadarack was taken by surprise and felt a little uncomfortable. He had never been introduced like that before. As a matter of fact, he had never been introduced at all, especially not to a powerful Viridi king.

"I take my leave," continued Riktlan. "I'll keep an eye out for Queen Cerathorn and bring her here as soon as she returns." Riktlan turned for the exit. Before he left, he looked back at King

Sturklan. "If she returns." A moment later, he was gone.

After a somewhat awkward silence, King Sturklan spoke. "Prince Thadarack," he said in a distinguishably gruff voice. "I am humbled to have King Thax's heir, Thrifsaer's kin, in my Sanctum. Please, feel at home here."

"I appreciate you hosting us," Thadarack said, trying to quell the bubble forming in the back of his throat.

"Of course," said the King. "But let's get right to business. Riktlan briefed us on the current situation. I would like to hear from you, however, exactly what has happened."

The bubble in Thadarack's throat quickly got the best of him, as he found himself unable to speak. He tried to find his voice, but the words got stuck when he opened his mouth.

The King was extremely intimidating. That, and the fact that there were four other equally imposing Stegokin staring at him, caused Thadarack to freeze. He was in a different place, and the gravity of the situation at claw overwhelmed him.

He had barely been outside Scythadon, never mind all the way to a new kingdom without his father or mother. The Stegokin waited patiently for the Prince to speak, but luckily, he had Thexis by his side.

"King Thax and his companions were ambushed when they were about halfway to Stegodor," Thexis said. "We have come to warn you that the Carne have broken through the Wall and request both Stegodor and Ceragorre send aid immediately."

King Sturklan and those around him looked toward Thexis, almost as if they hadn't noticed her presence until now. "And your name is Thexis?" asked King Sturklan.

"Yes. I'm a good friend of Prince Thadarack's. I will be his

175

Left Claw when he ascends to the Scythadon throne."

"That's quite an honor," said the King.

"I believe you knew my grandfather, Paxtorr. He was among the slain in the fighting. As was our Queen. Please, you must send your army. We beg you for the sake of our kin and alliance."

"Alliance?" The Stegokin to the immediate right of the King scoffed. "What—"

"Silence!" King Sturklan bellowed.

The Stegokin didn't finish his thought.

In a much calmer tone, King Sturklan continued. "I'm sorry to hear about your grandfather. Paxtorr was a good friend of mine. Without him, this parley wouldn't have taken place. I am also saddened to hear about Queen Luxren. She was as good a queen as there could be and will be sorely missed."

The King turned and glanced at the Stegokin to his right. "Scythadon is and has always been our ally." He turned his gaze back toward Thexis. "I understand why King Thax has stayed out of this war. I don't hold that against him, not in the slightest. How is he? Does he live?"

Thexis gave Thadarack a brief look before turning back to the King. "He's been gravely injured," she said. "When we departed the city, he was recovering at our Mending House."

"I hope he makes a full recovery," said King Sturklan. "Now, let's discuss this Carne threat that Riktlan has briefed us about. How did they break through the Wall?"

Just when Thexis was about to answer, Thadarack broke his silence. He couldn't speak to bring the news of the Carne army, nor explain what happened on his father's trip to Stegodor. His anxiety about what had happened didn't allow him to speak, but

176

the pain he had for his mother's death and his father's eventual demise did.

As he opened his mouth, he heard someone approaching from behind. When he spoke, he turned around and saw Riktlan enter the Sanctum accompanied by four Trikin. One of them was the Trikin from the front gate earlier. "He's dying," the Prince said softly. "My father…King Thax…is dying."

All present were silent as somber expressions passed over their faces. It was evident that Riktlan was about to announce Queen Cerathorn, as his mouth was frozen half open. But he didn't say a word.

Without saying anything, the four Trikin walked to the other side of the Sanctum as far from King Sturklan as possible. Thadarack, Thexis, and Kylesia were standing in between them.

"Are you sure?" Thexis whispered.

"Yes," said Thadarack in a barely audible whisper. "Medicus confirmed the news with me just before we left."

"This is most troubling," said King Sturklan, glancing across the room at the Trikin. "Carne ambushed King Thax while he was on his way here. He still lives but is gravely injured."

Thadarack looked at the Trikin and thought he knew which one was the Queen. This Trikin's sheer size and intimidating demeanor were enough to convince the young Prince of her station. She was a little bigger than King Sturklan, and her entire body was a deep mahogany. One of her two longer horns was shorter than the other but was resharpened back to a razor-sharp point. A small crack ran down the left side of it. *I wonder if it broke during battle,* Thadarack thought.

After another awkward silence, the Queen spoke. "How

exactly did the Carne get past the Vlax Pass Wall?" she asked rudely. "And I wonder even more, how could they have *ambushed* King Thax? How was he so oblivious to the fact that there were Carne on the mainland?"

"We aren't entirely—"

"I'd like to hear it from the Prince," interrupted the Queen abruptly, cutting Thexis off before she could finish her answer. She stared directly at Thadarack with eyes as cold as ice.

Just when Thadarack thought his uneasiness would once again get the best of him, Thexis gently nudged his arm. "You can do this," she whispered.

With a lengthy sigh, Thadarack found his voice. "We're not sure how they got north of the Wall. But we believe they snuck around Scythadon to cut us off from you."

"That would make sense," said King Sturklan. "They knew if they attacked Scythadon first, then your father would have immediately reached out to us. They didn't want to give him that chance."

"Exactly," said Thadarack. "Or at least, that's what we think. We barely got through their perimeter on our way here. We took an old path through the Great Forest in an effort to go unnoticed, but a group of Carne attacked us."

Thadarack gestured toward Kylesia with his right claws. "Had it not been for the help of Kylesia's kin, we…" his voice trailed off after realizing he didn't want to finish his thought.

"Yes, Riktlan told us," King Sturklan said. "He mentioned the Carne have also ventured west and ran the Pachykin from their homes." He looked toward Kylesia. "I was sorry to hear of what happened. Please know that your kin are welcome in Stegodor if they need sanctuary."

"Thank you," said Kylesia.

Queen Cerathorn sneered. "How gracious and noble of you."

King Sturklan narrowed his eyes on the Queen. Having most likely sensed tension, Thexis spoke quickly. "We think the Carne have also gone west to attack the Longneck tribes. When the Pachykin were forced from their homes, they retreated east and hoped to find safety with our kin. But when they saw the Carne here too, they sought refuge in the Great Forest. Both Carne armies have thousands of warriors."

"Carne armies?" Queen Cerathorn asked. "What do you mean by Carne armies?"

"The Carne have formed two armies," said Thexis. "Well, at least we think so. Our leaders think they have united behind a new High King. The armies are of mixed—"

"What nonsense is this?" Queen Cerathorn interrupted again. "There's no High King of the Carne. They're savages, unable to even live among themselves. We have all heard the stories about how they kill and maim one another. It's probably just some rabble that got past the Wall."

Quiet murmurs filled the room.

"Are you sure about that?" King Sturklan asked. "You've never visited the Wall. Neither of us know what the Carne have been up to. We must trust this intel and act. At the very least, investigate. You really think some "rabble" could overcome King Thax and his company?"

"We?" Queen Cerathorn asked. "I'm not falling for this. How do I know this isn't some ruse that you and King Thax have devised to distract us? We both know where his loyalties lie. I will not be taken for a fool!"

"No, please listen," said Thexis. "We are not trying to deceive you. This is real." Thexis held up her bloody but now dried claws. "We fought Carne on our way here and our friend Gwon has the wounds to prove it. Do you really think we'd lie about Queen Luxren's death? And claim that King Thax is dying just to trick you?"

"Tell my Queen *what* your friend is," said the Trikin that they ran into at the front gate.

"That's not important," said Thexis. "We also traveled with another. He—"

"It's a Carne," interposed the Trikin. "Their so-called friend is a Carne. I would have mentioned it before, but I assumed he'd be here so you could see for yourself."

Queen Cerathorn glared at Thexis and then at King Sturklan. "A Carne?" she said with resounding anger in her voice.

"I know this Carne's father," said King Sturklan. "I've never been comfortable with King Thax harboring Carne, but I can vouch for him."

"Of course you do," said Queen Cerathorn. "This is incredible. You invite us here under the pretense of peace when, in reality, you're trying to dupe us into a false sense of security. What are you planning? To attack us once we've let our guard down?"

"That's not true," said Thadarack. "Listen to us. My father would try anything to avoid going to war with the Trikin. And so would I. We don't want war; we want peace. Now that the Carne are back, we all need to work together."

"We let this happen," said King Sturklan, glancing at Queen

Cerathorn with sorrowful eyes. "We brought this upon ourselves."

Queen Cerathorn stared cold-eyed back at the King. "Is that so?" she asked.

"We've been so focused on our quarrel that we forgot who the real enemy is," said King Sturklan. "I bet that's why the Carne were able to break through the Wall. King Thax has been so focused on us that he let his guard down."

"Even if any of this is true, how does it have anything to do with us?" the Queen asked. "You don't speak on behalf of the Trikin. Besides, the Scythekin failed. It was their charge to keep the Carne at bay."

King Sturklan gave the Queen another nasty look. "How can you say that? Our ancestors all vowed to guard the Wall together. It was our struggle with one another that led to us deserting it. We made it the sole responsibility of the Scythekin. This is just as much our fault as it is theirs."

"That was hundreds of years ago," said the Queen. "The Trikin are not at fault here."

"My Queen," interjected one of the Trikin that accompanied her. "Why even entertain this folly? We should return to Ceragorre. They have clearly deceived us."

"Fools!" King Sturklan howled. "This mentality is the exact reason we are at war! You're so self-centered you can't even admit when you're wrong!"

"How dare you!" Queen Cerathorn shouted, putting her head down in a charge-ready posture. "I will spill your brainless guts right here in your own pathetic city!"

"I'd like to see you try!" the King roared, swinging his

thagomizer to the side and smashing it into the ground with fury.

"Stop!" Thexis yelled. "This ridiculous hate is what almost led to your demise a thousand years ago! We all need to work together to—"

"Ridiculous?" King Sturklan interrupted Thexis so loud he drowned out her voice. "These tri-horned beasts fled like cowards with their tails between their legs while my kin fought and died to protect them!"

Queen Cerathorn pawed the ground and readied herself to charge. King Sturklan slammed his thagomizer into the ground again so hard that the entire Sanctum shook. Pebbles and dirt shot in every direction.

"Maybe if your pathetic kin could fight better, they wouldn't have needed any saving to begin with!" the Queen shouted.

"Enough!" Thadarack screamed at the top of his voice. "The Carne are here! They are here to destroy everything and everyone! They want revenge against all of us! Do you think the Carne would consider coming to a place like this to discuss peace? While you two rip each other apart, the Carne march on my kin…"

His voice trailed off a bit before he continued on in a quieter manner. "They're your real enemy. Your ancestors realized it long ago." He paused briefly and looked at King Sturklan. "My kin came to your aid. Please, come to ours now when we need it most."

Thadarack then turned and looked at Queen Cerathorn. "Do I look like someone trying to deceive you? My mother is dead, and my father is dying. Ceraplazz realized he made a mistake when he abandoned the Stegokin. He later marched alongside

Thrifsaer. Together, Scythekin, Stegokin, Trikin…" He gestured toward Kylesia. "And Pachykin, with countless other Viridi tribes behind them, fought, bled, and died together, side by side, to destroy evil. An evil that didn't want peace. For the sake of everything we hold dear, I beg you, put aside your differences and help us."

Queen Cerathorn and King Sturklan calmed down, as did their guards beside them. The room fell completely silent. The Queen and King stared at Thadarack, probably too angry with one another to even share a glance.

Thadarack turned toward Thexis and saw her smiling at him, a smile so raw it warmed his entire body. A few more moments went by before King Sturklan broke the silence. He looked at the Stegokin to his immediate left. "Glathzolm," he said. "Muster the army." He then shifted his gaze back to Thadarack. "The Stegokin will march for Scythadon."

"But my King," said a Stegokin to his right. "What of the Trikin army?"

"I'm going to help the Scythekin," said the King before shooting a glance at Queen Cerathorn. "The Trikin can do as they please."

Thadarack looked at the Queen and saw she was still staring right back at him. After a short while, she shifted her eyes to the King. "I will uphold the truce for now," she said. "We will not attack Stegodor or any other Stegokin in the near future."

"And what of Scythadon?" Thexis asked.

"I will return to Ceragorre with my army," said the Queen.

"How can that be your answer?" Thexis asked. "We don't know for sure how many Carne are marching on our city. We may need all the help we can get!"

"Exactly!" Queen Cerathorn shot back. "You have no idea where the Carne are. What if they're on their way to Ceragorre right now? I must return to protect my city above all else."

"Of course," said King Sturklan. "This news doesn't shock me at all."

Queen Cerathorn once again glared at the King. "Watch it!" she roared.

"Or what?" the King asked calmly. "You'll attack a defenseless city?"

The Queen didn't say another word. She stormed out of the Sanctum with her guards following closely behind.

"But Queen Cerathorn!" Thexis yelled to no avail.

"Go!" one of the Stegokin screamed. "Cower behind your walls!"

"The Trikin's spinelessness has been passed down all the way from Ceraplazz!" another yelled.

"No Stegokin will fight alongside that of a Trikin!" a third shouted.

"This is madness," said Thexis.

"Never trust a Trikin!" Glathzolm yelled.

King Sturklan was silent. The disgusted look on his face did all the talking for him.

Although bitter at the Queen's departure, Thadarack was relieved King Sturklan agreed to aid his kin. "Thanks for helping us," he said. "We're eternally grateful."

"Don't thank me yet," said the King. "But hopefully, you will soon understand just how grateful *we are* that your kin helped our ancestors." The King gave Thadarack a slight smile. "You are welcome to march with us. For now, please go. I must speak with my council in private."

Thadarack, Thexis, and Kylesia nodded and left the Sanctum. They headed back down the corridor and exited the palace.

"We must catch up to Queen Cerathorn," said Thexis. "We need to convince her to reconsider."

"We'll try," said Thadarack. "But first, we need to find Gwon."

"Thadarack," said Riktlan from just outside the palace. "Follow me."

The trio followed Riktlan behind the palace to a small, secluded alleyway. There, they met up with their friend.

"So, what happened?" Gwon asked. "Are they going to help us?"

"Stubbornness happened," said Thexis. "King Sturklan is going to march to Scythadon without Queen Cerathorn."

"Well, that's good news, right?" asked Gwon.

"I don't know," said Thadarack. "It's something, but we have no idea what we're up against. We need all the help we can get."

"Let's go," said Thexis. "We must speak with the Queen."

"We'll escort you to the front gate," said Riktlan, gesturing his guards forward.

They headed in the direction of the front gate. On his way, Thadarack hoped more than anything that they could convince Queen Cerathorn to change her mind.

CHAPTER TWELVE

BONDS OF YORE

Just as the group exited the city, Thadarack saw Queen Cerathorn and her guards descend the hill a good distance away. "There she is," he said. "Come on."

"Wait," said Kylesia. "I must return to my kin. I will take King Sturklan up on his offer and bring my kin to Stegodor."

"I'm not sure that we ever thanked you for what you did in the forest," said Thadarack. "We will forever be in your debt."

"You have no need to thank me," said Kylesia. "I just wish we could come with you, but we are so few. I'm not sure whether we would make a difference, and we have also been through so much. I couldn't ask that of them right now."

"We wouldn't expect you to," said Thadarack. "May we cross paths with you again."

"I hope we do," said Kylesia.

Thadarack, Thexis, and Gwon said goodbye to their new friend. Kylesia took off toward the forest, while they ran in the direction of Queen Cerathorn. When they came upon the top of the hill, Thadarack saw the vast Trikin army scattered across an open field for as far as he could see.

There had to be thousands of Trikin below, many of which were thankfully facing the other direction. Fortunately for Thadarack and his friends, not many noticed that they were there. The ones that did see them did double takes and froze in place. They stared at the three friends with mixtures of confusion and concern across their faces.

"There she is," said Thexis, pointing toward Queen Cerathorn with her right index claw. "Let's hurry before more Trikin spot us."

They descended the hill and headed toward the Queen. It wasn't long before they reached her. She was talking to a group of Trikin on the outskirts of the army encampment.

"Queen Cerathorn," said Thexis. "We need to speak with you."

The Queen slightly turned her head, but not far enough to see them. She then straightened up.

"Sound the march," she said. "We leave for Ceragorre at once. Jearspike, travel west with your party and then head north. Ensure there are no Carne bound for Ceragorre. If you should come across any, report back as soon as possible. Make haste!"

"Move out!" Jearspike shouted as she and about ten other Trikin stampeded away.

"Please reconsider," said Thexis. "You must—"

"I mustn't do anything!" the Queen snapped as she turned aggressively around, interrupting Thexis before she could finish her thought. She then glared at Gwon. "And how dare you bring this abomination here!"

The Trikin to her side eyed Gwon and lowered their horns

viciously.

Thexis jumped in between her friend and the Trikin. "This is Gwon," she said, raising her claws in a peaceful way. "He means you no harm. He's our friend."

"Friend?" The Queen scoffed. "He's a Carne! Have you forgotten what his kind did to us?"

Before Thexis could answer, Thadarack spoke calmly in an effort to transition the conversation from Gwon and ease the tension. "Please Queen Cerathorn," he said. "We need your help. I swear we are telling the truth about what has happened. We wouldn't be here otherwise."

The Queen's aggression subsided as she turned her head slightly. "At ease," she said before looking back at Thadarack.

As she spoke, the Trikin raised their horns but kept their eyes locked on Gwon. "I'm sorry to hear about Queen Luxren," she said. "And I do hope your father recovers. Although we haven't been on the best of terms, he kept his word and didn't involve himself in the war. Because of that, I will honor the peace for now."

"So you do believe us?" Thadarack asked.

"At first I didn't," said the Queen. "But I can tell when someone is sincere."

"Then why won't you help us?" Thexis asked.

"You know very little about this threat," said Queen Cerathorn. "I know even less. How do I know that Carne haven't already flanked Ceragorre? How do I know that my city isn't under siege as we speak? I must return home. Ceragorre is my number one priority."

"You know the stories about the Great War," said Thexis.

"Without the Scythekin, the Viridi would have perished. The Carne know that, and they are trying to get rid of us first. And what if they already knew that you and the Stegokin were at war? What if they're counting on your hate for one another to be your very downfall?"

The Queen was silent for a moment and appeared to be deep in thought. "How could they know that?" she finally asked. "They've been locked away south of the Wall for a thousand years. It's probably some rogue Carne that you can easily dispatch on your own anyway."

"If that's true, then help us!" pleaded Thexis. "What do you have to lose?"

"I won't take that risk," said Queen Cerathorn sternly. "Not when Ceragorre may be in danger."

"You're scared," said Thexis. "We all are, but——"

"How dare you!" the Queen roared. "Watch how you speak to me, lest I change my mind about keeping the peace!"

"My apologies, Queen Cerathorn," said Thexis. "I didn't mean to offend you."

"My Queen," said a Trikin to Queen Cerathorn's right. "Forgive me for speaking out of turn, but maybe we should stay for a while longer and wait to hear back from Jearspike. If the Carne aren't heading toward Ceragorre, perhaps we can help."

The Queen turned her head slowly and looked menacingly at the Trikin that spoke. She glared at him for an awkward moment when another Trikin approached from behind. "My Queen," the Trikin said. "The army is ready to depart."

Queen Cerathorn turned back toward the trio. "You have my answer," she said as she turned around and began walking away.

The Trikin around her quickly followed suit, except for the one that suggested they stay. Just when he opened his mouth to speak, Queen Cerathorn turned her head and shouted. "Hornbrigg! Let's go!"

The Trikin closed his mouth and locked eyes with Thadarack. The young Prince saw the sadness behind them and the slight frown across his face. It was evident that Hornbrigg wanted to help, but what was he to do? The Queen had already decided she was returning to Ceragorre. Even so, Thadarack was hopeful the Trikin before him would somehow change the Queen's mind.

Right as Hornbrigg turned around and began following the Queen, Thadarack spoke loudly. "My father told me that Ceraplazz regretted not helping the Stegokin. He told me not a day went by that he didn't feel remorse for forsaking them. From that day forward, he pledged to always aid his fellow Viridi, no matter what kin."

The Queen stopped walking but didn't turn her head. "He knew who the enemy was. Don't make the same mistake that he did. There may be no second chance this time."

Hornbrigg then said something to Queen Cerathorn, but the distance made it too difficult for Thadarack to make out what it was. The Queen didn't respond, and after a short while, she started walking again. The trio watched as the Trikin army began to march in the opposite direction of Scythadon. It wasn't long before they had disappeared from sight.

"It's hopeless," said Thexis. "She's not going to change her mind. My grandfather wasn't kidding when he told me how stubborn the Trikin are. I believed him, but I never imagined they'd be like this."

"Maybe Hornbrigg will convince her to change her mind," said Thadarack optimistically. "I think he wants to help."

Thadarack glanced at his Carne friend and saw the defeated look on his face. Gwon was staring blankly in the direction the Trikin had gone. Thadarack recalled how Queen Cerathorn had referred to him as an "abomination." His heart broke for his friend, having to endure such cruelty. "Are you alright Gwon?" he asked.

In an instant, Gwon's demeanor changed. "Yes, I'm fine."

"She shouldn't have called you that," said Thexis. "That's not you at all."

"It's okay," said Gwon. "I know where my heart is, and that's all that matters."

"As do we," said Thexis as she gave him a warm smile.

Gwon returned it. "What's next?"

"I suppose we return to Stegodor and wait," said Thadarack. "There's really nothing else we can do in the meantime."

The three friends began walking back toward Stegodor. As they approached the walls, Thadarack heard orders being yelled and the sounds of Stegokin thagomizers smashing into the ground. Right when they entered the city, Riktlan approached them.

"Prince Thadarack," Riktlan said. "King Sturklan wants you to join him in the Sanctum immediately."

Thadarack, Thexis, and Gwon followed Riktlan back through the city toward the Sanctum. Although Gwon was once again the target of many angry and disgusted looks, the group was able to make their way to the palace courtyard with no issues. Once there, Riktlan turned around and addressed Thexis and Gwon.

"Both of you, wait here. The King wants to see Prince Thadarack alone."

Before Thadarack could say anything, Thexis spoke. "Go, we'll be fine."

Thadarack followed Riktlan through the palace corridor and into the Sanctum.

"I'll be outside, my King," said Riktlan before he departed.

King Sturklan was alone in the Sanctum with his back toward Thadarack, looking at a spike from a Stegokin thagomizer. It was suspended on the wall right behind where King Sturklan was standing during the meeting earlier.

Thadarack didn't see it before. The King must have been right in front of it, blocking the Prince's view. It was difficult to tell from where Thadarack stood, but it looked stained. It had a red tint as if it had been soaked in something. Thadarack immediately thought he knew what that "something" was.

The tip was no longer pointy as a chunk was missing, and there was what looked like a long crack that ran three quarters down the right side. Although it was damaged, it was still large, bigger than the largest spike on the King's tail.

Something about the spike mesmerized Thadarack. He was unable to take his eyes off it. He couldn't quite place what it was, but it looked so majestic and had a similar appeal to that of the colossus he had seen on his way into the city.

It was the only thing on the wall, and it was held up there by a good amount of cob. Thadarack's trance-like state was suddenly broken when the King spoke in a low, almost inaudible voice.

"This is all that's left of her," he said with his back still toward Thadarack. "This is all we have." He turned around and locked eyes with the young Prince. "It's one of Pyklania's spikes. It's all we have left from when Kezmirin brutally killed her on that fateful day."

Kezmirin? Thadarack thought. He had never heard that name before, and he was reluctant to ask King Sturklan who Kezmirin was. The King, however, prompted his question for him. "Do you know of Kezmirin?"

Thadarack shook his head.

"Kezmirin the Malevolent," said King Sturklan. It's said that his wrath and terror were only second to that of Orzligorn's. He was a Spinekin and one of Orzligorn's most trusted lieutenants in the Great War...pure evil."

King Sturklan turned back toward the spike. "You have Thrifsaer's body buried just outside Scythadon. The Trikin have Ceraplazz's body. This is all we have of Pyklania's. It's said that her body was so brutally maimed during the Battle of Tarned Hill that after it was impossible to determine what...parts were hers. They only knew that this spike, soaked in the blood of our enemies, was hers because of the royal marking."

Thadarack hadn't noticed before, but now he could see the marking etched into the spike across the crack. It was faint, and he couldn't actually make out what the marking was. The crack split it right in half. This, paired with the fact it was barely visible, made the details very difficult to see.

"Had Thrifsaer and your kin not shown up when they did that day, we wouldn't even have this. Not only that but we wouldn't be here. My only solace is taking note of the fact that Kezmirin was slain by our ancestors years later during the Battle of Vlax Pass."

King Sturklan turned back around and looked into Thadarack's eyes. "We are eternally grateful for what the Scythekin did for us." He then raised his head high. "We are a proud species, and I will be the first to admit that we can be stubborn as spikes. I know what my kin's resolve would have been at the Battle of Tarned Hill, but we...but I...am not too proud to state that Stegokin only draw breath today because of the Scythekin."

The King walked closer to Thadarack. "You have my word, Prince Thadarack. I will not rest until I free Scythadon from the jaws of the savage beasts at its gate, or so help me Hallowed Lumina, I will die trying."

King Sturklan's words sent shivers down Thadarack's spine. The feelings of pride and thankfulness that rushed him all at once were almost too much to bear. He could sense a tear forming, a tear he tried so hard to quell so he wouldn't look weak in front of the great Stegokin king.

The Prince's only reservation was wondering if it would be enough. Was the Stegokin army enough to save his city? Could they defeat the Carne that were already most likely attacking Scythadon? *I hope so...more than anything,* he thought.

"I have ordered my First Commander, Glathzolm, to hasten the readiness of the army. We will march for Scythadon within the hour."

"Thank you," Thadarack said. "From the bottom of my heart. I am beyond grateful and know that my father will be too."

Will be, he thought. He believed his father was still alive, and maybe Medicus was wrong after all. Perhaps he was going to survive, and he was already doing better. Thadarack wanted more than anything to return home so he could see for himself.

"You have no need to thank me," replied the King. "My forebears pledged to help the Scythekin should they ever need it. I'm simply honoring that pledge and will do all I can to aid King Thax in his fight against this evil enemy. It's my honor to aid you as the future King of Scythadon."

"Is there anything I can do to help right now?" Thadarack asked.

"I don't know what I am marching into," said the King. "Do you have any other intel you can share with me? Any idea who might be leading the army or what Carne it's composed of? Do we have any idea how many Carne there actually are?"

Thadarack thought to himself, trying hard to remember exactly what Clarrius had said when he returned to Scythadon. "I don't believe our scouts gave a specific number," he said. "All they said was that they saw the army from a distance and that there were thousands of Carne. I know very little, unfortunately, for we left before the army reached the city. I believe the Carne that attacked my father were Tarbokin, Carnokin, and Allokin."

"What about the Carne you and your friends fought in the woods? What were they?"

Thadarack had been so focused on making it to Stegodor alive that he realized he hadn't even talked to his friends about what happened—not just during the fight but after as well. "I'm not sure," he said.

"If I could only speak to your father," said King Sturklan. "I know very little about the Carne. I've heard of those three kins but don't know much about them."

"I wish I could tell you more. I'm sorry."

"No, you have nothing to be sorry for. I should be the one to apologize to you. The Stegokin abandoned the Wall long ago. Our quarrel with the Trikin became our focus. A quarrel that I believed was necessary up until now. Queen Cerathorn won't admit it, but I see now. We have gotten so distracted with our hate and contempt for one another that we have let the real enemy regroup and walk through our back door. It's no surprise they are attacking Scythadon first. With the Scythekin defeated, who will stand against them? Two Viridi tribes that have been at war with one another? What have either of us accomplished?"

King Sturklan's posture and demeanor quickly turned into that of rage.

"How did we let this happen?" he yelled. "How could we be so petty? The Carne are out for blood, revenge for what we did to them a thousand years ago!" He calmed down a bit before letting out a long sigh. "This is our fault, not yours. I should have tried to change Queen Cerathorn's mind. Instead, I let my disdain for her takeover and watched her walk out of here."

"We caught up with her," said Thadarack. "We tried to persuade her to help again, but she refused. She's worried that the Carne may also be on their way to Ceragorre."

"They're not," said the King. "The Carne aren't worried about us. At least not right now. I know what their plan is. It's to destroy the Scythekin and the Longnecks first. Then they'll march on us."

Hearing "destroy the Scythekin" didn't sit well with Thadarack. He couldn't let that happen. But after all, what could he do? He was one Scythekin, not even a seasoned fighter. His only hope rested upon the Stegokin's spikes.

Just when Thadarack opened his mouth to speak, Riktlan entered the Sanctum. "My King, the army is ready," he said. "Glathzolm is waiting for you at the city gate. She's leaving her brother's company to help defend the city should it be attacked while we are away."

"No," said King Sturklan. "We bring the entire army. Leave only the reserves for now."

"But my King," challenged Riktlan. "What if the Carne flank around us or the Trikin—"

"They won't," interrupted the King hastily. "The Carne aren't expecting us to show up. They made that clear when they set up this perimeter around Scythadon and ambushed King Thax. Their sole focus is there, not here. And the Trikin won't attack. That I'm sure of."

Riktlan still didn't look convinced, but King Sturklan made up his mind. Thadarack watched as Riktlan bowed his head and departed the Sanctum.

"Well," said King Sturklan. "I believe it is time. Let's get ready for our journey to Scythadon. My only hope is that we aren't too late."

Thadarack thought about his father, Girozz, Beroyn, and Rhinn. He thought about Septirius, Medicus, Haelicus, and all those that he had known and grown up with. He envisioned the city and its beautiful, transplanted mushrooms and impressive walls.

The young Prince saw the farm full of greens and seeds. He saw the cultivators working hard as if they were right before him. The magnificence of the palace flashed before his eyes. He was ready to return home. "Me too," he eventually said.

"The Scythekin are exceptionally skilled fighters," said King Sturklan. "They will put up one heck of a fight. You can count on that."

Thadarack was hopeful but still worried about Scythadon. He had never been this far from home or away for this long. It had only been a few days since he and his companions had left their home, but it felt much longer than that.

Not knowing how Scythadon was doing during such a catastrophe was eating away at him. However, Thadarack was glad he came and was able to persuade the Stegokin to send an army. He couldn't help but feel like his journey was just beginning, though.

"I must take my leave," said King Sturklan. "We will march for Scythadon soon."

The King walked past Thadarack and exited the Sanctum. Thadarack looked back at Pyklania's spike. It was so surreal to look at it, this thousand-year-old spike from the most famous Stegokin ever to roam Valdere.

The Prince hoped he would be remembered like Pyklania and Thrifsaer. *What will be my great deed?* he thought. *How can I make a difference in this world?* He then remembered what his father had told him about how his legacy would be showing the Carne that they could live peacefully side by side with the Viridi.

Thadarack vowed that he would fulfill his father's wish. *I'll do everything I can,* he thought, turning to depart the Sanctum. He then walked out and went to find his friends.

CHAPTER THIRTEEN

FEAR NO ENEMY

As Thadarack approached his friends a little way outside the palace, he saw them watching a large group of Stegokin warriors. Although the warriors looked determined and impressive, he couldn't help but notice that there didn't seem to be that many.

Thadarack immediately thought about how there might have been more if the Stegokin and Trikin hadn't been at war for the last three years. It upset him to think this, especially because the future of his city might depend on the Stegokin.

"I was expecting more," said Thexis. "I hope this is enough to defeat the Carne."

Thadarack tried to look past the warriors to see if there were any others in the distance. All he saw were some other Stegokin bystanders. "Is this all of them?" he asked nervously.

"I think so," said Gwon. "We haven't seen any others."

Thadarack grew even more worried. He remembered how scared Clarrius looked when he told them how massive the Carne army was. To see such a small Stegokin force before them didn't go a long way toward making Thadarack feel confident that they could defeat the Carne.

"All we can do is hope," said Thexis. "Hope that our kin will hold out long enough and that together with the Stegokin, we can defeat them."

"I can't believe that Queen Cerathorn left," said Gwon. "She's acting ridiculous. All she had to do was send some scouts back to Ceragorre, make sure that all is well, and agree to march with us back to Scythadon. You saw how fast the Trikin are. If they hurried, they could have gotten to Ceragorre and back in no time."

"She's definitely just scared," said Thexis. "Did you see her face? When we first told her about the Carne army, she was frightened."

"I'm scared," said Gwon. "King Sturklan is probably scared. Everybody is scared. Are we cowering or running?"

Thinking about how he was scared, Thadarack remembered his level of fear in the Great Forest when the Carne attacked them. It replayed in his mind how he didn't partake in the fighting.

He didn't want to talk to his friends about it but felt like he should. After all, his inaction could have ended up getting them killed. "I wanted to apologize," he said. "For how I acted in the Great Forest when the Carne attacked."

Both Thexis and Gwon looked at their friend, cocking their heads slightly.

"What do you mean?" Thexis asked.

"Apologize for *what?*" Gwon asked.

Thadarack quickly regretted saying anything. Had they not even noticed? Maybe in the heat of the action, they didn't realize

Thadarack wasn't fighting. He wanted to come up with some kind of lie, but he decided he owed his friends the truth. "I hesitated. When you charged at the Carne to help Arkonius, I froze." He looked at the ground, too ashamed to look his friends in the eyes.

"You have nothing to apologize for," said Thexis. "You're the Prince of Scythadon. You need to survive."

"Yeah, don't apologize," said Gwon. "I was actually hoping you would run. Getting to Stegodor was the most important thing at the time."

"We would have given our lives to protect you," said Thexis. "And besides, you didn't run. You could have, but when we thought the Pachykin were more Carne, you stood by our side."

Thadarack looked up at his friends and saw the sincerity in their eyes. He immediately realized how lucky he was to have them, two companions that he knew he could count on and trust. It was evident that no matter what they faced, they could face it and prevail together. "Have I ever told you how awesome you two are?" he asked.

"Well, I think that goes without saying," said Thexis.

"Of course I'm awe..." Gwon paused and smirked at Thexis. "Of course *we're* awesome."

"I'm just glad I have you two by my side," said Thadarack with a smile on his face.

"Forever and always," said Thexis.

"Always and forever," said Gwon.

Thexis playfully glared at Gwon. "You're such a pain," she said.

The three friends laughed as they turned back toward the

warriors. Laughing felt good, considering everything that had happened. A moment later, however, he stopped laughing as he remembered his concerns about the size of the Stegokin army. It was hard to tell, but he estimated the Stegokin army was less than half the size of the Scythekin army back home.

"We should have tried harder to convince Queen Cerathorn," said Thexis. "I should have tried harder."

"It's not your fault," said Gwon. "It didn't help our cause that I was there. I shouldn't have gone."

"No, it is my fault," said Thexis. "I am to be the Left Claw. If I can't convince Queen Cerathorn to help us when we need it most, what good am I? I bet my grandfather would have been able to persuade her."

"You said it yourself, Queen Cerathorn is scared," said Thadarack. "That's why she left, not because you weren't convincing enough. Nobody would have been able to change her mind."

Thexis sighed. "You might be right. Her fear is causing her to repeat the very same mistake that her ancestors made. I just hope the consequences aren't worse this time."

Consequences, thought Thadarack. He didn't want to think about the consequences. The very existence of his home hung in the balance. He then had a realization, a thought about something that made him distressed.

If Scythadon, and possibly the Stegokin army, were destroyed because the Trikin abandoned them, he'd never forgive Queen Cerathorn. The current war between Ceragorre and Stegodor started to make a little more sense to the young Prince. Was this abandonment any different from the Great Forsaking during the

Great War?

"Maybe she'll change her mind," said Gwon. "Maybe she'll help us after all."

"I doubt it," said Thexis. "Besides, she's already marching back to Ceragorre. If she decides to come back, it may be too late.

Too late, thought Thadarack. *Consequences.* This was all making the young Prince distraught. They were talking about how Scythadon may be destroyed by the time they returned. It was too much to bear and most certainly too devastating to contemplate.

"You know what I was thinking," continued Thexis. "What if there really *are* other good Carne? What if you and your father aren't the only ones that feel the fighting between us and them isn't right?"

"Where are they?" Gwon asked. "In the last thousand years, only two Carne have approached the Wall peacefully. If there are other good Carne like us, where have they been?"

"That is a good point," said Thexis. "It's just hard to believe that you and Girozz are the only good ones."

"My father believes there are others," said Thadarack. "I will do everything I can to make the Carne see that we don't have to be enemies. That we can live together peacefully."

"And how are you supposed to do that?" Gwon asked. "The Carne ambushed your father. They are attacking Scythadon, and they have all but destroyed the Pachykin. They don't seem like they'd consider talking about peace, never mind living alongside Viridi."

"Well, I'm with King Thax," said Thexis. "We have to try.

Otherwise, we'll be fighting until one of us…" She paused. "The fighting might not end the way it did last time. We may not be as lucky."

"I'm not sure luck had anything to do with it," said Gwon. "Good will always best evil."

Thadarack hoped Gwon was right. That good would always prevail over evil. And what were the Carne if they weren't evil? They wanted to enslave or kill all Viridi. How much more evil could they be?

"Has Girozz ever talked about where he came from?" Thexis asked. "Did he ever say anything about the possibility of there being more Carne like you?"

"No," replied Girozz. "He never likes discussing where we came from. I've tried asking him many times, but he always changes the conversation. Honestly, I've never liked how annoyed he got anyway."

Although Girozz was good, Thadarack knew that Carne were known for their short tempers and aggressive nature. Even Girozz, from time to time, would grow aggravated at the smallest of things. It was for the best that they lived in a house behind the palace, far away from the other homes. Even through the palace walls, Thadarack could hear Girozz overly frustrated every so often.

The fact that the Carne had been able to join forces to begin with was surprising. Thadarack thought about how evil this so-called "High King" must be for the various Carne tribes to obey him. He also wondered where he was. Was he the one leading the army toward Scythadon? Was he in the West?

"I'm sure it's very difficult for Girozz to talk about his past," said Thexis. "Especially considering what happened before he brought you to Scythadon."

Thadarack glanced at Gwon, wondering if he'd be angry with him for telling Thexis about his mother. To his surprise, Gwon didn't seem shocked at all.

"Yeah, it is," replied Gwon. "It's a shame that all this hate exists. I know that if the Carne would give the Viridi a chance, they'd see that we could live side by side."

"I have hope," said Thexis. "If King Thax believes it's possible, then so do I."

The three friends continued watching the Stegokin army prepare. Although not a huge army, they still looked like they would be a force to be reckoned with. Thadarack watched as the Stegokin methodically swung their thagomizers in sync, hitting targets painted on stumps in front of them.

The Prince's gaze was broken when Riktlan spoke to the friends from behind. "Pretty impressive, huh? We weren't always this disciplined, especially not during the Great War."

"What do you mean?" asked Thadarack.

"Many Stegokin would never admit it, but we have had to adapt a different, more defensive fighting style because of our lack of speed. And as such, we must rely heavily on the accuracy and strength of our thagomizers. It's the first of the two most important lessons taught to new army recruits."

"What's the other lesson?" asked Thexis.

"Learning how to be as agile as possible. Although we are slow runners, we have learned how to shuffle our feet quickly."

Thadarack watched as the Stegokin before him, one after another, shuffled in unison as they struck the targets. He noticed there were two rows of Stegokin, each performing a different movement.

"It's actually how we defeated the Trikin during our last engagement," continued Riktlan. "Even after three years, they still haven't figured out how to fight us effectively."

"What are they doing now?" Thadarack asked.

"Ah, our most effective battle formation," Riktlan said proudly. "Due to our inability to charge, our warriors mostly fight in a defensive, two-battle-line posture. The first line, spaced just far enough from one another, swings their thagomizers at the charging enemy simultaneously. Their main goal is to hit the enemy's legs or torsos, ultimately trying to slow and hinder their advance."

Riktlan paused and gestured with his head to a few Stegokin on Thadarack's right. "There, see what they're doing? That's what they're practicing right now."

"And what does the second battle line do?" Thexis asked.

"The second battle line shuffles as quickly as possible and places their hind legs on their fellow warriors' backs, swinging their thagomizers upward straight toward the enemy's face. Right there, see what they're doing?" Riktlan gestured toward a group of Stegokin to his left.

Thadarack watched in awe as the Stegokin practiced their battle formations. For a kin that relied on their defensive capabilities, it seemed critical that they were trained to fight effectively together.

"When done in sync with one another, our two battle lines are almost impenetrable," continued Riktlan. "Due to our defensive fighting style, the Trikin typically don't charge at us head on.

They'll try to flank us using their speed." Riktlan smirked. "Fortunately for us, that tactic failed miserably for them during our last battle. The Trikin rely too heavily on their charge, and they aren't very effective at close range."

"But what about when fighting the Carne?" asked Thexis. "You've never fought them before, right?"

"I'd assume it's similar," said Riktlan. "The Carne charge too, don't they? I foresee a similar fight to that of the Trikin. Well, the difference being the Trikin charge with their horns, while the Carne charge with their teeth."

"My father said that fighting Trikin isn't all that different from fighting Carne," interjected Gwon. "He said if you can fight one, then you can learn how to fight the other."

Riktlan glanced at Gwon and nodded.

"And might I just add," continued Gwon. "You have a very impressive army. If I was fighting the Stegokin, I would be fearful."

Riktlan slightly smiled. "You're beginning to grow on me, Carne," he said.

Thadarack saw a gigantic smile spread across Gwon's face. Having heard Riktlan speak this way made the Prince hopeful. If Riktlan came around so quickly and warmed up to his Carne friend, then maybe the other Viridi could too.

Riktlan looked back at the army. "If our battle lines falter, though, it's very difficult for us to regroup. That's why it's so critical that all who fight in the army are in top shape, and able to carry out their duties without issue."

"Well, let's hope that doesn't happen," said Thexis.

"It can't," said Riktlan sternly. "We are throwing everything we have at the Carne. We are leaving few reserves here to defend the city and should we fail…" Riktlan's voice trailed off. "I must report to Glathzolm," he said eventually, turning toward the trio. "I'll see you three later."

"Before you go," said Thadarack. "How quickly do you think we can make it to Scythadon?"

Riktlan narrowed his eyes at Thadarack. "Are you insinuating that it's going to take us a long time?"

The young Prince didn't mean to seem disrespectful, but after all, it was common knowledge that the Stegokin moved slowly. Even Riktlan himself admitted as much not but a few moments ago. "Um…I," Thadarack stammered. "No—"

Riktlan smiled and interrupted the Prince. "I don't blame you for asking. You'd be surprised at what our agility training has done for our endurance. We can go long distances fairly quickly without needing to stop or take breaks. We'll be there in no time. Don't you worry about that."

"Thanks for everything, Riktlan," said Thadarack.

Riktlan nodded, said goodbye, and walked away. Just as he did so, another Stegokin approached.

"Prince Thadarack," he said. "My name is Tryzolm. I am one of Glathzolm's captains. King Sturklan said that you and your friends can march with my company. The King will be in the front leading the army alongside Glathzolm. He wants you with my company in the center for your safety should we run into any Carne on the way."

"We can march with him at the front," said Thadarack, trying to appear brave. "After all, you're marching to Scythadon to help us."

"It is not a request," replied Tryzolm.

Just when Thadarack was about to challenge him, he heard King Sturklan begin to speak from atop the ramparts just over the city gate.

The King's stature was even more impressive now that he overlooked the army. His voice was stern, and his words were clear and crisp. Thadarack decided it was more prudent to listen to the Stegokin king than to argue with Tryzolm.

"My fellow Stegokin, today is the day!" the King shouted. "The day that we honor our forebears' pledge and march to the aid of the Scythekin!" He scanned the army and subtly nodded his head proudly. "Many of you have never been to Scythadon. Indeed, many of you don't personally know any Scythekin. Your family and friends are here, safe behind the walls of Stegodor. You may be wondering if this march is worth it. If this march is necessary at all. You might even question my decision and intentions as your king."

He paused, once again scanning all those who intently watched him. "But I ask you now, what would those that came before us do? Those that have passed down the stories from generation to generation. We all know what happened that fateful day atop Tarned Hill. We all know how our ancestors faced certain death and extinction. To face the fear that they would no longer exist and would be forgotten. To have been all alone and think that nobody was coming to help them as the enemy closed in…I say to you now, if Thrifsaer hadn't shown up with the Scythekin army, our kin would be but a distant memory, a faint whisper in the wind. All of this…"

He looked around at the city before returning his gaze to his army.

"Would not exist. Our heroine, Pyklania, would have given her life in vain. Her memory lost to all." He scanned for Thadarack and locked eyes with him. "That is why we march. We march to aid those that saved us a thousand years ago. Those who selflessly gave their lives for a kin they never knew and never met. Those whose very descendants face the same threat that we did on Tarned Hill. We will march and face this enemy with them, together."

King Sturklan's voice grew louder and bolder with each coming word. "Now come, my kin! March with me to Scythadon and show the Scythekin that they do not face the Carne alone! Show them that we honor our forebears' pledge! Show them who their friends are and that we will never, ever forsake them! We march for honor! We march for Thrifsaer! We march for Pyklania!"

The army roared and smacked their thagomizers on the ground with such thunderous force that the very ground they stood upon shook. It was a speech for the ages, a speech so filled with sincerity and fervor it sent shivers down Thadarack's spine.

He was proud to be Thrifsaer's kin and a Scythekin. For a brief moment, his fear melted away. He wasn't anxious or worried, for he was among friends. Friends that were willing to give their lives for him and his kin.

"March forth!" King Sturklan yelled as he descended from the ramparts. "And fear no enemy!"

The King, with Glathzolm by his side, reached the city gate. As the pair exited the city, the army followed closely behind. The synchronized marching of the Stegokin was magnificent.

"I have hope," said Thadarack quietly to his friends.

"Me too," said Thexis.

"As do I," said Gwon.

Thadarack, Thexis, and Gwon walked alongside Tryzolm's company. After a few moments, Stegodor was in the distance behind them. Thadarack looked back at the city and watched as it became smaller. He turned around and looked at the army before him. *I'm coming, Father*, he thought. *We're coming.*

CHAPTER FOURTEEN

MARCH TO SCYTHADON

It had been over a day since the three friends departed Stegodor with the Stegokin army. They marched quickly along the Eastern Road, and only stopped a few times to eat and drink when they came across water.

The night before had been an interesting experience for Thadarack. He grew worried that they'd have to stop marching for the night. He voiced his concern to Tryzolm, and hoped that there was some way they could continue. Tryzolm grinned, but didn't say anything.

When it got so dark that they could barely see a few feet in front of them, dozens of Stegokin across the perimeter of the army lit up like bonfires in the night. Thadarack then understood why Tryzolm grinned as he gazed upon the fascinating contraptions atop the Stegokin's backs.

Mobile heat light pyres were fastened to their backplates. They lit up the landscape all around them and provided enough light that allowed them to continue marching all through the night. Thadarack was perplexed how the Stegokin got them on their backs but knew better than to question their abilities. Tryzolm, in particular, looked tough, and Thadarack didn't want to get on his bad side.

It became evident that King Sturklan had every intention of reaching Scythadon as quickly as possible. Although they marched at a steady pace, Thadarack could tell that the army was not tired, confirming what Riktlan had told them about their endurance. As a matter of fact, Thadarack himself grew tired but pushed on due to his determination to return home.

They marched all morning and through midday, and when dusk approached, Thadarack was surprised that they hadn't seen any Carne yet. Surely the Carne would have been patrolling the Eastern Road, wouldn't they? They had already been walking for about a day and a half. At their steady pace, Thadarack knew that they would be upon Scythadon soon.

Suddenly, the Prince heard someone yell from a few rows in front of him. "Halt!" The army came to a stop just as he saw a Stegokin walking in his direction.

As Thadarack began to look around, he immediately recognized where they were. His heart dropped when he scanned the vast valley sprawled out in front of him that he gazed upon with his father only a few days ago.

He squinted and saw the overlook far in the distance that they stood atop, watching the beautiful and majestic sunset. He wished more than anything he could go back to that night, even if just to spend a little more time with his father by his side.

"Prince Thadarack!" the approaching Stegokin shouted. "King Sturklan insists that you join him at the front lines." He then turned toward Tryzolm. "And you too, with haste!"

"Go," said Thexis. "We'll wait for you here."

Thadarack and Tryzolm made their way to the front with the Stegokin. The army was standing still, and Thadarack could hear quiet murmuring among the warriors as he walked past.

When they reached King Sturklan, he and Glathzolm were engaged in conversation with Riktlan. Thadarack grew concerned because of the serious looks on their faces. He immediately looked across the open valley but didn't see anything.

"Tell Prince Thadarack what we've learned," King Sturklan said.

Thadarack looked at the King and saw him glancing at Riktlan.

"A few hours ago, we saw some Carne in the distance," Riktlan said. "We were about to order a halt, but as soon as they saw us, they fled. We haven't seen any other Carne since. But now…" Riktlan's voice trailed off as his expression turned somber. "Our scouts just returned and said a very large Carne army is approaching. It will reach the valley at any moment and appears to greatly outnumber ours."

Thadarack's heart dropped as he turned his head toward the other end of the valley. He still didn't see anything, but the anticipation of what Riktlan had told him was almost too much to bear. How far away was this Carne army?

Something then dawned on him, shooting waves of fear through every part of his body. It became difficult for him to breathe, almost to the point of hyperventilation. *What does this mean for Scythadon?* he thought. If "a very large Carne army" was on its way here, did Scythadon fall?

He immediately turned back to Riktlan. "Did your scouts

happen to see Scythadon?" he asked. "The city is only a few miles from here."

"They didn't get that far," said Riktlan. "But do not lose hope, Prince Thadarack. I refuse to believe that Scythadon has fallen."

Thadarack wanted to feel the same way, but how could he? Surely, if a Carne army was marching toward the Stegokin, then Scythadon was most likely destroyed. Or was it? It didn't make much sense that Scythadon could still be standing if a Carne army was marching toward them. Could it?

He closed his eyes and focused on his breathing. He desperately tried to calm himself, but the gravity of the situation at claw overwhelmed him. Although he was scared, he decided he needed to go see the city for himself. He opened his eyes and looked at Riktlan.

"I need to go to Scythadon," he said distraughtly. "I need to see it."

"And how do you expect to get there?" King Sturklan interjected. "You said it yourself, there are Carne everywhere in these parts. I'm sure they are watching us right now."

"I made it to Stegodor," said Thadarack. "I can sneak past them again."

"You were lucky," said King Sturklan. "And if I recall, you barely made it to Stegodor. Didn't the Pachykin help you? I forbid it. You are not going."

"I have to," said Thadarack. "I have to see it."

"You will do no such thing, and that's an order," said King Sturklan. "I need you to—"

Sheer panic set in as Thadarack drifted away from the conversation in his mind. He continued looking at the King, but

215

the Prince didn't hear a word he was saying. Thoughts of his mother, father, Girozz, Beroyn, and everyone else he knew in Scythadon flashed before his eyes.

He feared the worst; Scythadon had fallen and all those within were either killed or enslaved. The thought of his father being defenseless as the Carne were upon him filled him from head to tail with terror.

"Prince Thadarack!" King Sturklan yelled. Thadarack jumped, as the King's yell was enough to bring him back to reality. "You must go seek cover! I will not let you stay here and take part in the coming battle!"

Seek cover? Thadarack thought. He quickly realized going to Scythadon wasn't reasonable, but could he really turn around and hide? If he was being honest with himself, he wanted to. But he couldn't. No, he wouldn't. Especially not now.

He felt his fear transform inside of him, and he was no longer panicking. That fear and panic transitioned into anger. He thought about Arkonius and how he had given his life to save them. He again thought of his father and the fact that Scythadon might be gone. Rage boiled up inside of him, a feeling he had never had before. "But I want to fight!" he yelled. "I've already left my kin to die! I will not leave you too!"

King Sturklan smashed his thagomizer into the ground with such force that Thadarack took a step back. Even Riktlan, Glathzolm, and Tryzolm jumped slightly at the King's aggression. "Get out of this valley!" the King roared. "King Thax would never forgive me if I let you stay here, nor would I forgive myself! You are the Prince of Scythadon, you need to survive!"

King Sturklan took a deep breath and calmed down, subtly

shaking his head. "I hate to say this, but you might be among the last of your kin. You must live."

Thadarack's emotions flooded him so strongly that his body physically ached. King Sturklan's words struck a chord with the Prince. His anger now transformed into full-on grief. Were he and Thexis really some of the last Scythekin?

A few tears began to form as he looked down at the ground. Thadarack had never felt so defeated in his entire life. He longed for his mother's warm embrace and the simple life he had before all of this. He now realized he took it for granted.

"I need you to be strong," said King Sturklan. "I know none of this is fair. But we need to push on, even in the face of such adversity."

The King scanned the surrounding area. "Up there," he said while gesturing with his head. "That hill looks like the perfect place to take cover. There are dense trees and bushes up there."

Thadarack desperately tried to fight back his tears as he turned and looked up at the hill.

"Should things look bleak, you and your friends must return to Stegodor and warn my kin," continued the King. "Do not linger too long, for if it even so much as looks like there's a chance we're to be overrun, make haste back to Stegodor. Do you understand me?"

Thadarack tried to speak, but he couldn't. He instead nodded slightly in understanding.

"I will need every last Stegokin in my army to fight. I am relying on you and your friends. If things should go south, bring the news back to my kin. Tell them we fought bravely, and for those left to prepare for the Carne to attack. Then, travel far and wide. Tell every Viridi tribe that you can find that the Stegokin came to the aid of the Scythekin. That we gave our lives to help them. Use this day, this very moment of despair, to unite the rest of the Viridi world against this evil. Do this Prince Thadarack, you must promise me!"

Just as Thadarack was about to answer, the ground began to shake. At first, it shook lightly. But with each passing moment, it grew more and more intense, quickly becoming a fierce tremble. Thadarack could hear murmuring from throughout the ranks of the army behind him.

He once again looked in the distance across the valley, but he still didn't see anything. Although nothing was there, he knew what was causing the trembling. It was coming from the very direction he so desperately wanted to go.

"Prince Thadarack," said King Sturklan sternly. "You must understand what I am telling you to do. Our very existence may depend upon it."

"I…I," Thadarack stammered. "I understand."

"Good," replied King Sturklan, seeming to be completely unfazed by the growing trembling.

Thadarack couldn't believe that the very valley he had visited with his father would be the site of a great battle that was to come. The battle between the Stegokin and the Carne would occur in the very place that filled Thadarack's heart with warmth not even a week ago.

As dusk fell, Thadarack saw the same beautiful shades of yellow, orange, and red that he had seen with his father. He remembered that when his father was telling him of the Great War, he questioned how such evil could exist in such a peaceful-looking world.

"Glathzolm," said King Sturklan. "Go forth and get the army in battle-ready formation. I want the army to make up the center. Riktlan's guards will cover the flanks. We can't let the line falter, no matter what!"

"Yes, my King!" Glathzolm shouted. She then turned around and shouted orders at the army behind them.

The King looked at Riktlan. "Split up your guard and make ready on the flanks as close as possible to the hills on both sides."

He turned to Tryzolm. "You are to command the left flank while Riktlan commands the right. Do not let the Carne get behind us! I know they are many, but we must keep them in front at all costs!"

"Right away, my King!" Riktlan and Tryzolm shouted simultaneously. As Riktlan walked past Thadarack, he shot the Prince a glance. "Stay safe. I *will* see you after the battle."

Thadarack watched Riktlan and Tryzolm run toward the army. It wasn't long before he heard them shouting commands.

"Prince Thadarack," said King Sturklan. "It's time for you to go." The King turned toward his army as it shuffled about into battle-ready formation. He then looked out across the valley.

Although the sounds of the Carne army grew louder, they still hadn't emerged from around the bend at the opposite end of the valley. The King looked back at Thadarack. "It is my sincerest hope that Scythadon hasn't fallen," he continued. "But know this. We will not surrender. We will fight to the death rather than become slaves to the Carne. They will have to take every inch of this valley, and by the Hallowed Lumina, we will make them take it with their blood. If Scythadon really has fallen, I will make them pay. But be on your way now and keep a keen eye. Do not delay, nor hesitate should we fall. I must go to my army now. You have your orders."

King Sturklan gave Thadarack one brisk nod before he turned around and headed toward his army. It was still being formed, and Thadarack could hear the orders being shouted among the frantic whispers of the warriors. He made his way back to his friends, who by this time, were standing all alone a good distance from the back of the army.

"They told us to wait here," said Gwon. "Where does the King want us? When will the Carne be here?"

Thadarack turned and watched the army continue mobilizing into their positions. For the time being, the trembling caused by the Carne army was masked by the shuffling of the Stegokin. Soon, a two-Stegokin-deep battle line was formed from one hill across the valley to the other.

"Thadarack!" Thexis yelled. "Tell us what we're to do!"

Startled, Thadarack turned back toward his friends. "We're to go up there and take cover," he said while gesturing toward the hill with his right index claw.

Both Thexis and Gwon looked at the hill and then back at Thadarack with confusion across their faces.

"No!" Gwon said firmly. "I want to stay and fight!"

"Calm down, Gwon," said Thadarack. "This is the order I was given by King Sturklan. We are to hide, and if things don't look good, we must head back to Stegodor as fast as we can. The King wants us to warn the city should they be...defeated."

"He needs us to," said Thexis. "None of the Stegokin would

be able to make it back."

The realization that, if defeated, the Stegokin would all perish, tugged at Thadarack's heart-strings. There wasn't any retreat for them. There was no regrouping and no second chance. If they lost this coming battle, they would all die.

He immediately regretted asking the Stegokin to come. If Scythadon really had fallen, the Stegokin were here for no reason. They left the safety of their city, the safety of the walls that could have aided in their defense should the Carne have attacked them. Would they have attacked? Did he lead the Stegokin to their certain death? These thoughts were too much for Thadarack to handle.

"What does this mean for Scythadon?" Thexis asked. "Do we know the city's status?"

"We don't," said Thadarack. "The army is coming from the direction of Scythadon. The scouts that saw the army didn't make it to the city."

"Well, we can't assume anything," said Thexis. "That doesn't mean anything."

"But it does," said Gwon. "How could the army be marching from Scythadon if Scythadon hasn't already fallen?"

"Don't say that," said Thexis. "I still have hope."

"Do we know how big the Carne army is?" Gwon asked.

Just as Thadarack was about to tell them what the scouts said, he realized it might be better if he told a little white lie. He could tell that they were both disheartened already, especially Gwon. And besides, they would soon see for themselves once the army arrived. "They didn't say," he said. "And I felt the same way you do. I wanted to stay and fight. But King Sturklan needs us to survive."

"We have no choice," said Thexis. "If we don't make it out of here, Stegodor won't know what happened until the Carne army is at its gate."

"Exactly," said Thadarack.

Gwon sighed. "You're right. I'd prefer to fight, but I understand."

"We also have another important job to do," said Thadarack. "Should the Stegokin be defeated, we are to spread the word of what happened here today. King Sturklan thinks it will inspire the other Viridi tribes to join forces and fight. Much like it did a thousand years ago when the Scythekin came to the aid of the Stegokin."

"Who are we going to tell?" Gwon asked. "The Carne have already invaded the West. We have no idea if the Longnecks are still alive. Queen Cerathorn has forsaken us."

"Come on, Gwon," said Thexis. "We need to stay positive, especially now."

As Thadarack was about to chime in, he caught a glimpse of movement coming from the far side of the valley. "Let's go," he said. "We need to hurry."

Thadarack, Thexis, and Gwon ascended the hill. Once they reached a thick oak tree and some dense brush, they crouched low to the ground. Thadarack watched in terror as the Carne funneled around the bend and into the valley. Row after row, the Carne kept coming, and for a time, it didn't look like there would be an end.

They formed lines like the Stegokin, stretching across the valley from hill to hill. After six battle lines formed, the Carne finally halted their advance.

One Carne emerged from the first line and let out a mighty roar that sent shivers down Thadarack's spine. Then, all at once, every Carne in the valley roared so ferociously that they were most likely heard for miles in all directions.

Thadarack could tell that the Carne army was three times the size of the Stegokin army. Roar after roar, the sound that permeated from the army was horrifying, much more so than anything Thadarack had ever encountered.

The Prince watched as the Carne that emerged from the first line stopped roaring. Instead, he stood there with a scowl and sinister look on his face, staring across the valley at the Stegokin. For what felt like an eternity, the Carne behind him continued with their deafening roars.

"Oh, my Hallowed Lumina," said Gwon. "How are the Stegokin going to stand up to that?"

"Have faith," said Thexis. "We need to have faith."

Thadarack didn't say a word. He watched as the Carne continued roaring nonstop. He looked up for a brief moment, and saw the last of the birds fly away. There was probably not another animal for miles. The sheer stature of the Carne army was enough to instill terror in even the most courageous of the Stegokin.

"What do we do?" Gwon asked, breathing heavily. "They can't win against this. Should we go now?"

"I think we should do what King Sturklan asked us to," said Thexis. "We wait and see what happens. If the Stegokin begin to falter, we head straight back to Stegodor without delay. But I believe in them. The Stegokin are fighting for something. What are the Carne fighting for? We'll prevail."

Thadarack was unsure which camp he was in. He somewhat agreed with Gwon that the Carne army would overwhelm the Stegokin. But part of him had hope, just like Thexis, that the Stegokin would win. "Do you know what kind of Carne they are?" Thadarack asked. "They look like the same ones we came across in the forest."

"The one that stepped forward is a Tarbokin," said Gwon. "They are the bigger ones and the Carne that Arkonious was fighting in the forest. The horned ones are Carnokin, and the others with the bumps above the eyes are Allokin. I'm not entirely sure about the smaller Carne. I never heard my father talk about them."

From down in the valley, King Sturklan started shouting at his warriors. "This is the hour!" He began to trot up the Stegokin lines. "The hour that we go to battle! The hour that we show these beasts what the Stegokin are made of! The hour that we rout them from this valley and march onward to Scythadon!"

The King's voice quieted a bit, but Thadarack could still make out what he was saying. "You may feel like our chances of victory are slim. It is true; we are outnumbered. The enemy is many, and we are few. But let me tell you a story. Stegokin, starving, surrounded, and outnumbered, stood upon Tarned Hill with no chance of victory. The Carne closed in around them from all sides. Did they give up? No, they did not."

The King paused and turned to look at the Carne across the valley. A moment later, he continued on, more animated and louder with each sentence. "They fought. They fought on and we all know the stories. The stories of how each Stegokin took with him or her at least four Carne! Pyklania is said to have slayed more than twenty Carne by herself before she fell! If we fight with that same determination and fervor, we will prevail this day! The descendants of those very Scythekin that saved our kin, all those years ago, are only a few miles away! Let's throw down this enemy and march to their aid!"

Just when the army cheered and roared with renewed vigor, Thadarack saw the Carne begin to charge. The Stegokin smacked their thagomizers on the ground with such thunderous strength, that the land behind them caved in.

The ground shook so fiercely that it was tough for Thadarack, even atop the hill, to keep his balance. He watched as the Stegokin got ready, courageously standing their ground amid such a perilous calamity. All at once, the Carne began charging at them ferociously.

After he was done inspiring his army, King Sturklan turned to face the enemy. He backed up into the center of his first battle line and filled the gap there. Although they looked scared, the Stegokin had determination and defiance in their eyes.

The Carne roared and snarled as they approached the patient, battle-ready Stegokin lines. Thadarack watched ever so intently, hoping that his fellow Viridi could hold their ground and beat back the enemy.

The larger Tarbokin led the assault, while the smaller Carnokin and Allokin kept at a steady pace behind them. The much smaller Carne were scattered all through the army, and they were desperately trying to avoid getting trampled.

Thadarack looked at the Carne leader intently and wondered who it was. Could it be the High King? He definitely looked menacing enough. *Is it him?*

Thadarack closed his eyes and prayed for victory while the Carne got closer and closer to the Stegokin battle lines.

CHAPTER FIFTEEN

AN IMPROBABLE FEAT

When Thadarack opened his eyes, the Tarbokin were almost upon the Stegokin. He quivered at their deafening roars and fearsome appearance. In a unified fashion, they lunged forward—jaws wide open.

The front Stegokin battle line spun quickly on their feet and struck, flailing their thagomizers like thunderclaps. Most met their marks, smashing into the Tarbokin in such a violent clash that Thadarack's stomach turned.

Countless Tarbokin were hit in their midsections, coming to an abrupt halt. Others stumbled to the side, while many more fell to the ground amidst sounds of pain and agony. Quite a few were struck in their legs, causing them to weakly, but forcibly, fall forward past the first Stegokin battle line due to their forward momentum.

Some Stegokin missed—the Tarbokin having successfully dodged their attack. They quickly latched onto the Stegokin's tails, unharmed from the spikes, and viciously shook their heads, tearing into the Stegokin's flesh. The Stegokin warriors howled in pain as they desperately tried to break free from the aggressor's devastating jaws.

Almost immediately, following closely behind the first Stegokin battle line, the second line spun forward and planted their hind legs on their fellow warriors' backs. They swung their thagomizers upwards, striking the Carne in the face.

Quite a few of the approaching smaller Carne leaped through the gaps in between the Tarbokin line. Thadarack saw them get impaled with spikes as they did so, their lives ending immediately, while their frail bodies flew through the air. Thagomizers met the jaws of countless Tarbokin, disfiguring their faces and piercing their skulls, leaving them limp as they came crashing to the ground.

The Carnokin and Allokin were shortly upon the Stegokin, and due to their overwhelming numbers, surrounded many of them fairly quickly. Any Stegokin that ventured too far from the battle line was ferociously ganged up on and killed in a mere instant.

Thadarack looked on as carnage ensued. Although significantly outnumbered, the Stegokin held their line well, working in tandem with one another to keep the Carne at bay as best they could. It soon became apparent that, had they not had in-depth battle training and effective tactics, they would have been overrun quickly.

Thagomizers swung from side to side, spraying blood and dirt in all directions. The Carne lunged at the Stegokin, latching onto their necks as they powerfully shook their heads. Shrieks soon overwhelmed the roars as the battle raged on under the setting sun. The bodies of both lifeless Carne and Stegokin lay upon the valley, tainting the land beneath them a burgundy red.

Although the Stegokin were outnumbered, it appeared as if there were more dead Carne on the battlefield. The Carne themselves seemed surprised at the tenaciousness of the Stegokin. Many backed away and approached the Stegokin in a more reserved manner.

Based on how they charged at the Stegokin, it seemed to Thadarack that the Carne thought they could easily overwhelm them. The Carne's initial charge proved futile, however, as the Stegokin were doing a good job of holding them back. He did fear, though, that the sheer numbers of the Carne would eventually lead to a Stegokin defeat.

It wasn't long before the Stegokin army started getting pushed back toward the end of the valley it had emerged from. Thadarack watched in despair as the left flank of the army began to falter and cave inward. Many of the smaller Carne had also gotten behind the Stegokin. Even though they seemed too small to bring them down on their own, they were enough of a distraction, helping the larger Carne gain the advantage.

"They're getting overrun!" Gwon yelled. "We need to help! We need to do something! I can't just sit here and watch as they get slaughtered!"

Thadarack watched King Sturklan kill Carne after Carne, swinging his thagomizer with incredible strength and speed. He and Glathzolm were putting up the greatest resistance in the center.

Riktlan, on the right flank, was also fighting heroically. He kept the Carne at bay although Stegokin lay dead all around him. Even though many of the Carne he was fighting were bigger than him, his skillful use of his thagomizer proved too great a challenge for them to overcome.

On the left flank, Tryzolm was fighting valiantly amid Stegokin falling all around him. Then, in the blink of an eye, two small Carne jumped on his back and latched their small jaws around his neck.

A Carnokin then rammed him from the side just as a Tarbokin clenched its jaws down on his right arm. With one final attempt at breaking free, an Allokin lunged for his thagomizer, pinning it to the ground. Thadarack watched as Tryzolm stumbled and fell. A short moment, his wriggling stopped, and the Carne ripped into his lifeless body.

The bulk of the Carne army was funneling to the two Stegokin flanks in an apparent strategy to overwhelm them. It was happening the worst on the left flank, especially where Tryzolm had been killed. Although this was occurring, the Carne center was still matched up evenly with the Stegokin due to their sheer advantage in numbers.

King Sturklan must have noticed the left flank was being overrun because he led a small contingent behind the line to reinforce it. Glathzolm stayed in the center and continued putting up a courageous fight, throwing down Carne all around her. Her speed and mobility were incredible to witness as she swung her thagomizer around like it was a twig.

Just as King Sturklan and a group of Stegokin closed the left flank, Thadarack saw the right begin to fall apart. Riktlan, seemingly tired and injured from numerous wounds, stumbled backward. He swung his thagomizer at an approaching Tarbokin, sinking it deep into the Carne's head, causing him and the

Tarbokin to fall to the ground together.

Thadarack watched as Riktlan was swarmed by another Tarbokin, three Allokin, and countless smaller Carne that jumped onto his back. With one last ditch effort by a few close Stegokin to save him, and one final, albeit weak, strike of Riktlan's thagomizer, he became motionless.

Many other Carne descended upon him, and soon, Riktlan's body had been torn apart. The right flank was slowly overrun, and with Riktlan gone, had nobody to rally it and lead a counterattack. Thadarack watched in horror as the line collapsed.

No...Riktlan, Thadarack thought. *This can't be happening.* The Prince turned away in despair. The trees behind him were blowing in the wind peacefully as the setting sun cast its colorful rays down upon them. *How can this be happening...here?*

He didn't want to turn back toward the battle. He had seen enough. Watching the Stegokin get killed one after another was too much to handle. Although he had a bit of hope before it started, he now realized that the battle was over before it began. This realization was hard to accept but nevertheless true.

Just when he turned back around, he watched with dread as the Carne slowly pushed the left flank back again. King Sturklan put up a heroic fight, but it wasn't enough for the outnumbered Stegokin.

With many dead on the battlefield, the Carne force grew more disproportionate to that of the Stegokin. The center was holding, but soon both flanks were overrun. The Stegokin were now fighting for their very survival on all fronts.

In a roar louder than any that had preceded it, the Tarbokin that led the attack shouted from behind the surrounding Carne army. "Leave none alive! Kill them all! Let not one Stegokin out of this valley nor draw further breath!"

Thadarack watched as King Sturklan locked eyes with the Tarbokin leader. Only a few Carne stood between them. All hope seeming lost, King Sturklan broke rank and charged at the Tarbokin, swinging his thagomizer with a mighty roar, pummeling and impaling those that stood in his way.

Surrounded, the King made his attempt at striking him down just as the Tarbokin lunged forward and latched onto his tail, thwarting his strike. He chomped deep into the King's tail, sinking his teeth deeper and deeper into the flesh.

Thadarack wondered if most other Stegokin would have been helpless against such a ferocious clench and grip, but the strength of King Sturklan was clearly unmatched among them on the battlefield. Seeming all but impossible to Thadarack, he broke free with a mighty whip of his tail, forcibly dislodging the Carne's teeth. The Carne stumbled to the side and almost fell over.

Just as the King was about to swing his thagomizer at the off-balance Tarbokin, an Allokin leaped at him, latching its teeth around the King's neck. Another jumped forward, biting down on King Sturklan's right arm, causing it to buckle. The King fell forward on the right side of his head and neck.

A Carnokin then charged right into the King's vulnerable left abdomen, painfully impaling him with its horns and knocking him to the ground. Thadarack flinched as he watched King Sturklan desperately try to free himself from his aggressors.

The Stegokin King was on the brink of defeat. Thadarack almost couldn't watch as King Sturklan grew closer and closer to death. Held back by the Carne, his surrounding kin were powerless to help. Glathzolm fought valiantly and tried to get to her King but couldn't break through the thick Carne battle lines.

King Sturklan's life slowly drained away as he became limper with each passing second. The Tarbokin leader, after regaining his balance, approached the weakened and defenseless King.

"He's mine!" he snarled as the other Carne backed out of the way. "How does it feel? How does it feel to be the leader of the pathetic Stegokin and know that you will be erased from history? Something that should have happened a thousand years ago!"

King Sturklan trembled as he tried to get to his feet, a task that proved too difficult due to his arms and legs buckling under his weight. He gave it his all, trying to find what strength he had left to get up but such a feat proved impossible.

The Tarbokin leader got closer to King Sturklan and said something else to him, but from his distance, Thadarack couldn't make out what it was. The King soon gave up and lay there motionless, appearing to have accepted his fate. Thadarack watched the remaining Stegokin decrease in number.

"We need to get going," said Thexis in a shaky, barely audible voice. "It's over."

Thadarack nodded, and with one final look of sorrow at the King and his army, turned around. Just as they took their first steps, Thadarack felt a rumbling coming from the direction they were heading.

His heart sank in his chest and panic quickly consumed him. Something was most definitely coming toward them, and whatever it was, it was moving fast. With the battle raging on behind them and approaching footsteps, the three friends were trapped.

"We've lingered here too long!" Thexis cried. "They must've seen us and flanked around to ensure we can't escape!"

"Get ready to fight!" Gwon yelled.

At first, Thadarack felt like turning around and hiding in the thick brush behind him. He was shaking uncontrollably, and had Thexis and Gwon not been by his side, he knew he would have tried to hide. But where would he go? Could he *really* hide in the brush? The Carne would surely find him.

Then, something unexplainable happened. A vivid image of his father flashed before his eyes. He saw him as if he were right in front of him, the way he looked when he returned to the city. His mind raced with what might have happened to those he loved and cared about back in Scythadon.

He recalled the discussion he had with his father about the Great War, and he thought about Thrifsaer; how he threw down Orzligorn so many centuries ago. Something spoke to him, an echo that was so light, so quiet, it wasn't anything more than a whisper.

What would he do? it said to him. *Would he cower in fear, or would he stand and fight, inspiring those around him?* With newfound bravery, Thadarack clenched his claws, stood right in front of his friends, and shifted his feet into battle stance. *Duck, dodge, and strike*, he thought. *I'll make Arkonius proud. Even if I go down slashing.*

Thadarack waited and watched with his friends by his side. The surrounding foliage was dense, making it hard for him to see the enemy. The rumbling grew more intense and louder with each passing second. He realized it was pointless to try to hide anyway. The sounds that approached were coming from every direction.

Was this really the end? Were the Carne closing in around them too? Just like they were to the Stegokin down in the valley? Gwon let out a mighty roar just before what was approaching emerged from the dense foliage before them.

Thadarack closed his eyes briefly, took a deep breath, and opened them with courage and determination in his heart.

CHAPTER SIXTEEN

THE TIMELY ARRIVAL

Thadarack hesitated and stopped himself from lunging forward. What he saw wasn't an army of Carne, nor was it anyone who wanted to hurt him and his friends. His tenseness gave way to feelings of relief and hope. He stared at whom he saw, speechless and completely frozen.

"Prince Thadarack," said Queen Cerathorn. "And your two companions."

Queen Cerathorn stood before Thadarack, Thexis, and Gwon as the vast Trikin army slowly emerged from the trees and dense foliage. It stretched across the hill in both directions for as far as Thadarack could see. As he scanned the army, he saw Hornbrigg staring directly at him with a slight smile across his face. *He must have done it,* Thadarack thought. *Hornbrigg must have changed her mind.*

The Queen walked past the three friends and looked down upon the valley at the carnage below. The army followed behind her and stopped just in front of the trio.

As the Queen continued peering over the edge of the hill, Thadarack saw her shift her head in the direction of King

Sturklan. She then turned around and gave Thadarack a quick glance before turning her gaze to her army.

"Fellow Viridi are dying upon the field below!" she shouted as she traversed slowly in front of the Trikin. "Viridi with whom we have been at odds with for the better part of the last millennium!"

The Queen's voice then quieted down a bit as she stopped moving, turning back toward the battle below. "Viridi that we have fought against and killed for the last three years. But…" She turned back around and shot Hornbrigg a look before glancing back to her army, raising her voice once more. "Viridi nonetheless! Just like us! Those Carne beasts in the valley below are our enemy! Our one true enemy! Now, my fellow Trikin, charge with me into the fray! Charge forward in the redemption of Ceraplazz! Charge forward to the Stegokin and fight this evil by their side! Honor the alliances of old! Onward! With haste!"

Queen Cerathorn, with flames of fury in her eyes, descended the hill. Like an avalanche, the Trikin army stormed down right behind her. They roared and howled with such ferocity that Thadarack was shaken to his very core.

The three friends approached the edge of the hill and watched as the Trikin stampede grew louder and more thunderous with each passing stride. With Queen Cerathorn at the helm, the Trikin army formed a flying wedge aimed straight toward where King Sturklan lay on the battlefield.

The Carne turned and began to form ranks in an attempt to withstand the charge, but their efforts appeared to be in vain. The Trikin descended upon them at a speed and fierceness that Thadarack didn't think anyone could withstand.

The Trikin smashed into the Carne like a tsunami upon sand, impaling the Carne with their horns and throwing them to the side with incredible ease. The smaller Carne didn't stand a chance and were flung through the air as the Trikin plowed straight through them.

Blood and dirt sprayed in all directions as the Trikin barreled forward to the sounds of painful screams and howls. They didn't stop, their momentum carrying them further and further through the Carne battle lines. Even the larger Carne couldn't withstand the power of the Trikin charge. Many were gutted and tossed to the ground the instant they were struck.

It wasn't long before the Carne army began to waver. Thadarack saw many begin fleeing from the devastating assault. The Tarbokin leader tried to rally the army, but it was to no avail. The Carne were quickly overwhelmed and began routing in a panic while the Trikin pursued.

The Trikin pushed on and easily caught up to many of the Carne. It was obvious that they were tired from having already been engaged in battle. As the Trikin reached the Stegokin, they adjusted their pursuit right around them, chasing the Carne from the valley in every direction.

In the chaos that ensued, Thadarack watched a Trikin ram the Tarbokin leader, thrusting its two long horns deep into his abdomen. Almost simultaneously, another Trikin struck the leader's left thigh, causing him to collapse to the ground.

The Tarbokin wailed in pain as he desperately tried to fight back, but his efforts quickly proved helpless. The Trikin twisted their horns deeper into his wounds. Once incapable of fighting back at all, the two Trikin released and flung him to the side. He lay on the battlefield, convulsing and trembling in pain, not far from King Sturklan.

Thadarack looked on with renewed spirits as he watched the last of the Carne disappear from the valley. The trio descended the hill and quickly made their way toward King Sturklan. Thadarack ran past what must have been hundreds, if not thousands, of dead Carne and Stegokin on the way. It was more gruesome a sight than anything he had ever seen.

Queen Cerathorn gave up her chase and also headed in the direction of the King. On her way, Thadarack saw her finish off countless wounded Carne she came across. They howled and screamed in pain before becoming limp and lifeless.

"My King!" Glathzolm shouted as she rushed to King Sturklan's side. "By the Hallowed Lumina, are you alright?"

As Thadarack approached, he realized how badly injured King Sturklan really was. His body was soaked in blood from his head to his tail. He had too many wounds and bite marks to even count, and his neck was a mangled mess.

The deepest wounds he suffered were still bleeding; although, surprisingly not as much as Thadarack would've thought. Even so, he was losing a lot of blood and for an unfortunate moment, Thadarack feared the worst. Was he going to live? Was he going to make it out of this mass graveyard alive? The young Prince wasn't sure.

"I..." The King struggled to speak. "I am now." He painfully turned his head toward Queen Cerathorn, who was now standing beside him. "Thank you...Q...Queen Cerathorn," he said in a raspy and barely audible voice.

The Queen gave King Sturklan a sympathetic look and

nodded.

Thadarack looked at Queen Cerathorn's bloodied horns, the two longer of which had flesh still hanging from them. Although shaken from the carnage all around him, he was glad that the Trikin were on his side. Having witnessed the ease with which the Trikin charged through the Carne army made him optimistic.

Queen Cerathorn turned toward a large group of Trikin in the distance. "Hornbrigg!" she shouted at the top of her voice. "Call them back! Don't pursue past the valley's edge!"

Thadarack saw Hornbrigg shout at some far off Trikin. They turned around and started heading back to where the bulk of the Trikin army was. There were also quite a few Trikin walking around the battlefield, finishing off wounded Carne one after the other. To the pleading sounds of agony, they thrust their horns deep into the Carne, instantly ending their lives.

"What changed your mind?" King Sturklan asked weakly. "Why did you decide to come?"

Queen Cerathorn turned and looked at Thadarack. "He did," she said, gesturing toward the Prince with her beak. "You're quite convincing, Prince Thadarack."

She then looked out in the distance toward Hornbrigg before turning back to the King. "I also have a persuasive commander."

"Well, whatever the reason, we are most fortunate you came," said the King.

"P...pitiful," choked the Tarbokin leader from behind them.

Queen Cerathorn turned around and approached him. "Funny you should say that since you're the one dying," she said as she lowered her horns toward him.

"Wait," said King Sturklan just before the Queen struck the

Tarbokin. "He's the leader. He was commanding the army. Maybe we can learn something from him."

Queen Cerathorn raised her horns and scowled at the Tarbokin. "You're the leader, huh? Your army has been obliterated, and you'll be dead soon enough. *You're* pitiful."

The Tarbokin tried to laugh, but choked on a mixture of blood and spit.

"Who are you?" the Queen asked. "The so-called High King of the Carne?"

"M...me?" the Tarbokin gagged weakly. "I'm nobody. Just a Carne among many."

"A nobody? Some leader you are."

The Tarbokin grimaced. "I'm not the leader. I'm but a taste of what's coming for you. He...will come for you all...and eradicate this world of your kind." He laughed sinisterly as blood dripped from his mouth.

"Who will come?" the Queen asked. "Who will come, you swine of a beast? The High King? Where is he?"

The Tarbokin's life then slowly faded away. He became motionless and no longer choked dreadful sounds. The only movement came from the slowly dripping blood out of the corner of his mouth.

"He must have been talking about the High King," said Queen Cerathorn, turning back around toward King Sturklan. "That's the only thing that makes sense."

A taste? Thadarack thought. *The Carne army looked massive. How could this have only been a taste?* Having been distracted by the arrival of the Trikin and the events that followed, Thadarack immediately thought about his home.

241

"We must go to Scythadon!" he blurted out as everyone turned toward him. "It's a few miles from here!"

Queen Cerathorn scanned the Trikin around her and in the distance. "Horngorre!" she shouted as loud as she could. "Take your scouting party ahead toward Scythadon and report back what awaits us there!"

"Yes, my Queen!" Horngorre shouted from a good distance.

Thadarack watched as a group of about ten Trikin sprinted away at a great speed. It wasn't long before the Trikin were well out of sight, disappearing beyond the edge of the valley in the direction of Scythadon.

"The city hasn't fallen," said King Sturklan. "Scythadon still stands."

"How can you be sure?" asked Queen Cerathorn.

King Sturklan looked at the dead Tarbokin leader. "That abomination told me as much," he said while wincing. "He said after we were defeated, they were going to return and finish off the Scythekin."

Waves of relief poured over Thadarack. He had never been so happy about something in his entire life. Did that mean his father was still alive? Were Girozz, Beroyn, Rhinn, and everyone else he knew still alive? He desperately wanted to know. "I need to get there!" he shouted. "I need to get to my kin!"

"We can't be too hasty," said Queen Cerathorn. "We don't know what awaits us, and chances are, there are still Carne there. They wouldn't have fully abandoned the siege."

Thadarack caught himself just before he took off. Queen Cerathorn was right, and although he wanted to go to his father right now, he decided it wasn't worth acting rashly.

242

"I want to go too," said Thexis gently from right behind him. "But we should all go together."

"I agree," said Gwon.

Thadarack nodded reluctantly. "You're right," he said. "When will we depart for Scythadon?"

"We'll begin our march to the city soon, but we should wait to hear back from Horngorre before we rush in," said Queen Cerathorn as she turned toward Hornbrigg. "Form up the army."

Hornbrigg shouted commands at the Trikin who quickly began to form ranks. In the blink of an eye, the Trikin army was ready, standing shoulder to shoulder with one another in three columns and facing in the direction of Scythadon.

"Glathzolm," said King Sturklan quietly. "Form up what's left of our army. You are to lead them alongside Queen Cerathorn and Hornbrigg."

"You've done enough," interjected Queen Cerathorn. "Let us finish this."

King Sturklan tried to respond, but for the moment, he couldn't muster his strength. He glanced at Glathzolm and nodded.

"We will not back down now," said Glathzolm. "We're going to see this through. We will march to Scythadon with you."

King Sturklan glanced at Queen Cerathorn and nodded once more. The Queen returned the gesture. "So be it," she said. "We shall fight this calamity together." She then headed toward the Trikin army.

"Will you be okay, my King?" Glathzolm asked.

"Yes. I'll be alright."

"At least let me leave someone with you."

"No," said King Sturklan. "You need every able warrior to go to Scythadon. You do not yet know what awaits you there. Now go, prepare the army."

Prepare the army? Thadarack thought. *There's not much of an army left.* He watched as Glathzolm said goodbye to her King with pain in her eyes. She hesitantly turned away and walked over to what was left of the Stegokin army.

Thadarack didn't know how many Stegokin warriors had come to the valley, but he estimated it was at least a thousand. It looked like there were no more than a couple hundred left, and many of them were wounded to some degree.

His heart dropped as he looked out across the field of corpses. He saw a few Stegokin here and there that seemed like they might still be alive. They were wailing and weeping in the distance from their debilitating wounds. He thought about what that meant for them. How did the Stegokin care for their wounded? Was there anything they could do?

Thadarack watched as a few Stegokin knelt down beside some of the wounded. They talked but didn't do anything to tend to their injuries. They merely stayed beside them and kept talking.

The Stegokin then stood back up, and with a quick strike of their thagomizers, they ended their lives in a split second. Thadarack, Thexis, and Gwon gasped as they watched many more across the valley do the same thing.

"What are they doing?" Thexis asked. "Why are they killing them?"

"We have no way to care for them," said King Sturklan. "And if they wish to be freed from their pain and suffering, we pray with them and fulfill that wish."

"There's nothing you can do?" Thadarack asked. "What about the Scythekin healers?"

"It's their choice," said King Sturklan. "Some may choose to wait and see if help will come, but for others, the pain might be unbearable."

The horrific sight made Thadarack queasy. Watching Stegokin kill their own wasn't something he had expected. But then again, what *had* he expected? He realized at that moment that he hadn't fully grasped the gravity of the situation. Not until now.

Death was all around him for as far as his eyes could see. There were a few Trikin that fell at the jaws of the Carne, but the overwhelming majority of the corpses were Carne and Stegokin. Thadarack looked up toward the sky and could already see countless vultures circling high in the air.

I caused this, he thought sorrowfully. *I had no other choice, did I?* Guilt started to flood Thadarack's mind as he watched more and more Stegokin die. He brought the Stegokin here, and had the Trikin not shown up, he would have brought them all to their certain death. The realization that the entire Stegokin army would have been annihilated sent chills down his spine.

Thadarack *was* relieved that Scythadon was still standing. He hoped his allies would get there in time. But he couldn't kick this newfound guilt that weighed heavily on his heart. He thought again about his trip to the valley with his father. Never in a million years would he have foreseen the events that had transpired since that night.

"Prince Thadarack!" Queen Cerathorn shouted from a good distance away. "It's time to go! You can march with me at the head of the army!"

"Go," said King Sturklan. "And save your city."

"I'm so sorry this happened to you," said Thadarack.

"Don't be," the King said quietly. "I would do it all over again. Besides, I knew the Trikin would show up. They realized they'd be better off with us alive than dead." He tried to smirk but quickly coughed and choked on his own blood. "But go, don't worry about me. I'd like to stay here and keep my fallen company anyway."

Thadarack watched King Sturklan scan his fallen warriors. He saw the sorrow in the King's eyes as his gaze moved from one dead corpse to the next, some of which were so mutilated there was no way to tell who they once were. It was a horrific sight.

"We will see you again," said Thexis.

"Thank you, King Sturklan," said Gwon.

"We'll send healers as soon as we can," said Thadarack.

King Sturklan nodded softly and lowered his head. A moment later, he closed his eyes. The trio started making their way toward the head of the Trikin army.

As he walked, Thadarack heard Glathzolm shout orders to the scattered Stegokin. He watched them form ranks behind the Trikin army, and in a few moments, they were in formation and ready to begin marching toward Scythadon.

He looked around at the thousands of lifeless Carne and Stegokin that littered the landscape. It was almost impossible to wade through the dead bodies without stepping on them. The disfiguration of some was so brutal that it was almost too difficult to determine if they were Carne or Stegokin.

Thadarack, Thexis, and Gwon joined Queen Cerathorn, Hornbrigg, and Glathzolm at the head of the two armies. Queen

Cerathorn glanced at Gwon, as did everyone else that was within view. "I will allow you to march with us because Prince Thadarack has vouched for you," she said. "Do *not* make me regret it."

"You won't," said Gwon shakenly. "I swear, my allegiance lies with the Viridi."

"Very well," said Queen Cerathorn as she looked at Hornbrigg. "Sound the advance. We march for Scythadon at once."

"Advance!" Hornbrigg shouted.

Everyone began walking toward the end of the valley in the direction of the city. Thadarack turned around and glanced one final time at King Sturklan. He saw the King slowly crawl to a tree and collapse beneath it. The Prince hoped he would survive, especially considering what he did for his kin...what he sacrificed. Thadarack turned back around, and with a few final strides, the valley was behind him.

CHAPTER SEVENTEEN

THE FATE OF THE EAST

It wasn't long before Thadarack heard the sounds of battle coming from the direction of Scythadon. The distant roaring and thunderous stomping grew louder the closer they got to the city. Soon, all that stood between them and Scythadon was about a mile of the Eastern Road, and an upcoming bend around the Great Forest that led into the Scythadon Glade.

"Who is that?" Thexis asked, pointing with her right index claw. "I see someone coming."

Thadarack squinted and looked far in the distance. A moment later, he saw Horngorre and the other Trikin scouts running full speed at them. She shouted something from a good distance away, but it was too difficult to hear what it was.

As she grew closer, she yelled again. This time, there was no mistaking what Horngorre said. "The Carne broke through the walls!" she howled. "They're in the city! The Scythekin fight on, but the Carne are many! We must hurry!" She and the other scouts were quickly upon them, desperately trying to catch their breath.

A multitude of emotions passed over Thadarack. At first, he was relieved that his kin were still fighting. He was hopeful that they'd prevail, especially now that the Trikin and Stegokin were so close. He pictured his father and wondered if he was alive.

Then, the doubt and fear took hold of him. *How many Carne are there?* he thought. The Carne army they'd defeated in the valley was large—at least a couple thousand strong. How could there still be so many Carne?

"How is that possible?" Glathzolm asked. "We must have already killed thousands in the valley."

"They split their main army when they learned of your advance toward Scythadon," said the Queen. "That's what I would have done, especially with greater numbers."

"How many Carne did you see?" Hornbrigg asked.

"At least a few thousand," said Horngorre to the gasps of everyone within earshot. "But it was hard to tell because they were already in the city. At first, we thought Scythadon had fallen, but once we looked from atop a hill, we could see the fighting all throughout the city."

"What's the plan?" Hornbrigg asked. "We should have the element of surprise."

"Did the Carne spot you?" Queen Cerathorn asked.

"No, they didn't," said Horngorre. "But it looked like some of the Carne that fled from the valley had just rejoined the army when we arrived."

"So they'll know we're coming," said Glathzolm.

"Not necessarily," said Queen Cerathorn. "If they're fighting across the city, it would be impossible for the Carne that returned to warn them all. If we hurry, we should still be able to catch most of them by surprise."

"And we'd be fighting them on two fronts," said Hornbrigg.

"Let's march without delay," said Queen Cerathorn. "The Scythekin have probably been fighting for at least a few days already. We don't know how much longer they'll hold out, especially now that the Carne have breached the walls."

The Queen turned toward Thadarack. "I know you want to fight, but you need to stay out of the coming battle as well."

Queen Cerathorn was right. Thadarack wanted to fight. He really did. But he now knew he'd be no match for the Carne. Having witnessed the previous battle firstclaw in the valley, he knew if he fought alongside the Trikin and Stegokin, he would surely die. After all, he wasn't even fully grown yet, nor did he have adequate battle training.

"Okay," Thadarack said reluctantly.

"And that goes for the two of you as well," said the Queen. "Especially you." She gestured toward Gwon with her beak. "I've trusted Prince Thadarack's judgment about you, but on the battlefield, my warriors will mistake you for the enemy. You must stay out of the coming battle if you want to live."

Gwon opened his mouth, but then he closed it and nodded. Thadarack agreed that Queen Cerathorn's reasoning made sense, and although he knew Gwon wanted to fight, it was a smarter move to stay away. Thexis then also nodded in agreement.

"Very good," said Queen Cerathorn as she turned toward Hornbrigg. "Sound the advance. We march for Scythadon with haste."

"Advance, double time!" Hornbrigg shouted.

The two armies were moving faster than before but weren't

in a full out run, allowing the Stegokin to keep pace with the Trikin. It wasn't long before they approached the bend in the road and turned the corner around the Great Forest, funneling into the Scythadon Glade. Thadarack caught his first glimpse of the Carne army and the city far in the distance.

By now, the sun had set, but the full moon that came after it shone brightly. Although this allowed for decent visibility into the clearing, it was difficult to tell how many Carne there were. If he had to guess, Thadarack estimated at least two to three thousand. That didn't include the Carne he couldn't see inside the walls. Like the valley, the army appeared to be a mixture of Tarbokin, Carnokin, and Allokin. The Prince also saw smaller Carne mixed in here and there.

"Look!" one of the Stegokin warriors yelled. "The Scythekin fight on!"

"The Scythekin can't be conquered!" another shouted.

"Even against so many, the Scythekin prevail!" a Trikin warrior yelled.

The Trikin and Stegokin armies soon erupted in cheers. To see his kin still fighting on, after what had to have been at least a day or two, gave Thadarack confidence that they could win.

As the cheering continued, Thadarack, Thexis, and Gwon snuck off to the side and hid behind a raised outcrop on the outskirts of the clearing, just within the Great Forest tree line. From there, they were hidden and high enough that they could see not only the armies before them but also Scythadon far in the distance under the beaming moonlight.

Thadarack saw two areas of the wall that had collapsed. The Carne were funneling into the gaps and although he could see over the walls slightly, he couldn't tell what was happening inside the city from this far away. Even though the wall had collapsed in those two areas, the gaps weren't very wide.

It didn't appear many Carne would have been able to get inside the city at once. That, coupled with the difficulty of traversing over the massive logs from the collapsed areas of the wall, most likely made for a tough assault on the city. It was evident that the Carne had a difficult time breaking through the walls. Dead Carne littered the clearing in all directions.

The slingers had done their job well. Countless corpses had scythes lodged deep inside them. Unfortunately, it looked like the Scythekin had to abandon them now that the Carne had broken through the wall. Thadarack's heart raced as he watched the Carne descend upon his city with hope and fear at the same time.

"I can't believe they've held out for so long against so many," said Thexis as she scanned the vast Carne army. "Before the Carne split their army, double this was besieging the city."

"And they were all alone," said Gwon with a ghastly look on his face.

They were alone, Thadarack thought. *Not knowing if anybody was coming to help.* But his kin weren't alone, not any longer. The Prince of Scythadon had returned, and with him, he brought the Trikin and Stegokin armies. Well, what was left of the Stegokin army at least.

Thadarack glanced at the two Viridi armies just as they finished funneling into the clearing. Fresh off their victory in the valley and fueled by the resolve of the Scythekin, the Prince could see the determination in the warriors' eyes.

Thadarack grew proud of his kin. Even against such superior

numbers, they'd endured. He looked upon the attacking Carne and saw many were wounded with slash marks all across their bodies. Many more had been struck by the scythes and appeared to be in excruciating pain.

But then Thadarack saw numerous Carne that had bloodied jaws; blood that he knew once flowed through the veins of his kin. He grew enraged, glaring at the menacing Carne before him. Strangely enough, he was no longer scared. He was mad. Mad that such wicked beings dared to attack his home.

Queen Cerathorn began issuing orders to the Trikin army. Hornbrigg took a contingent of Trikin and moved further down the left side of the clearing, staying close to the fringe of the Great Forest. Horngorre then took about the same amount of Trikin warriors to the right side of the clearing.

Queen Cerathorn stayed in the center while the Trikin army spread itself from one bank of the Scythadon River to the other, stretching like a crescent all the way across the clearing. Glathzolm shouted orders to the Stegokin warriors. They began to spread out in one single line right behind the Trikin.

Thadarack watched as more and more Carne turned around toward the Trikin and Stegokin. He saw quite a few of the Carne trying to get the attention of others, but the chaos of the battle made it difficult. They tried to reform a second front facing the Viridi, but it was disorganized with numerous gaps.

"If they attack now, they'll catch the Carne off guard!" Thexis said animatedly. "Many haven't noticed them yet!"

Just when Thadarack was about to voice his agreement, Queen Cerathorn screamed in a fit of rage. "With me! Charge! To the Scythekin! To Scythadon!"

The Trikin, with Queen Cerathorn, Hornbrigg, and Horngorre at the forefront, formed three flying wedges aimed straight at the enemy's flank. They charged defiantly at the Carne, many of whom were still unaware of their advance. The Stegokin followed behind the Trikin and tried their best to stay as close as possible, but the speed difference between the two created a rather large gap.

The ground shook like an earthquake as the Trikin grew nearer to the Carne. When the Trikin got closer, other Carne must have felt the stampede. Hundreds turned around and desperately tried to establish a more continuous battle line outside the city walls.

Some Carne began to charge back, roaring and howling as they went. But the fear across the faces of many, most likely due to the surprise and ferocity of the Trikin charge, was unmistakable.

In a few mere moments, the three Trikin flying wedges smashed into both the oncoming Carne and the army's flank. The Trikin warriors drove their horns deep into the Carne they encountered, pushing through the thick Carne lines as far and as fast as they could.

The sounds from the clash were so great that they could have been heard for miles in all directions. Thadarack looked on as carnage unfolded before him and his friends once again, watching in horror as more and more Carne turned around to meet the Trikin in battle.

Although the Trikin's charge was powerful, and many Carne were impaled and killed immediately, it didn't prove as devastating as it had earlier. A majority of the Carne were caught off guard, but the Trikin didn't have the momentum they had from charging down the hill in the valley.

The fighting ensued, and in a terrifying twist of events, the Carne began overwhelming the Trikin. Even though the Carne were now fighting on two fronts, their sheer numbers proved problematic.

Thadarack remembered Riktlan had said that Trikin relied too heavily on their charge, and they weren't great at close-range combat. What he was witnessing before him proved this to be true. Although the charge caused significant damage, the Carne rebounded fairly quickly.

At the best possible time, the Stegokin finally arrived. In a unified and strategic movement, the Trikin fell back just enough for the Stegokin to swiftly shuffle and smash their thagomizers directly into the Carne, halting their advance.

The Trikin then re-engaged with a small but effective charge and fought alongside the Stegokin, the arrival of whom seemed to help even the odds. The battle raged on for what felt like an eternity.

Although barely visible through the blood spray, dirt, and dust, Thadarack watched as both Viridi and Carne corpses fell at an even rate. Neither appeared to be gaining an edge in the chaotic battle.

Shrieks and sounds of agony filled the air as each side struggled for superiority over the other. Bodies dropped everywhere, piling up on one another, eventually making it hard for the combatants to fight.

Thadarack tried to scan the battle for the Queen and anyone else he knew, but his vantage point and the mayhem all around made it difficult to see. A moment later, Thexis shouted, "The Carne are getting the upper claw! Horngorre has been killed and her line has been overrun!"

Thadarack looked to the right side of the Viridi army and saw it falling apart. It wasn't long before the Carne pushed through and flanked the Trikin and Stegokin. Slowly, the Trikin and Stegokin were pushed further left, closer and closer to the Scythadon River.

Carne began pouring out of the two gaps in the city wall, and for a moment, it seemed like they'd never stop. A jolt of terror coursed through Thadarack's veins, thinking about how his kin might all be dead. Otherwise, how could so many be swarming out of the city?

"There's just too many of them," said Gwon. "How were they supposed to win against such overwhelming evil?"

Thadarack watched with dread as one by one, the Trikin began to retreat. He saw many of the Trikin outrun the Carne that pursued them, but watched countless Stegokin get maimed by the jaws of their enemy as they closed in all around. *They're all going to die*, he thought. *Every last Stegokin is going to die.*

Amidst the chaos, Thadarack watched Glathzolm courageously fight for her life, throwing down Carne after Carne with vicious strikes of her thagomizer. The speed and power with which she was capable of thrashing it around didn't look Stegokinly possible. As he watched her fight for her very life, he thought the worst. *It's over...we've lost. What do we do now?*

Thadarack began to panic as his allies fell apart in front of him, the army now in complete disarray. He scanned the routing Viridi army but didn't see Queen Cerathorn or Hornbrigg anywhere. He glanced back at where he saw Glathzolm, but there were so many Carne in his line of sight that he couldn't see her any longer.

"We have to get out of here," said Thexis. "We need to leave now."

"And go where?" Gwon asked. "We're to just leave them to their certain deaths?"

"I don't like it any more than you do," said Thexis. "But if we stay here, we'll all die."

"I'd rather fight and die here than run like a coward!" Gwon yelled, standing up on top of the outcrop.

"Our most important job is to keep Thadarack alive!" Thexis challenged. "You are not a coward if we leave to that end!"

Gwon sighed as he continued looking out at the mayhem across the clearing. By now, the retreating Trikin had almost made it to where they were hiding. Just when it looked like Gwon was reconsidering, Thadarack caught a glimpse of movement from his right. He immediately thought the Carne had somehow circumvented the Viridi army and were now also attacking from behind.

He turned in fear but saw something unexpected, something that filled him with an intense passion he had never felt before. Kylesia and Fulgro, with only a hundred or so Pachykin behind them, charged straight into the fray.

"They'll be massacred!" Thexis cried. "What are they doing?"

The Pachykin howled and yelled, displaying such valor that it inspired Thadarack, transforming his fear into courage. He then saw many of the retreating Trikin slow down and do a double take, watching the Pachykin run right past them.

In an instant, Gwon leaped down from the outcrop and started charging right after the Pachykin. Thadarack then saw Queen Cerathorn, not far from their hiding place, throw down a Tarbokin she was fighting with. She struck it right through the gut and threw the large Carne off her horns with such ease that one could be fooled into thinking it didn't weigh more than a feather.

"Don't retreat!" Gwon screamed as he charged forward. "Fight! Fight! Fight alongside the Pachykin! Don't give up! Never give up!"

Thadarack watched as his friend ran through the retreating Trikin, many of which stopped dead in their tracks and watched him go by. Gwon was soon right next to Queen Cerathorn, and together, with a quick glance and nod, they took off side-by-side straight toward the pursuing Carne.

Although Thadarack was too far away to hear at this point, Queen Cerathorn yelled something, and suddenly, the routing Trikin turned around and charged alongside the Queen, Gwon, and the Pachykin.

The Pachykin rammed into the Carne, while the Trikin re-engaged the bulk of the Carne army. Thadarack tried to keep his eyes on Queen Cerathorn and Gwon, but he couldn't see them now that the battle was again in full swing.

The Prince saw some Stegokin fighting far in the distance, but they were surrounded. Glathzolm was somehow still at the forefront, fighting valiantly as Carne closed in all around her.

Bravery and determination having now taken hold of him, Thadarack emerged from his hiding place. *I can do this,* he thought, standing ready to charge. *I must do this.*

"You aren't a coward if you stay here," said Thexis. "As a matter of fact, it's the right decision for you to make. You know you can't fight the Carne. At least not yet."

Thadarack looked at his friend and knew she was right. He turned back toward the battle, and although he wanted to follow his friend and fight courageously, he knew he couldn't.

"I'll stay here with you," continued Thexis. "We'll stay here together."

If Thexis had followed Gwon, Thadarack would have as well. He knew that much to be true. A few days ago, that might not have been the case, but today it was. Knowing that made him feel much better.

The Carne that pursued the Trikin were slowly pushed back toward the wall of the city. After a long while of harsh fighting, the Carne were one army again, fighting the Trikin, Stegokin, and Pachykin all at once. They began to waver, and one by one, started trying to escape.

"They're retreating!" Thexis yelled. "And look! Our kin!"

The Scythekin began emerging from the walls, having pushed the Carne out of the city. Thadarack watched as many of the Carne tried desperately to fight their way through the Trikin, Stegokin, and Pachykin, as they were now in a rout.

Although the Carne army was surrounded, the Viridi lines were thin, allowing for countless Carne to make it through. They headed for the Great Forest, while others made their way toward the Scythadon River, having had no other choice.

The Trikin, Stegokin, Scythekin, and Pachykin chased after them in all directions, and soon the entire clearing was in pandemonium. Smaller skirmishes were occurring all over and at times, it was difficult to tell who was winning.

As Carne ran in their direction, Thadarack and Thexis crouched behind the outcrop to remain unseen. Carne began to run around them, weaving in and out of the dense forest trees as quickly as they could to escape the onslaught.

After it appeared no more Carne were going to run past him, Thadarack peered over the outcrop just in time to see the Carne begin struggling in the river. Before a single Carne made it to the other bank, the river began to run red in what looked like a bloodbath. Unable to fight effectively in the water, the Carne were getting ripped apart.

The pursuing Viridi stopped at the riverbank and watched as the Carne painfully flailed around in desperation to make it to the other side. Cheers among the Viridi lines began to erupt as they watched their enemy get torn to pieces from those that lurked in the depths of the river.

"It's the Seaborne!" Thexis shouted as she and Thadarack came out of their hiding place. "They've come to help us!"

Thadarack watched as some Carne put up a fight, but a majority of those who tried to cross the river stood no chance. Bodies of mangled Carne floated down the river, and although some eventually made it to the other side unscathed, most were killed with the river becoming their watery tomb.

As the Seaborne continued devouring the dead Carne, the cheering began to wane. The Viridi warriors soon dispersed across the clearing and began finishing off any wounded Carne they came across. Although Thadarack knew it needed to be done, the sight disturbed him. Many pleaded for their lives to be spared. Others tried to fight back, snapping their jaws at their executioners, albeit in vain.

By now, the last of the Carne had fled from the battle, and Thadarack saw the Scythekin healers emerge from Scythadon. They started caring for the wounded: Trikin, Stegokin, Scythekin, and Pachykin alike. Many others emerged from Scythadon and sobbed as they came across their slain loved ones. Sounds of agony and cries for help permeated from among the hundreds, if not thousands, of wounded.

Thadarack and Thexis stood on the outcrop, scanning the horrific sight before them. Corpses laid across the clearing for as far as the eye could see. Although they had won, it didn't feel like it. Thadarack wanted to be happy, but the death all around him made it difficult to be.

"Do you see Gwon?" Thexis asked. "I don't see him anywhere."

Thadarack didn't see him either. He desperately scanned the clearing and looked for his friend, but couldn't spot him anywhere. His heart sank into the pit of his stomach.

"Come on!" Thexis said. "Let's go find him!"

CHAPTER EIGHTEEN

THE PERILOUS SECRET

As Thadarack walked through the battlefield with Thexis looking for his friend, the death and destruction all around was almost too much to bear. The sounds of weeping and wailing Viridi sent chills down his spine as he carefully traversed past their mangled bodies.

He wanted to stop and care for them, or at least let them know they weren't alone, but the urgency he felt to find his friend forced him to keep going. He did see quite a few Scythekin healers tending to the wounded, but there were so many that it would most likely take hours before they were all treated.

For what seemed like an eternity, they scoured the battlefield looking for Gwon. With each passing minute, Thadarack grew more and more concerned. It would have been undoubtedly hard for the Trikin, Stegokin, and Pachykin to distinguish Gwon from the enemy. Or would it have been? That fear ate away at the young Prince while he desperately searched for his Gigakin friend.

Then, Thadarack heard a familiar voice call to him from a

good distance away. "Thadarack!" the voice yelled. "Thexis! Over here!"

Thadarack turned around and saw Gwon standing beside Queen Cerathorn, Hornbrigg, and Glathzolm. His relief consumed him as he quickly made his way toward them. All four were bloody from head to toe and except for Gwon, had numerous wounds.

Glathzolm looked the worst, but despite her wounds, she was still standing. Queen Cerathorn and Hornbrigg looked like they showered in a waterfall of blood, as their horns and their faces were soaked dark red. Gwon's jaws were dripping with blood, but thankfully, he didn't appear to have any major wounds. *Maybe the Carne mistook him for an ally?* Thadarack thought as he ran to his friend.

When Thadarack and Thexis reached Gwon, they threw their arms around him. "Ouch!" he blurted as they both hugged him close. "Watch your claws!"

They backed off and laughed, an act that the young Prince welcomed in the face of everything that had transpired. Just then, Kylesia and Fulgro approached. They were also bloody, but just like Gwon, they didn't appear to have major battle wounds.

Queen Cerathorn turned and addressed the two Pachykin. "Thank you," she said. "If you hadn't come when you did…" Her voice faded as she looked at the nearby corpses of her kin.

"We saw you marching while on our way to Stegodor," said Kylesia. "We decided after all that we couldn't sit back and do nothing. Especially considering everything they've taken from us."

"We are forever in your debt," interposed Glathzolm. "It was because of your bravery that we prevailed."

"Your courage inspired us all to keep fighting," said Hornbrigg.

Kylesia nodded.

"You," said Queen Cerathorn gruffly as she narrowed her eyes at Gwon. "Recklessly charging straight into the battle. We could have killed you. What were you thinking?"

Thadarack looked at his friend and could tell he was caught off guard, probably surprised that the Queen wasn't more appreciative of what he did. After all, many of the Trikin turned around because they saw the courageous Pachykin *and* Gwon fearlessly trying to rally them.

"Um…I…" Gwon stammered.

"I shouldn't have doubted you," said Queen Cerathorn warmly. "You showed your true colors today."

Gwon's smile stretched across his entire face. It radiated from him, and despite everything that had happened, witnessing this amiable interaction warmed Thadarack's heart. It also appeared Gwon didn't know what to say. He just stood there and smiled as Hornbrigg, Glathzolm, and countless other nearby Trikin and Stegokin alike, thanked him for what he had done.

Thadarack glanced at Thexis and donned his own smile, once again realizing how lucky he was to have such good friends. Friends that he knew would always look out for him, no matter what they faced.

As he listened to everyone discuss the battle, and how proud they each were of one another, Thadarack heard a familiar voice call to him from behind. "My Prince!" the voice yelled.

Thadarack turned and saw Rhinn making her way toward him.

As with everyone else who had been fighting the Carne, her face was bloody, and she had what looked like numerous bite marks on her neck, arms, and legs. Although she was limping toward him, it was apparent that her injuries hadn't debilitated her. "Thank the Hallowed Lumina you are alright!" she yelled as she got closer.

Not being all bloody began to make Thadarack uncomfortable. For a moment, he became concerned that everyone who saw him would look down upon him due to the fact he wasn't engaged in the battle. He soon realized, though, that everyone was happy he was alive.

His concern soon fluttered away as he gazed into Rhinn's thankful eyes. "You've returned," Rhinn said, now standing right before Thadarack. "And you brought help."

She glanced at everyone present and nodded. "Thank you all. If you hadn't come when you did…" She briefly paused as sorrow passed across her face. "Well, we can talk more later." She then turned back toward Thadarack. "King Thax will want to speak with you right away. He's still recovering in the Mending House."

Thadarack breathed a sigh of relief. His father was still alive? Did that mean he was going to survive after all? Or was there still a chance he was going to die? Regardless, Thadarack was more than ready to go see him, even if it was for one last time.

"Have you seen my father?" Gwon interjected. "I've looked all around, but I haven't seen him anywhere. Is he okay?"

Thadarack was so caught up in thinking about his own father that he hadn't even thought about Girozz. He knew that the Scythekin would be able to discern Girozz from the enemy but wasn't sure about the others. After all, Queen Cerathorn said herself that Gwon must stay out of the battle for that very reason.

That realization hit Thadarack and seemed to have hit Thexis at the same time. They both turned around frantically and peered in all directions, but Girozz was nowhere in sight.

Rhinn was deep in thought for a few moments before responding. "You know what, I haven't seen Girozz since shortly after you left for Stegodor," she eventually said. "I'm not sure where he is, but I'm sure he's alright." Rhinn gave Gwon a slight smile before turning around and walking toward a group of nearby Scythekin.

Worry spread across Gwon's face. After all, how could such a large Carne among the Scythekin simply vanish? Did his father order Girozz to hide so there wouldn't be any confusion during the battle? Wherever he was, Thadarack wished that he was okay.

"I'm sure he'll turn up," he said in an effort to cheer up his friend. "Let's go see my father. He might know where he is."

The friends said their goodbyes to everyone around them and made their way toward the front gate. For the time being, Thadarack forgot about Girozz as he walked past the mutilated bodies on his way to the city. When he entered Scythadon, he froze.

The entire farm looked like a battlefield. Hundreds, if not thousands, of dead Carne and Scythekin were piled on top of one another. All the trees and plants had been trampled for as far as Thadarack could see. Most of the homes had been demolished, and although it was a good distance from them, the city hub looked to be utterly destroyed. It was hard to tell from this far away, but Thadarack thought the palace might still have been intact.

After a few moments of gazing at such horror, Thexis broke the silence. "This is awful," she said quietly. "I still can't believe it came to this. I don't..." She paused for a moment, pointing at a body not far inside the wall. "Is that..."

The three friends gasped as they looked upon Beroyn's dead body, mangled and deformed almost beyond the point of recognition. A couple of his soldiers stood around him, murmuring words too quiet for Thadarack to hear.

Rhinn soon walked past them and approached the gathered Scythekin. "Help me lift him," she said. "He shan't lie here among these beasts any longer."

Rhinn and the guards picked up Beroyn and carried him out of the city.

"I wonder where they're taking him," said Gwon. "And where is my father?"

"Come on," said Thadarack as he started making his way in the direction of the Mending House. *I bet my father knows,* he thought. His friends followed closely behind.

The dead bodies became fewer and fewer the closer they got to the Mending House. It wasn't that surprising to Thadarack, considering the Mending House was near the back of the city. Once they got there, the surrounding area remained untouched. The Prince didn't want to think about how many dead Scythekin they had passed on their way. *One is too many,* he thought.

"Go ahead," said Thexis. "We'll wait out here."

"Give the King our best," said Gwon. "And please ask him about my father."

"I will," said Thadarack.

Just as he was about to walk into the Mending House, Medicus exited. He was covered in blood from head to tail. Fortunately, none of his numerous wounds looked to be life-threatening.

Medicus' gloomy expression turned cheerful when he set his eyes on the Prince. A big, warm smile quickly passed over his face.

"Prince Thadarack!" he shouted excitedly. "You've returned not a minute too soon! I knew you'd succeed!"

Thadarack returned the smile. "I couldn't have done it without them," he said, gesturing toward his friends. "I would have never made it without their help."

Medicus nodded at Thexis and Gwon. "Well, I'm glad you're all back," he said before turning back to Thadarack. "The King is awake for now, but he is very sleepy. Go to him."

"Have you seen my father anywhere?" Gwon asked. "Rhinn said she hasn't seen him in days."

Medicus cocked his head in bewilderment. "I actually haven't either," he said. "Girozz is a tough Carne, though. I'm sure wherever he is, he's fine."

Thadarack was nervous. *Did something happen to Girozz?* he thought. *How have Rhinn and Medicus not seen him?* He looked at Gwon and saw panic in his eyes. How could a Carne among the Scythekin just disappear?

Gwon sighed. "I'm going to look for him. I'll meet you both back here later."

"I'll come with you," said Thexis. "We'll see you later."

"Okay," said Thadarack. "We'll find him, Gwon. I'm sure of it."

Thexis and Gwon took off in the direction of Gwon's home. "How has nobody seen him?" Thadarack asked once his friends were out of sight.

"I'm not sure," said Medicus. "It is peculiar. I haven't seen him in a few days myself. I think not since the Carne arrived. I'm positive he didn't fight in the battle. But go speak to your father. Maybe he knows something. I'm glad you're home, Prince Thadarack. I must get going, though. I should go look after the wounded."

"King Sturklan is very hurt," said Thadarack. "He stayed behind in the valley. I'm sure the Stegokin have gone to find him, but can you please care for his wounds when he returns?"

"I will," said Medicus. "If they haven't left already, I will accompany them."

Medicus departed just as Thadarack entered the Mending House. When he approached his father in the back room, he could see that his eyes were barely open. They were dark and bloodshot, and he looked much more fatigued than he did when Thadarack saw him last.

The King hadn't moved at all since Thadarack left for Stegodor. He also noticed his left arm had been amputated. All that was left was a stub, charred black from the cauterization process. He tried not to let the sight bother him, but he became a bit nauseous.

"My son," said King Thax gently. "You made it home. I knew you would."

"I did, Father," said Thadarack.

"You did good," the King said. "I heard the Trikin, Stegokin, *and* Pachykin came...they saved us...you saved us. I couldn't be prouder of you, my son."

Thadarack was caught somewhere between a smile and frown. It was difficult to feel happy in the presence of his incapacitated father. "I couldn't have done it without my friends. Thexis and Gwon came with me."

"And they're okay? They made it home safely?"

"Yes."

"And what about Arkonius?"

Thadarack's heart dropped at the mention of Arkonius' name. *Was there a chance that Arkonius was still alive? When we left him, he hadn't died yet.* He immediately wanted to return to the Great Forest to look for him.

But Thadarack quickly realized that the chances of Arkonius having survived were very slim. He recalled how there were Carne charging straight toward them when they ran away. If Arkonius hadn't died from the wounds he'd incurred, the incoming Carne would surely have finished him off. "We came across Carne on our way to Stegodor," he said, glancing toward the ground. "Arkonius gave his life to protect us."

King Thax sighed. "I'm sure he fought bravely."

"He did," said Thadarack as he looked back at his father. "If he wasn't with us…" He paused and decided he didn't want to finish his thought.

"But he was," said King Thax. "And that's all that matters. I'm deeply saddened to hear of his death, but I'm glad the three of you made it home."

"Me too," said Thadarack. "Do you know where Girozz is? Rhinn and Medicus haven't seen him since before the battle."

King Thax's already melancholy look quickly became more

pronounced. "What I'm about to tell you must stay between us. Nobody else can know, especially not Gwon."

The ominous tone in his father's voice made Thadarack uncomfortable. What could have happened that was so bad that not even Gwon could know? Thadarack was unsure he even wanted to know himself. "Why?" he asked. "What happened? Is Girozz okay?"

"Promise me you won't tell anybody," said King Thax. "Not even Gwon."

"I promise," Thadarack said reluctantly.

King Thax breathed an exceptionally long sigh. "Girozz has left us," he finally said. "He returned to the Carne."

Thadarack didn't know what to say. Confusion and a hundred different questions flooded his mind. *Returned to the Carne? Why would he do that?* He thought about Gwon and what he would think if he found out. "What do you mean?"

"He came to us under false pretenses," said the King. "With a purpose that I had originally considered but lost sight of. He came to learn as much about us as possible. To discover our weaknesses and our strengths. And to ensure that we let our guard down so the Carne could regroup and attack when we were at our most vulnerable."

Thadarack shuddered at his father's words. If his father wasn't the one telling him this, he wouldn't have believed it. Was he saying that Girozz was a spy for the Carne? It didn't seem possible, but the look on his father's face confirmed that what he was saying was true. Or at the very least, he believed it to be.

"Girozz loves Gwon," the King continued. "He means the world to him. He had no other choice but to follow orders to keep him safe…and…keep his mother alive."

"His…" Thadarack stammered. "Mother? Gwon's mother is alive?"

"Yes, she's alive. She was being held captive and had Girozz not followed through with his task, she would have been put to death. He had no choice but to do what he did."

Thadarack became speechless and stared blankly back at his father. He had a million questions he wanted to ask but was unable to open his mouth to ask them. Gwon's father was not only a spy for the Carne, but his mother was still alive? On top of that, Thadarack wasn't supposed to tell him anything? How was he going to keep this secret from his friend?

"He was the reason the Carne were able to invade so easily," continued the King. "And why we were so blindsided."

Thadarack's next realization was enough to force his mouth open. His bout of shock transitioned into anger. "What does that mean, exactly?" he asked. His heart raced as he put more and more pieces of the puzzle together. "Is he the reason that nobody made it back to Scythadon from the Wall to warn us?"

King Thax slightly nodded. "He—"

"He killed Scythekin!" Thadarack interrupted aggressively. "How did you find out about this?"

King Thax closed his eyes. "You must calm down."

Thadarack didn't understand how his father was so calm. Girozz was responsible for the horror he and everyone else had endured for the last few days. He thought about Arkonius, Beroyn, and all the other Scythekin who had died. He thought about all the dead Stegokin and Trikin that were scattered around both the valley and Scythadon.

Then it dawned on him...something that made his heart throb with not only anger, but immense and searing pain.

"What about my mother?" he asked slowly. "Was he responsible for the ambush?"

King Thax opened his eyes and hesitated before answering. "Yes," he eventually said.

Thadarack's heart dropped so far in his chest that for a time, it seemed like it might fall right out. His anger and pain transitioned into a fit of rage. He clenched his claws together and gritted his teeth, feeling as if he might explode.

"You must calm down," continued his father. "I will explain what—"

"Calm down?" Thadarack yelled so loud that others outside surely overheard him. "He's responsible for mother's death...your mate...our Queen! How am I to calm down? And what about you? You almost died!"

King Thax didn't have the strength or energy to challenge Thadarack's rage. The King tried to raise his voice, but instead, he started coughing, and was unable to say more than a few unrecognizable words.

Thadarack then realized something that did in fact calm him down a bit. He remembered how Girozz was the one who brought his father home after the ambush. The sight of Girozz by his father's side flashed before his eyes. "But he saved you," he said in a much calmer voice. "Didn't he?"

After a few moments of desperately trying to stop his coughing fit, King Thax spoke gently. "When he saw your mother die, he realized that what he had done was wrong. He began this task with two goals in mind: to free the love of his life from bondage and keep his son safe. Those goals grew hazy the longer he was here…for we showed him that we are not evil…that we are good, and if given the chance, we are willing to live peacefully alongside the Carne. In the end, even after all he had done, he realized his allegiance was here. He fought by my side and killed more Carne than I could count when we were ambushed. Without his change of heart, I would have been slain. Not only that, Scythadon would've had no idea that a Carne army would soon be at its gate."

Most of what his father said didn't register. Thadarack was so distraught at Girozz's betrayal and his mother's death that it was hard for him to fully grasp the details.

"But he caused mother's death," he said as tears formed behind his eyes. "It's because of him that she's gone and never coming back. We don't even have a body to say goodbye to."

"The Carne would have invaded regardless of what Girozz did," said King Thax. "He may have caused her death, and I will never forgive him for that, but we all die eventually. It's only a matter of when."

King Thax reached out his right arm and interlocked his claws with Thadarack's. "I would have done the same thing if I were him. You know that to be true."

Thadarack tried to hold back his tears, but thinking about his mother's death made it too difficult. Tears began to roll off his beak as he stared back at his dying father. Although Thadarack had hoped Medicus' diagnosis was wrong, it was more apparent now than ever that it wasn't.

He didn't want to believe it was true, but he could tell from looking in his father's eyes that he was slowly fading away. "How did you learn all of this?" he asked.

"Shortly after you left, Girozz came to me and disclosed everything. He threw himself upon my mercy and told me to do with him what I saw fit."

"And what did you do?"

"I told him to go," said the King. "To return to the Carne immediately and free the love of his life."

"But why?" Thadarack asked. "Why would you let him go?"

"He's already being punished. He will live with the guilt of what he did for the rest of his life. I saw it in his eyes and sensed it in his pained voice."

"But how do you know the Carne will release her?" Thadarack asked. "We won the battle."

"He did his part," said King Thax. "It was apparent that had the Stegokin and Trikin not shown up, we would have been overrun. When I told him to return, he offered to stay and fight, but I knew he couldn't bear to witness what he had a huge part in setting in motion. And after all, he hoped you three would be successful...the one group he let slip away from the city."

Let slip away from the city, thought Thadarack. He wondered how many Scythekin Girozz had a tooth in killing. His heart palpitated at the thought, especially when he realized how the Scythekin would have let their guard down around Girozz.

They would never have suspected him to be a killer, and for that, they would have paid the ultimate price. "I can't believe he told you all of this and you just let him walk away...after all he's done...after all this time," Thadarack said distraughtly.

"He could have killed you," the King said quietly. "My son...the Prince of the Scythekin."

Thadarack saw his father's eyes swell with tears. "He was among the very few who knew exactly where the four of you were headed. He could have killed you, Arkonius, and Thexis. He could have taken Gwon with him and sealed the fate of Scythadon. But he didn't. Out of his grown respect for me and his love for Gwon, he let you leave."

"How do you know he didn't try to have us killed? We were attacked on our way to Stegodor."

King Thax sighed. "There are few I believe would be able to defeat Arkonius in combat. Girozz is one of them. If he wanted you dead, he would have done it himself."

"But still, why did you let him leave? You just let him walk away?"

"Yes," said King Thax. "I told him to go save the love of his life. I told him to tell the Carne that he killed me while I lay weak on my deathbed. That he shouldn't wait one moment longer to save her. I hope that he walked out of here with his head held high, despite everything he's done…Yes, he almost brought the destruction of our city. And…yes, he caused the death of many honorable Scythekin, including your mother…but he was also a good Carne. Just like we know Gwon is."

The King paused for a moment, catching his breath before continuing. "And I say to you, my son, the experiment that Carne and Viridi can live peaceful lives, side by side, was a success. That war is not the only way. I only wish he had told me sooner. That he had told me everything. I would have tried to help him. He saved my life. A Carne saved the life of a Viridi king. A Scythekin king, nonetheless. But the past is in the past. We can only look to the future now. And know that before he left, he pledged he would help the Viridi however he can for the rest of his life. I believed him."

"But what about Gwon?" Thadarack asked. "Where does this leave him?"

"Gwon is why nobody can know. If others find out, they will take it out on him. I told Girozz I would protect Gwon until the day I die. That he will always be welcome among our kin. I have no regrets from that day when Girozz and Gwon showed up at the Wall. I was deceived, but that doesn't make me regret my decision. Carne and Viridi *can* live together."

Thadarack tried hard to see things from his father's point of view, but there was one thing that made it difficult. One thing that, each time he thought about it, caused a burning pain to fester in his heart. "But he is the reason mother is dead. He is why she's never..." His voice trailed off as he wept.

"I know," the King said gently. "But we both knew your mother. She would have understood. You know she would have wanted him to go save his mate. She loved Girozz, and I truly believe that Girozz, in the end, loved her too."

Thadarack understood what his father was saying, but it didn't help him feel any better. He was furious at Girozz, and although he knew it wasn't fair or right, a part of that anger extended toward Gwon. He didn't think Gwon would ever betray him, but then again, he never in a million moons would have thought Girozz would either.

Then, another realization sent shivers down his back. He thought about how Girozz was a spy for the Carne. Did this mean that, when he returned to the Southern Peninsula, he was in fact colluding with the High King? "Does he know the High

277

King?" Thadarack reluctantly asked.

Thadarack's father looked at him for a few moments. After what felt like an eternity, he finally spoke. "Yes," he said. "The High King is the one who imprisoned Gwon's mother."

Thadarack was unsure when the devastating news would stop. There seemed to be one thing after another. Every bit of information was worse than the last. Girozz was planning their demise all this time. For fifteen long years, he was plotting how to most effectively destroy Thadarack's kin. It was too much to handle for the young Prince, especially considering he couldn't tell Gwon anything.

He knew Gwon would go after his father if he found out. Not only that, if anyone else in Scythadon found out, Gwon would no longer be welcome. He knew he had to keep this a secret, but he recognized such a feat would prove difficult. Not to mention, what was he going to tell Gwon? That his father just up and disappeared?

"Gwon will wonder where his father is," continued the King. "You are to tell him that Girozz has left with the intention of reasoning with the Carne. That he's attempting to stop any further bloodshed. Tell him that he has left to find the High King and that his aim is to achieve peace. And that I forbid him from going after his father."

"Okay," Thadarack said. "But I'm still so confused. Why Girozz? Why did the High King imprison *his* mate?"

"He told me that the Carne had been planning to attack the Wall for decades," said the King, briefly pausing before continuing. "You can't tell anybody any of this, remember that."

"I won't."

"At one time, Girozz vied for the high kingship. He fought a Rexkin for it and lost. He was the last one strong enough, or brave enough, to challenge him. Before they fought, he was the leader of the Gigakin. But because of his defeat, he lost their respect and loyalty. They submitted to the Rexkin, who in turn was named the new High King. He had no choice but to do what was demanded of him if he wanted his mate and Gwon to survive."

Thadarack wondered what would have happened if Girozz had become the High King. *Would Gwon have grown up to be my enemy?* The thought was deeply distressing and he quickly tried to forget about it. "So who is the High King?" he asked.

"His name is Skorzo. He's a direct descendant of Orzligorn. Girozz said that he is just as ruthless."

Skorzo. Orzligorn. Both names made Thadarack shudder. "In the valley, a Tarbokin told us that someone would be coming for us. He must have been talking about him."

"Most likely," said King Thax. "Girozz also told me what their plan is. Skorzo sent the Tarbokin, Allokin, and Carnokin east to fight us. And as we assumed before you left, they planned to isolate us and finish us off first. The Rexkin, Gigakin, and Spinekin, under Skorzo's leadership, went west to deal with the Longneck kingdoms. He said—"

"Spinekin?" Thadarack interrupted. "I thought they were extinct?"

"It was believed they were. But we were very wrong. Girozz said that there are still many. It may not seem like it, but we were fortunate that they didn't all come here first. Their fear of the Longnecks may have very well saved us."

"So, we were right," said Thadarack. "We guessed that they split up. We didn't think they'd want to give us a chance to join forces."

"Exactly. They were hoping to destroy us in the East and destroy the Longnecks in the West. Then, they would finish off any other Viridi tribes that have the means to fight back."

"Like the Stegokin and Trikin?" Thadarack asked.

King Thax nodded. "With all the Viridi tribes that could fight back gone, they would subjugate the rest and rule all Valdere. But speaking of the Stegokin and Trikin, where are King Sturklan and Queen Cerathorn? Are they here? We must discuss our next plan of action."

"Queen Cerathorn is, but King Sturklan was wounded during the battle in the valley. He couldn't make his way here and was resting under a tree when we left him."

"I hope he lives," said the King. "And although we must focus on the future, I have grown very tired. Please give me some time to sleep. Afterward, we will all convene and deliberate where we go from here."

Thadarack had so many questions he wanted to ask, but could tell his father was tired. After all, his eyes were already half shut.

"I love you, my son. I'm so proud of you."

"I love you, Father."

"Now go, let me rest. Summon everyone who should be present for the meeting. Send for them to come here first thing in the morning. I also want you, Thexis, and Gwon to be here."

"But who should I summon? I'm not sure who..." Thadarack's voice trailed off when he noticed his father had already fallen asleep. He wasn't kidding when he said he'd grown tired. The Prince turned around and quietly headed for the exit.

Before he walked out, he turned and glanced one more time at his father. He looked at the stub where his left arm used to be, and sadness consumed him. He didn't want to leave. He wanted to stay by his father's side and look after him. He looked so frail. But eventually, Thadarack turned around and exited the Mending House.

CHAPTER NINETEEN

HEROIC DEEDS

A cool, brisk evening greeted Thadarack as he exited the Mending House. Almost immediately, he could hear sounds of celebration echoing throughout the city. Laughter and joyous songs were coming from the direction of the city hub.

Although the sounds were pleasant, Thadarack had a hard time reveling in them. He was glad everyone was now so happy. He wished that he could also feel that way, but couldn't, especially not now.

"Thadarack," said Gwon. "How is King Thax?"

When Thadarack glanced at his friend, his heart pulsed so sporadically that for a moment, he grew concerned for his health. *Please don't have a heart attack,* he thought, for it really seemed like he might.

He looked Gwon in the eye and for a split second, he believed he was going to tell him everything. Lucky for him, Thexis spoke before he opened his mouth. "How is he?" she asked. "I'm sure King Thax was glad to see you."

"He...he's...doing okay," stammered Thadarack. "He's

sleeping." *What are you doing? Act normal.* Then he wondered what *normal* was. Nothing about what had happened this past week was normal. He looked back at Gwon and for a moment, strongly considered telling him. After all, if the roles were reversed, he'd want Gwon to tell the truth…wouldn't he?

Then, he remembered the promise he made to his father. And not only that, he remembered why he couldn't tell him. Although there were many reasons, one stuck out in his mind. He knew if he told Gwon the truth, the young Gigakin would go looking for his father…and his mother. Or at least, Thadarack thought he would, so he decided not to risk it.

"Are you okay?" Thexis asked.

"Yes," said Thadarack. "It was just hard to see him in his current state. He's doing alright, all things considered. He's glad we made it home safely."

"Well, not all of us," said Gwon. "Did you tell him about Arkonius?"

"Yes," said Thadarack.

"I'm relieved he's doing alright," said Thexis. "Did you happen to ask him about Girozz? We looked everywhere but couldn't find him. Everyone we talked to gave us a similar answer. Nobody has seen him since before the battle."

Here we go, Thadarack thought. *Here's when the lie begins.* Although he knew it had to be done, knowing that didn't make him feel any better. His only solace came from the fact he knew he was protecting Gwon; not only from what he would do himself, but from everyone else around him.

"I did," he said. "My father sent him to reason with the Carne. He's hoping that, once they learn that Carne have been living

283

peacefully among Scythekin, they will understand we don't have to be enemies."

"He's...gone?" Gwon asked, wrinkling his snout in confusion. "He went to the Carne?"

"To try to reason with them," said Thadarack. "He's trying to help us."

Gwon's harrowing expression was unsettling. Thadarack's only consolation came from believing that the truth would have garnered a much worse response.

"I'm sure he'll be okay," said Thexis as she put her right claws on Gwon's back. "Girozz will get through to them."

Gwon's silence troubled Thadarack. It pained him to not be honest with Gwon, but he knew it was for the best. He quickly decided to change the topic in the hope that he'd distract his friend. "We are to summon everyone for a meeting in the Mending House first thing in the morning," he said. "My father wants the three of us there too."

"Who's everyone?" Thexis asked.

"That's what I was wondering," said Thadarack. "He dozed off before I could ask."

"Well—"

Gwon interrupted before Thexis could finish her thought. "He's really gone?" he asked. "And we have no idea when...or if he's coming back?"

The pain in Gwon's eyes was unmistakable. Although it was a lie, Thadarack began to think about it as if it were actually the truth. He wondered what the Carne would really do if Girozz tried to plead with them.

Would they consider what he had to say? He doubted it,

especially knowing now what he knew about the High King. It was much more likely that the Carne would imprison him. Or worse, end his life.

"I'm sure he'll come back," said Thadarack in an effort to comfort his friend. "Girozz can be very convincing. I have hope that the Carne will consider his opinion."

Thadarack caught Thexis giving him a doubtful look but only for a split second. He assumed she realized it wouldn't help Gwon feel any better if he saw her, but thankfully, he didn't think his friend did.

Thadarack knew Thexis' skepticism was warranted. After all, it was common knowledge that Girozz, and Gwon for that matter, weren't very...diplomatic. At the end of the day, no matter how good they were, they were still Carne.

"I guess you could be right," said Gwon. "I just can't believe he left."

To Thadarack's relief, it finally seemed Gwon was appeased. He was ready to tell him that his father forbade him from going after Girozz, but thankfully, the thought didn't even appear to cross Gwon's mind.

"Well, let's try to be optimistic," said Thexis. "I have total faith that Girozz will not only convince the Carne to end the fighting but will return soon. For now, let's go try to enjoy ourselves and celebrate."

Celebrate? Thadarack thought. He didn't understand how anybody could be celebrating, especially with all the deaths that had occurred. He understood they were victorious, and that it could have been far worse, but even so, he wasn't in a celebrating mood.

"Come on," continued Thexis as she glanced at Thadarack. "I'm sure our kin will want to see you."

"Alright," said Thadarack reluctantly, turning toward Gwon. "Are you okay?"

"Yes," said Gwon. "Thexis is right, we should join the others in the celebration. Giving everyone hope is the most important thing right now."

"Is saying I'm right even necessary?" Thexis smirked. "After all, I am always right. It should simply be inferred."

"I won't argue with that," said Gwon with a smile on his face.

The trio made their way to what was left of the city hub, having by now been cleared of the dead. There must have been hundreds of Scythekin there. They were dancing, singing songs, and enjoying well-deserved meals. Despite everything that had happened, everyone Thadarack saw looked so happy, relishing in their hard-fought victory. His mood quickly changed when he realized that, even amid so much evil, happiness had its place.

"My Prince!" a nearby Scythekin yelled. "We are so glad that you have returned!"

"Prince Thadarack!" another shouted. "Our savior!"

All the Scythekin began to quiet down as they shifted their eyes toward Thadarack, watching him intently. The nearby balladeers stopped singing and the joyous conversations ceased. All those in the city hub looked upon their young Prince with heartfelt gratitude in their eyes.

"Speech!" a few Scythekin echoed all at once. "Speech!"

"You can do this," whispered Thexis. "I'll be right beside you. We both will." She gestured toward Gwon with her beak.

"Go ahead," said Gwon. "You got this."

Thadarack walked toward the front of the city hub. The Scythadonians before him steadily moved out of his way. As he walked, he thought about all the anxiety, fear, and pain he had felt in the last few days.

He remembered how he lost his voice in front of King Sturklan in the Sanctum and how he froze in the Great Forest when his friends fought the Carne. He remembered how Thexis had come to his rescue when his fellow Scythekin were yelling at him at the front gate.

As he made it to the front and turned to look at the hundreds of Scythekin before him, he didn't feel anxious. He wasn't fearful or in pain. He was confident not only in his kin and their stoic resolve but in himself. He looked at Thexis and Gwon beside him and felt empowered.

After a few moments of silence, he looked out at all the Scythekin in front of him and spoke. "My fellow Scythadonians," he said passionately. "Our beloved city was in grave danger, but you all fought bravely. You beat back the enemy time and time again, showing your steadfastness and resilience. My father and I could not be prouder to be Scythekin, to be among you, and to lead you during this time of great strife."

He paused and scanned the area, gazing deep into the eyes of hundreds of Scythekin. "We won this battle, but the war is not yet over. However, on this day, this very night, you have earned the right to celebrate and honor all of those who gave their lives, so we could continue living ours. I say to you, to all of you, live your life to the fullest in honor of our fallen. And I will do everything in my power to defend and keep this city safe."

Thadarack's voice grew louder with each word that came. "If

all of us pledge to defend our home and protect our loved ones, there is nothing the Carne can do to us! No army, however vast, will be able to conquer us! We will prevail and the stories of your triumphs will live on for generations to come just like our kin of old! Thrifsaer will look down upon us and smile knowing that what he did, as well as what thousands of others had sacrificed, was not in vain! I say to you, here and now on this sacred ground, we *will* prevail, we *will* triumph, and we *will* achieve victory!"

The crowd erupted in deafening cheers, howling and yelling excitedly as they gazed back at their Prince. At that very moment, the moon breached a few thick clouds overhead and cast its radiant glow straight down upon where Thadarack stood.

He looked up, and for a mere moment across the moon's surface, he thought he saw the faces of two Scythekin smiling back at him. *My mother and Thrifsaer*, he thought wishfully. With a smile across his face, he looked back out at his kin before him with pride in his heart.

"May the Hallowed Lumina bless you, Prince Thadarack!" an onlooking Scythadonian yelled.

"We couldn't have won without you!" another shouted. "You saved us!"

Countless other onlookers shouted at Thadarack while he looked at Thexis and Gwon, both of whom nodded at him. He was proud, proud of himself and his kin. It was an incredible sight to behold, hundreds of Scythekin cheering and yelling with such vigor that the sounds must have echoed for miles in all directions.

Thadarack, with Thexis and Gwon by his side, walked back through the cleared path of Scythekin. With their eyes glued on their Prince, they cheered on, transitioning back into dance and song. As the friends made their way out of the city hub, Rhinn and another Scythekin were waiting for them.

"That was some speech," Rhinn said. "And exactly what they needed to hear."

"I hope it helped," said Thadarack. "I couldn't have done it without these two by my side."

Rhinn glanced at Gwon. "Did you ever find your father?"

Gwon sighed. "Not quite. King Thax sent him to the Carne in the hope that he could convince them to stop this war. I don't know when, or even if, he's coming back."

"He will," said Rhinn. "And if things don't go as planned, he is more than capable of protecting himself."

"I hope so," said Gwon.

"I believe that all fighting across Valdere will one day come to an end," said Rhinn. "That one day in the future there will be eternal peace. Maybe Girozz will be the one to achieve that."

"Why can't that day be tomorrow?" Thexis asked.

Rhinn shot Thexis a glance. "Because righteousness wouldn't exist without calamity. And sometimes calamity is a long storm that must be weathered before the sun can rise."

Thadarack didn't want to believe it would take a long time to attain peace but knew Rhinn was right. This was just the beginning, and before peace could be achieved, they'd have to persist. He took some comfort in knowing, however, that the Viridi now had two victories and the Carne…well, at least in the East, had none.

"I still wish it was tomorrow," said Thexis.

"As do I," Rhinn said. "Anyway, this is Raddius." She

gestured to the Scythekin by her side. "With the loss of Beroyn, I'm now first in command of the army. Raddius will serve as my second in command. He has proven himself time and time again in both skirmishes at the Wall, and the recent defense of Scythadon."

Raddius was about the same size as Rhinn, and although he looked familiar, Thadarack wasn't sure if he'd ever met him before. There was something about him, though, that made Thadarack believe he knew him. He couldn't quite place it, but once Raddius spoke, he knew right away what it was.

"It will be my greatest honor to fight alongside Rhinn and lead your army into battle," he said. "While I draw breath, I will do everything I can to protect you and our great city."

"We both will," said Rhinn.

"And if you don't mind me asking," Raddius said. "I believe my father accompanied you to Stegodor. His name is Arkonius. I haven't seen him anywhere. Did he return with you?"

It felt like claws were being jabbed into Thadarack's back as he stared back at Raddius. He could feel Thexis and Gwon glancing at him, and only imagined what might be going through their minds. He realized he had no choice but to be honest with Raddius.

He had enough of lying, and after all, what lie would he tell? "I'm sorry, but he didn't make it," Thadarack said. "He gave his life to protect us from Carne while on our way to Stegodor."

Raddius exhaled deeply and Thadarack could see the sadness behind his eyes. "That sounds like him. My father's reputation was no secret. I knew firstclaw he could be tough and stubborn. But he was unwavering in his love for Scythadon, as well as for you, Queen Luxren, and King Thax. I'm sure he was content with giving his life so that you could make it to Stegodor safely."

Thadarack couldn't hold back his tears. They began to roll down his beak as he remembered his battle training with Arkonius. He thought about how he wanted more than anything for his session to end that day. Now, he wished he could go back in time and train with him all over again. This time, he wouldn't want such things.

"If I'm not mistaken," Raddius continued. "My father was training you, right?"

Thadarack nodded, wiping away his tears with his claws.

"I'd be honored if you'd allow me to pick up where he left off. He taught me everything he knew, and I can't think of a better way to honor my father's legacy than to pass all of that on to you."

"That sounds great," said Thadarack.

Raddius smiled. "Let me know when you'd like to begin."

"How about tomorrow? My father wants to meet with everyone first thing in the morning in the Mending House. So, maybe we can begin after that?"

"Sounds perfect," said Raddius.

"Speaking of the King," said Rhinn. "How is he? We were on our way to see him when we saw you."

Thadarack, not wanting to tell another lie, decided that Rhinn and Raddius deserved to know the truth. Besides, he felt their stations made them privy to such information. "He is still alive," he said quietly so the others nearby wouldn't overhear. "But he is dying. Medicus says he doesn't know how much longer he has left."

Rhinn and Raddius frowned as did Gwon. Thadarack realized his friend was hearing this news for the first time.

"That is devastating news," said Rhinn.

"He's sleeping now and asked not to be bothered," said Thadarack.

"Very well," said Rhinn as she turned toward Raddius. "We will head back to the garrison for now and review the status of the army." She glanced back at Thadarack. "Take care, my Prince."

Rhinn and Raddius took off in the direction of the garrison.

"I'm sorry, Thadarack," said Gwon. "I didn't know he was dying."

"We don't want the others finding out," said Thadarack.

"Especially now," said Thexis. "Everyone needs to have hope and a good mindset for what is to come. Knowing that King Thax is dying is not something that will help them."

"You knew?" Gwon asked.

"Yes," said Thexis. "But only because Thadarack shared it during our audience with King Sturklan and Queen Cerathorn."

"I would have told you earlier," said Thadarack. "I haven't had a chance."

Not only had Thadarack not told Gwon about his father dying, but he was also keeping information about his own father and mother from him. Thadarack felt even worse as he looked at his friend, knowing full well that if...or when he learned the truth, their friendship may never be the same.

"What do we do when he..." Gwon's voice trailed off.

"We'll cross that bridge when we come to it," said Thexis. "For now, they don't need to know. Knowing will only dampen their spirits." Thexis looked around. "For the time being, where is Queen Cerathorn? Where are both the Stegokin and the Trikin?"

With everything going on, Thadarack hadn't realized there were no Stegokin or Trikin present in the city. At least, not that he'd seen. "That's a great question," he said. "I'm not sure where they are."

Just as Thadarack began to look around, he saw Septirius approaching.

"Septirius!" Thexis shouted as she ran up and hugged him. "You're alright!"

"Of course I am," said Septirius, who surprisingly, didn't have that many wounds. "Did you think a few filthy Carne could best me?" He looked at Gwon. "No offense."

"None taken," said Gwon with a chuckle.

"That was a great speech, Prince Thadarack," said Septirius. "It was exactly what everyone needed at a time such as this."

"I was only doing what my father would have done," replied the Prince.

"Well, you did it just as well as he would have," said Septirius. "And you showed up with reinforcements in the nick of time."

"Speaking of reinforcements," said Thexis. "Do you know where the Trikin and Stegokin are? We realized we haven't seen them in the city."

Septirius sighed. "The Trikin have set up camp just before the tree line on the outskirts of the clearing. The Stegokin returned to the valley to find King Sturklan."

"Why don't the Trikin stay in the city?" Thexis asked.

"Who knows," answered Septirius. "Knowing how stubborn

they are, they probably don't want to be in the same place as the Stegokin when they return."

Thexis scoffed. "Well, I hope they will now put their grievances aside and work together from here on out. We all need each other in order to survive. Today couldn't have demonstrated that more."

"You couldn't be more right," said Septirius. "If the reinforcements never came, I'm not sure how much longer we'd have held out. They had broken through the walls only a few hours before you arrived. It was our last stand."

"I'm just glad we got here in time," said Thadarack.

"Me too," said Septirius.

"My father wants to meet with everyone tomorrow," said Thadarack. "Please go to the Mending House first thing in the morning."

"I will," said Septirius. He then looked around and stepped in closer to Thadarack. "The others can't know about him, not at a time like this."

"Medicus told you?" Thadarack asked.

"Not quite," said Septirius. "I delivered reports of the battle to the King throughout. I took one look at him and knew. Nobody else can know. We must keep it that way for now. It won't be good for morale."

Thadarack nodded.

"I'm afraid I need to go, though. I must oversee the city wall repairs. Those vermin did quite a job on it. We haven't heard of any other Carne activity in the East yet, but we ought to be prepared just in case. I'm glad you're all home."

"Before you go, do you know who that is?" Thexis asked,

subtly gesturing with her beak.

Thadarack turned to see who Thexis was looking at. It was someone Thadarack didn't know. The Scythekin had sleek silver feathers and sharp claws that gleamed in the moonlight. He was burly and tall, similar in stature to that of Beroyn. Well, when Beroyn was still alive, of course.

Septirius glanced at the Scythekin. "That's Kormalus," he said. "He's a lieutenant in the army. Why?"

"I'm only curious," said Thexis. "I've never seen him before."

"Well, he is an incredible warrior," said Septirius. "I wouldn't want to fight against him." The captain looked back at the trio. "But I really must go now. Take care." Septirius then turned and headed toward the front gate.

"Only curious?" Gwon asked. "Of all the Scythekin here, why him?"

"It's just something about the way he was watching Thadarack when he was speaking," said Thexis. "Everyone was so happy. Except for him. It was like he was…emotionless. I don't know, it struck me as odd."

Thadarack glanced back at the Scythekin in question. He sure looked happy now. Although he had his back toward them, the Prince could tell he was talking and laughing with a few other Scythekin a good distance away.

"Maybe he lost a loved one in the battle," said Gwon.

"Maybe," said Thexis.

Thadarack peered at the Scythekin one final time before turning back toward his friends.

"What happens next?" Gwon asked.

"I think for now, we *try* to get some rest," said Thexis. "There isn't anything else we can do."

The trio stood there on the fringe of the city hub and watched the crowd savor their victory. The celebration was still in full swing, and it seemed unlikely to die down any time soon.

"Well, I'm exhausted," said Gwon. "I could use some sleep."

"You also never ate," said Thexis. "You must be starving."

"I know this might sound…disturbing," said Gwon. "But during the battle…I—"

"Nope," Thexis interrupted hastily. "Don't want to hear it."

Gwon laughed. "Didn't think so. I'll see you both bright and early." He then took off in the direction of his home.

"That's so disgusting," said Thexis. "I wish I didn't even say anything."

"Well, just pretend *he* didn't say anything," said Thadarack.

Thexis shook her head. "He's fortunate his house is behind the palace," she said. "When we were looking for Girozz, we saw there was no fighting back there. He actually has a place to sleep."

Thadarack thought about how so many no longer had a home. *Where are they going to sleep?* he thought. *I guess that might be the least of their concerns right now.* He especially felt bad for Thexis. In a matter of days, she had lost her grandfather and her home.

The Prince recalled the story his father had told him about Thexis' parents. The story only now resonated with him. For her first birthday, they wanted to surprise her with her favorite food, leaves from a ginkgo tree. The morning of, they brought her to Paxtorr's house and left the city in the hope of finding one of the trees.

A short while later, a terrible storm erupted out of nowhere. Thexis waited with her grandfather all day, but her parents never came home. Since that day, she hasn't eaten a single ginkgo leaf, even though they're now grown on the city's farm.

Thadarack glanced at his friend, only now understanding how she must have felt...how she probably still feels. "You're welcome to come back to the palace if you want," he said. "There's more than enough room for you."

"That sounds great. I could also go for a good night's sleep."

Thadarack and Thexis walked to the palace and went inside. The total silence within saddened the young Prince as he thought about his mother and father. His mind, however, quickly shifted when Thexis spoke. "So, tell me the truth. I may have partaken in your lie for his sake, but you know I'm smarter than that."

Thadarack stared blankly back at his friend. He knew what she was talking about, but he didn't want to be the one to say it first. An awkward moment passed before Thexis spoke again. "I'm sure it was to protect Gwon, but I know it must weigh heavily on your heart. Don't carry that burden all alone. You can tell me. I promise the secret will stay safe with me."

Thadarack gazed at his friend for a few more moments, contemplating whether to tell her the truth. But she was right; more so than Thadarack wanted to admit. It *was* weighing heavily on his heart, and he did feel comfort knowing Thexis would keep the secret.

He told her all about what his father had shared with him, each and every last detail. Although she was surprised to a degree, she assumed as much when Thadarack first told them where Girozz had gone. Thexis was too smart, knowing all too well that Girozz would never attempt to talk peace with the Carne. All that mattered, though, was that Gwon believed it.

Thexis realized something that Thadarack had not, however. Girozz had killed countless Carne at the Vlax Pass Wall. If he was a spy, why would he have done that? The two Scythekin assumed it was part of his plan to earn King Thax's trust. At least, that was the only thing that made sense. But still, killing his own kind to achieve such an end made Thadarack's feathers crawl.

The pair entered Thadarack's chamber and wished each other a good night. Thadarack offered his bed to Thexis, and she laid down, quickly falling asleep. He considered going into his parents' chamber but decided to leave it be. *Just how they left it*, he thought. *That's how it will stay.*

He laid down on the floor beside his friend and closed his eyes. It took a little while, but eventually, he drifted off to sleep. As he did so, he wished with all his heart that when he awoke the next morning, he'd find his mother and father outside his room eating their breakfast.

CHAPTER TWENTY

IT'S ONLY THE BEGINNING

Thadarack woke up the next morning to the sounds of birds chirping. Thin rays of sunlight coursed through small cracks in his chamber wall. He lifted his head, and to his surprise, he saw Thexis was already gone. He was shocked that he slept for so long. It had to be well into the morning hours.

He arose and stretched, his back stiffer than he'd like from sleeping on the ground. As he came to, he quickly remembered the meeting his father had asked for the day before. As soon as he walked out of his chamber into the greens room, he heard a commotion coming from outside the palace entrance. When he exited the palace, he saw Thexis, Gwon, and Medicus gathered outside the Mending House.

He started walking toward them, and at first, he was curious as to what was going on. Then, his heart fluttered when he saw the foreboding expressions on all their faces. He stopped dead in his tracks as his mind introduced a thought that shot waves of dread throughout his entire body.

He heard raised voices coming from inside the Mending

299

House, but from his distance, he couldn't quite make sense of what was being said, nor decipher who was speaking. *Is he...dead?* he thought. *Surely they would have woken me up? Wouldn't they?*

A slight sense of relief passed over him once it registered in his mind that Medicus was standing outside. He assumed that if his father had indeed passed away, Medicus would have been by his side. At least, he thought so.

Thadarack saw Thexis turn and do a double-take once she saw him. Right when Thexis tapped Gwon on the shoulder, Medicus said something to them before walking into the Mending House.

Thexis and Gwon then made their way to Thadarack. As they did, the voices permeating from the Mending House grew louder. Whoever was inside began shouting angrily.

"I was about to come wake you," said Thexis. "I only woke up a few minutes ago."

By now, Thadarack had recognized that if his father had died, Thexis would have quickly retrieved him. His sense of worry for his father slipped away, but his concern for what was happening in the Mending House remained. "What's going on? Is my father okay?"

"Yes," said Thexis. "Medicus said he's doing well, all things considered." Thexis sighed, then shot Gwon a glance before turning back to Thadarack. "King Sturklan is dead."

Thadarack's concern swiftly transitioned into full-out sorrow. *King Sturklan is dead?* he thought. *Oh, my Hallowed Lumina.* Almost immediately, regret flooded Thadarack's mind as he remembered how he, as well as everyone else, left King Sturklan all alone in the valley.

"They brought him back to Scythadon during the night," said

Thexis. "Medicus did everything he could for him, but he said his wounds were too great. He died about an hour ago."

Thadarack then discerned one of the voices shouting from within the Mending House. *Glathzolm.* Not knowing what was happening inside the Mending House filled him with anxiety and trepidation.

Thexis looked at Gwon. "Tell him what happened. You've been awake since they returned to the city."

"Glathzolm is furious," said Gwon. "It wasn't always so. She was devastated when the King died but cordial to all. For a time, it didn't appear she'd hold it against the Trikin."

"So, what happened?" asked Thadarack. "Why is she so mad now?"

Gwon sighed heavily. "Glathzolm was expecting Queen Cerathorn, as well as all the Trikin, to be a bit more sympathetic. And a tad apologetic."

Thadarack now understood where this was going. Although he hadn't spent much time with the Trikin, he caught a glimpse of how stubborn and prideful they could be. "But they were just fighting side by side," he said. "What exactly happened?"

"Glathzolm didn't like something Queen Cerathorn said," answered Gwon. "I didn't hear it word for word, but it was something along the lines of "these things happen in war." The tone sounded very…unremorseful." Gwon briefly turned around and glanced at the Mending House before looking back at Thadarack. "It's been downhill from there."

"I mean, I can understand why Glathzolm would be mad about that," Thadarack said. "But surely the Queen didn't *mean* to come across in a bad way, right?"

"I don't know," said Gwon.

"Emotions are running high all around," said Thexis. "Glathzolm is clearly devastated by the loss of King Sturklan. I don't blame her, however, now is not the time to let emotions control things. We need to come together and focus on the problem at claw and on what we are going to do to ensure we have a future."

"I couldn't have said it better myself," said an approaching voice. The friends turned and saw Rhinn, accompanied by Raddius, walking toward them. "I hope for our future's sake, we can come together in the coming days," continued Rhinn. "But as for the present, things look bleak."

"What do you mean?" asked Thexis.

"We came from the clearing," said Rhinn. "The Stegokin are ready to march home."

"March home?" Thadarack asked. "But we need to discuss our next plan of action."

"I tried talking sense into them," said Rhinn. "The Stegokin aren't thinking clearly right now. Were you to peer over the walls, you'd think yesterday's battle was fought between the Trikin and Stegokin. The scowls and glares the warriors are giving one another from across the way are—"

"You've got to be joking," interrupted Thexis. "They fought side by side yesterday, and within a matter of hours, they've gone back to hating one another? This is unbelievable."

"I guess my kind have to be tearing them apart in order for them to get along," said Gwon. "Otherwise, their inherent hate for one another is at the forefront."

"They're seriously considering leaving?" Thadarack asked.

"They're not considering it," said Rhinn confidently. "The decision's already been made. When Glathzolm returns…oh look, here she comes now."

The trio turned and saw Glathzolm storm out of the Mending House with two Stegokin by her side. She had fury in her eyes, and the anger spread across her face was unmistakable. Although she had countless gashes from the battle, some of which were still slowly bleeding, her movement was unhindered by them.

As the three Stegokin approached, the one to Glathzolm's left whispered something in her ear. Thadarack couldn't make out what it was, but the glower upon the Stegokin's face made him feel uneasy. *Could they be mad at us?* he thought nervously. *What did we do?*

By now within earshot, Thadarack heard Glathzolm's response. "It is not the Scythekin we should be angry with. We will give Prince Thadarack a moment of our time."

Well, that's reassuring, Thadarack thought. He wondered if they'd be able to talk Glathzolm down. She was clearly mad, and her demeanor made Thadarack uncomfortable. He knew there was nothing he could have done that would have angered her like this, but regardless, her body language could've deceived him.

"We're so sorry to hear about King Sturklan," said Thexis in a soft voice once the Stegokin were before them. "Without him, who knows what would have become of Scythadon."

Glathzolm's grimace tapered down a bit as did her two companions'. She took a moment before responding. Thadarack assumed it was because she was trying her hardest to calm down.

After a brief, if somewhat awkward silence, she spoke gently. "Thank you. I am, and always will be, proud that we came to help your kin. If need be, we would do so again. But for now, we will return to Stegodor."

She turned her head around toward the Mending House and then back toward Thexis. "I can't be in her presence for one moment longer. She can say whatever she wants about why she decided to help us, but it's clear she only showed up because she realized that the Trikin would have to face the Carne alone if we were gone. She's selfish. That's the only reason the Trikin came. They didn't come because it was the right thing to do."

"I know what Queen Cerathorn said was distasteful," said Thexis. "But we need to decide what we're going to do now. Stay and meet with us."

Thadarack could tell that Thexis was trying to sound as non-confrontational as possible. For the time being, he was glad she was the one speaking. He remembered how quickly Riktlan's temper would get the best of him, fearing that Glathzolm might suffer from the same fate.

Riktlan, Thadarack thought. *I still can't believe he's gone.* Although he only knew Riktlan for a short time, the Prince had grown rather fond of him. Especially because Riktlan seemed to be the most accepting of Gwon after getting to know him.

"It's not just about what she said," stated Glathzolm. "It's also *how* she acts and the *way* she speaks. It's as if nobody else matters. The most important Stegokin is…" She paused briefly and looked toward the ground. After a moment, she glanced back up at Thexis. "Our King is dead. Our army has been reduced to a fraction of what it once was. We will return to Stegodor for now and keep in touch."

"Keep in touch?" Thexis asked. "But what if the Carne come

back? Or what if they attack Stegodor next? Shouldn't we come up with a plan?"

"We need to go on the offensive," interjected Gwon. "Carne are too proud to sit back, especially now. This defeat will not sit well with them. They'll be back, and I fear if we don't take the fight to them, they will attack again soon."

"How are we to take the fight to them?" Glathzolm asked passionately. "Have you not seen our army?" Her voice grew louder. "We are to return to Stegodor and mourn our fallen! Our kin don't even know that King Sturklan is dead! And although I agree we need to devise a plan, I will not sit here while that condescending…"

Glathzolm shut her eyes and breathed a long sigh. She opened them a moment later and spoke in a much more subdued way. "While I am truthfully grateful that the Trikin came, if they hadn't abandoned us in the beginning, my King, as well as many of my kin, might still be alive. Besides, you have scouts up and down the frontier now. They'll send news well in advance should the Carne be on the move. I appreciate your condolences, but we shall take our leave."

Glathzolm and her two companions started to walk away, leaving Thexis and Gwon looking exasperated. Although he was upset that Glathzolm was leaving, Thadarack, at least a little, understood why.

He put himself in Glathzolm's feet, realizing that he would feel the same way if what had happened to King Sturklan happened to his father. Especially if the Trikin were too stubborn to admit that they made a mistake.

"Thank you, Glathzolm," Thadarack said. "For everything.

We truly are sorry about King Sturklan and for everyone else who was lost. We will always remember what you all did for us. I vow I will honor our alliance and friendship no matter what happens."

Glathzolm turned her head slightly and nodded. She then turned back around and walked away. A few moments later, the Stegokin disappeared behind a few of the ruined homes.

"Well, this is great," said Gwon. "They despise each other again."

"It's ludicrous," said Thexis. "They need to work together."

Thadarack remembered the discussion he had with King Sturklan a few days ago in the Stegodor Sanctum. He thought about how thankful the King was that the Scythekin had saved his kin and how much he revered Pyklania's spike. *I hope they honor him the same way,* he thought. *For King Sturklan deserves nothing less.*

Losing his mother, and most likely his father soon, was hard for Thadarack to accept, as was the loss of every other Scythekin that had died. He mourned the deaths of Arkonius, Beroyn, and all the others that he sadly didn't personally know.

But the deaths of King Sturklan, Riktlan, Tryzolm, Horngorre, and all the other Stegokin, Trikin, and Pachykin affected the young Prince in a different way. For the rest of his life, he knew that every time he thought about them, he would feel a disparate kind of sorrow. Whether it was warranted or not, he couldn't help thinking their deaths were on his claws.

He knew that he had no choice in bringing them to Scythadon, and at the end of the day, his father was the one who sent him to Stegodor. But Thadarack was the one who convinced them to come. Knowing that hit him exceptionally hard.

"I'm surprised neither of you said anything," said Thexis as she glanced at Rhinn and Raddius. "Don't you believe the Stegokin should have stayed?"

"The Stegokin have given enough," said Rhinn. "The Carne are defeated for now, at least in the East. While it would have been nice for them to stick around for the meeting, I don't fault them for wanting to return home. They need time to mourn. And besides, Glathzolm was right. We know who the enemy is now and which direction they'll be coming from. We won't be taken by surprise again."

"I guess that makes sense," said Thexis. "I feel so bad for what has happened to them. They've lost so many."

"I wouldn't count the Stegokin out just yet," said Rhinn. "Their army may only be a fraction of what it was, but I know the Stegokin resolve. They can turn ordinary Stegodorians, both the young and old, into effective warriors. I've seen them do it in the war against the Trikin time after time. I don't believe for a second that the Stegokin are out of this fight."

"Well, that's comforting," said Thadarack. "I was concerned about that, especially if the Carne target Stegodor next."

"I'm confident in saying that we have not seen the last of the Stegokin," said Rhinn. "Nor the last of Glathzolm."

"When we first pushed the Carne out of the city, we climbed atop the ramparts to see what it was like over the walls," interjected Raddius. "We witnessed Glathzolm ferociously killing Carne after Carne. She was invincible."

"We saw her too," said Thexis. "I'm glad she's on our side."

Thadarack glanced toward the Mending House. "We should head in," he said. "Do you know who's in there besides Queen Cerathorn?"

"I saw Hornbrigg and Jearspike go in with the Queen," said Gwon. "I heard Septirius when we were standing outside. Other than that, I'm not sure if there's anyone else other than the King and Medicus."

"We should get Kylesia," said Thadarack. "Have you seen her anywhere?"

Everyone shook their heads.

"Okay, I'll go find her. You—"

"No," interrupted Thexis. "I will. It's more important for you to be there. I'll go find Kylesia and bring her back."

Thexis departed just as Thadarack, Gwon, Rhinn, and Raddius headed for the Mending House. The yelling had died down since Glathzolm had left, but as soon as they entered, Thadarack heard the discussion taking place.

As they walked to the back where the King lay, Medicus reapplied healing ointment on some of his wounds. The Queen, Hornbrigg, Jearspike, and Septirius were gathered around.

"You have my word," said Queen Cerathorn. "I will stand by the peace treaty between us and Stegodor. You kept your word and didn't intervene in the war. By my honor, I will keep mine."

"Very well," said King Thax gently. "Glathzolm is just upset. You have to understand."

"I do," said the Queen. "Even so, she had no right to speak to me that way. She was out of line. I will let it slide this time, but I may not be so forgiving if it happens again."

King Thax nodded. "I wish you safe travels back to Ceragorre. We will keep open close lines of communication and reach out to you as soon as we learn of any Carne activity."

"We will do the same," said Queen Cerathorn. She then

308

glanced at Thadarack, who by now, was standing at his father's side. She gave him one brisk nod. "Prince Thadarack."

As she turned around and made her way toward the exit, she gave Gwon a brief smile. Hornbrigg followed suit, and a moment later, the three Trikin were gone.

Although Thadarack was delighted by the amicable gesture toward his Carne friend, he was in total shock that Queen Cerathorn left. *But what about the meeting?* he thought. *Why is she leaving so suddenly?*

He glanced at his friends, both of whom appeared as puzzled as he was. He turned toward Rhinn and Raddius, but to his surprise, they didn't seem perplexed at all. The Prince then looked at his father and saw him slowly adjusting his head toward Thadarack. "My son," said the King, giving him a slight smile.

"Why did Queen Cerathorn leave?" Thadarack asked. "We still have to discuss what we're going to do."

"We've already discussed everything we needed to," replied the King.

"I know it might not be my place," said Gwon. "But shouldn't we go on the offensive? I think we should strike them now while we have the advantage."

King Thax glanced at Septirius. "Please explain," he said quietly.

"We're not in a position to go on the offensive," said Septirius. "At least not yet. This invasion caught us by surprise. We need to regroup and think strategically. We also need time to mourn our fallen. Only then will we be in a place to take the fight to the enemy."

Gwon sighed. "I guess that makes sense."

"What of the relationship between the Stegokin and Trikin?" Thadarack asked. "Glathzolm was enraged when she left."

"They'll be okay," said Septirius. "Both Glathzolm and Queen Cerathorn took King Sturklan's death very hard. They need some time to process it, that's all."

"But Queen Cerathorn didn't seem remorseful at all," said Thadarack. "It didn't look like she cared."

"You weren't here when she learned of King Sturklan's death," Septirius said. "One look in her eyes and you could tell she was in pain."

"But she—"

The King cut his son off from finishing his thought. "Everyone copes with loss differently," he said softly. "Instead of projecting what the Trikin perceive as weakness, Queen Cerathorn did the only thing she knows how…mask her regret and pain. Just like Ceraplazz, the death of King Sturklan will haunt Queen Cerathorn for the rest of her days. Of that I am certain."

"The Stegokin and Trikin know who the enemy is now," said Septirius. "When the time comes and it matters most, they will both fight the Carne by our side."

Thadarack was glad his father and Septirius seemed convinced that they'd work together. However, he still couldn't kick the cloud of doubt in the back of his mind. After all, he'd witnessed firstclaw how the Stegokin and Trikin felt about each other. His only hope was that the threat of the Carne was greater than their dislike for one another. "I hope so," he said.

"By the way, where is Girozz?" Septirius asked, glancing at Gwon. "Where is your father?"

"He's gone," Gwon said. "He went to reason with the Carne in the hopes that we can avoid further bloodshed and settle things peacefully."

"Settle things peacefully?" Septirius asked. "With the Carne?" He looked at King Thax. "You believe that's possible?"

King Thax slowly nodded.

"We have to try," said Thadarack. "And who better to do that than a Carne who has lived peacefully among us?"

"While I'll be the first to admit that Girozz and Gwon are our friends, they have lived here for over a decade," said Septirius. "The vile beasts that attacked us know only contempt and hate for Viridi."

"We don't know that," said a voice from behind. Thadarack turned and saw Thexis and Kylesia approaching. "We have to believe there are good Carne out there," Thexis continued. "Otherwise, the fighting will never end."

"I concede it's worth a shot," Septirius said. "But where is he? When did he leave? I haven't seen Girozz in days. The Carne still attacked us, and he hasn't returned."

Thadarack's heart dropped in his chest. Septirius was right. If Girozz left with the intention of reasoning with the Carne, he wouldn't have had to go too far. If that was what he had *really* left to do, where was he now?

He looked at Gwon and saw the baffled look on his face. What was his friend thinking now? What was he going to say or do? For a moment, Thadarack was worried his friend would figure out he lied. The Prince frantically tried to think of something to say just when his father spoke. "He's gone to find the High King," King Thax said. "He knows the High King is the only one who can stop this."

"That makes sense," said Septirius.

Thadarack's heart stopped pounding. He should have known his father would have an answer. His friend also looked convinced, and right now, that was all that mattered.

"While I agree Girozz's mission is important, we must decide what to do in the meantime," said Rhinn.

"Thadarack will share what he and I discussed yesterday," said the King. "Before Girozz left, he came to me and shared his thoughts on what he thinks the Carne are planning."

As Thadarack spoke, he was careful not to say that Girozz *knew* what he had told his father. He explained it in a way that implied it was mere speculation, and no more than Girozz's assumptions due to him knowing and understanding more about how the Carne thought. And of course, he didn't say anything about Gwon's mother.

"So, that's why there were no Rexkin or Gigakin here," said Rhinn. "They're all in the West."

"And the Spinekin too," said Kylesia.

"Spinekin?" Raddius asked. "Are you sure?"

"I saw them with my own eyes," said Kylesia. "They were terrifying."

As Thadarack listened to everyone's reactions and thoughts about what to do next, he started hearing some commotion coming from outside. Soon, everyone heard it, having grown silent and turning their heads toward the entryway. A moment later, Fulgro came charging in followed closely by two Scythekin guards.

"Forgive me, my King," said one of the guards. "This

Pachykin insisted on an audience, and when I tried to stop him, he unexpectedly ran past us."

"Fulgro!" scolded Kylesia. "What are you doing? This is a—"

"I apologize for barging in," interrupted Fulgro hastily. "But..." He paused, desperately trying to catch his breath as one of the guards reached her claws for him.

"Wait," said King Thax. "Leave him be."

The guard nodded and took a step back.

"What is it?" asked Kylesia.

"Magdro and Vendria are here," Fulgro said. "They arrived shortly after you left."

Kylesia's eyes widened, piquing Thadarack's interest regarding who Magdro and Vendria were. He waited for Kylesia to speak, but when it was apparent she was too in shock, Rhinn spoke instead.

"What's going on? Who are these two you speak of?"

"My brother and his mate," said Kylesia quietly. "They're alive?"

"Yes," said Fulgro. "When the Carne attacked us, they escaped and fled west. They found sanctuary with the Diplikin, but when the Carne overran them, they barely escaped again. They traveled east, searching for other Viridi. They ran into Scythekin scouts who pointed them in the direction of Scythadon. You should go to your brother now. He's at the front gate...he's gravely wounded."

Before anybody said anything else, Kylesia bolted out of the Mending House.

"Medicus," said King Thax. "Go tend to their wounds immediately."

Thadarack had forgotten Medicus was even there as he'd been standing far-off in the corner. The healer briskly nodded, grabbed a jar of healing ointment off a nearby boulder table, and ran after Kylesia.

"Wait, slow down," Septirius said. "Are you saying the Diplikin have been destroyed?"

After a brief pause and a lengthy sigh, Fulgro spoke. "Yes."

"Who are the Diplikin?" Gwon asked.

"One of the four Longneck kingdoms of the West," said King Thax.

"No, they were one of three," said Fulgro. "While in Dipliburgh, Magdro and Vendria learned of the Dredkin's earlier demise."

"Dredlind has been destroyed too?" Rhinn asked. "Two of the four Longneck kingdoms have already fallen to the Carne?"

"No," said Fulgro. "The Dredkin fell prior to the Carne invasion."

Thadarack's heart sank for what seemed like the hundredth time. Although Septirius, Rhinn, and Raddius began asking countless questions and speaking over one another, he soon found his mind drifting off.

He recalled how Kylesia had said that some Longneck kingdoms had been at war. She told them that she thought one of those kingdoms might have been close to defeat. As it turned out, she couldn't have been more right.

There are only two Longneck kingdoms left? Thadarack thought. *Will the other two survive?* He quivered at his own questions, desperately searching for some solace. He hoped good news would somehow find its way to him. Instead, his trance-like state was suddenly broken when his father began coughing out of control.

"My King," Rhinn said, putting her right claws gently on the King's shoulder. "Are you alright?"

"I'll go get a healer," said Thexis, but right when she took a step toward the exit, Haelicus barged in.

"Medicus asked me to come care for the King while he's gone," Haelicus said as she knelt by King Thax's side. "Everyone, I know you have important business to discuss, but I think it'd be best for the King to get some rest."

Thadarack watched his father's cough attack in anguish. The King choked and hacked in such an unpleasant way that Thadarack's stomach turned. He saw Haelicus trying to feed him herbs to help with the cough, but it was a difficult feat. His father tried hard to eat them, and after a few failed attempts, he was able to finally swallow some. Fortunately, his coughing ceased. His eyes closed, and his breathing became shallow.

"He needs rest," Haelicus said. "The medicine will knock him out anyway."

Everyone said their solemn goodbyes to the King and made their way toward the exit. Just before he walked outside, Thadarack turned around and glanced back at his father. Haelicus turned toward the Prince and gave him a warm smile.

Thadarack was unsure why she was smiling, especially at a time like this. But to his surprise, even amidst everything that had happened, he found comfort in it. He smiled back, turned around, and left the Mending House.

Once outside, Fulgro took his leave to return to the front gate. Rhinn also departed and headed in the direction of the garrison.

Septirius went the opposite way, toward one of the areas of the wall that had collapsed.

"Well, what do you say, Prince Thadarack?" Raddius asked. "It seems to me that we shouldn't wait a moment longer to resume where you left off with your battle training. Are you ready?"

"Yes," said Thadarack. "I'll meet you behind the palace in a little while."

With a nod, Raddius departed. Thadarack said goodbye to Thexis and Gwon, then he ran back to the palace for a quick bite to eat. Afterward, he headed for the small clearing behind it.

As the young Prince approached, he saw the stump that Arkonius had set up for him not even a week earlier. Raddius was standing beside it, gliding his claws across his father's claw marks. Although Raddius didn't say as much, Thadarack assumed he knew they were his father's. It was just something about the way he was looking at them.

When Raddius realized Thadarack was there, he turned and asked him where he left off with the battle training. Thadarack explained what he and Arkonius had done. After a few words of encouragement from his new trainer, the young Prince walked up to the stump and got in his battle-ready position.

Duck, dodge, and strike, he thought, eyeing the same mark he had missed when Arkonius was beside him. With motivation in his eyes and determination in his heart, Thadarack took a deep breath, ducked, rolled, jumped, and struck his right claws as hard as he could.

INDIE AUTHOR

Reviews help indie authors get noticed. As of now, this novel can be reviewed on Amazon and Goodreads.

You can sign up for my newsletter at michaelrobling.com. You can also follow me on Facebook and Instagram.

The second book in this series is scheduled for a release in the fall of 2025.

Lastly, I wanted to thank you for reading my debut novel. I *sincerely* hope you enjoyed it!

THANK YOU

Michael Robling

Made in the USA
Middletown, DE
04 August 2024

58237912R00198